About the author

Claire Smallman began her career as a tennis coach, running her own successful business for ten years and representing Suffolk as a player. She moved on to become publisher of *Community News,* a local Suffolk newspaper and then published tourist guides for English-speaking visitors to Germany. Claire lives in Lowestoft, Suffolk.

THE SATINWOOD BOX

Claire Smallman

Book Guild Publishing
Sussex, England

First published in Great Britain in 2014 by
The Book Guild Ltd
The Werks
45 Church Road
Hove, BN3 2BE

Typesetting in Sabon by
Norman Tilley Graphics Ltd, Northampton

Printed and bound in Great Britain by
CPI Group (UK) Ltd, Croydon, CR0 4YY

A catalogue record for this book is available from
The British Library

ISBN 978 1 909716 06 3

1

Spring 1869

'Yes, yes it is,' said Mr Harcourt in reply to his wife's question.

They were walking along the shore path at Lebritan, with their son Theo. Mrs Harcourt had remarked how peaceful it was there.

'But maybe not so peaceful for long,' said Mr Harcourt. 'The railway is not far from here and there is talk of a branch line connecting Lebritan to the main line.'

'I think the railway will be good for the town,' said Theo. 'Looks like the place needs livening up.'

Theo stood for a moment gazing out to sea, while his father and mother walked on. He had accompanied them on their visit to the south coast to buy property. One day the house they bought would be his, so they had insisted he should come and approve of their choices. 'But would I want to live in the south?' thought Theo. 'I am a man of the north country; it's so different here – as my mother said, so peaceful. Could I fit in to all this? Would I want to fit into all this?'

Theo had been brought up in Lancashire where his father owned a textile mill; they were a successful business family and already owned properties in the north. Theo's father, however, wanted his son to be a gentleman and to have a country seat in the wealthy south of England, something he had not been able to do, but to which he always aspired. If he couldn't have it, then he would make sure his son had the opportunity. Theo

1

was a partner in the business although his contribution was small; his father had insisted that he joined the local militia, and Theo took that as an opportunity for drinking and gambling, much to his parents' disappointment. Perhaps a move to the south would encourage Theo to do something useful with his life.

Two people appeared in the distance; a man, and on his arm a young woman. They walked slowly, stopping occasionally to take in the view. As they came nearer, the natural beauty of the young woman struck Theo; she was perhaps twenty-five – the man on her arm must be her father or uncle, the facial resemblance was noticeable. Theo was now twenty-eight and had sown many a wild oat. His father was anxious for him to marry and produce heirs, but Theo was happy to carry on with his carefree life. The young lady intrigued him; such loveliness yet there was a tinge of sadness about her, not just on her face but also in her demeanour. 'So young to be so sad,' he thought.

'Good morning,' said Theo. 'What a remarkable view and such a peaceful place.' He thought it best to use his mother's description of Lebritan rather than air his own thoughts; these people may live locally and it would be discourteous to criticise the area.

'Yes,' said the man, 'my daughter and I love this walk and often stroll along here to enjoy the tranquillity.'

'You must reside locally to be able to take advantage of such a lovely place so often.'

'Indeed,' said the man. 'We live just a short distance away in Bishopfield. And you, sir, you are not from these parts?'

'No, sir, my parents and I are visiting the area to buy property. We are from Lancashire.'

After talking for several minutes about each other's interests, the man said to Theo, 'Buying property, well now... I know the area well, maybe I can help you?'

'Let me introduce you to my parents, sir.' Theo called to his mother and father who were a few yards ahead.

'This gentleman and lady live near here and are knowledge-able of property in the area – they may be able to assist us.'

'That's most helpful, sir,' said Theo's father. 'We shall be pleased to have any advice available, we have little knowledge of local property and local people are always the best advisers. We have a textile business in Lancashire – Harcourt's, that's our family name, and have decided to invest in property here in the south for our son Theo. The north is very industrial; here it is much quieter, greener, and so different.'

'Let me introduce myself. I am William Gilman, and this is my daughter, Mrs Warner, who shares my home. We should meet again to talk about property, if you so wish. We live at Berg House, Bishopfield. Perhaps you would care to call on a Thursday afternoon and take tea with us?'

'That is so kind!' said Theo's mother, Mrs Harcourt. 'We shall be pleased to accept your invitation.'

'We are free next Thursday, if you would care to come then?' said Mr Gilman.

'Yes, we shall look forward to that,' said Mrs Harcourt.

Mr Gilman turned to his daughter. 'Come, Jessica – you look tired. We should go home now.'

'Yes, Papa.'

Mr Gilman and his daughter continued walking along the pathway, while Theo and his parents made their way back to their carriage to return to their lodgings in East Leah.

'What an interesting family!' said Jessica, who knew little of the north, having lived in the south of England all her life. 'I thought northern folk didn't like the south – I wonder why they want to buy property here?'

'I can guess why they want to buy property here; they want to buy position in society. I will help them as much as I can with property but I don't want to get too involved with them,' replied her father. 'The Barm House is still for sale, no one locally wants it… maybe I can persuade them to buy that, it will be doing everyone a good turn.'

'Why don't you want to get too involved with them?'

'My dear, will you never learn? They are in the textile business and are trade; we are not. They are from the north, and we are southerners. We have our place in society; they do not. Besides, I wouldn't trust them too far.'

'Why, you hardly know them! It seems you are making judgment with little knowledge.'

'My dear, you seem to be full of "whys"! I wouldn't trust them because I think that they are trying to be something they can never be – that is the way of people from the north who have money, but no breeding. Their methods of getting what they want are not the same as ours. Besides there is something about that son Theo… don't know exactly what, but be careful of him.'

Jessica sat quietly in the carriage as it meandered along the lanes on their way home. 'What a handsome man Theo is!' she thought. 'Such good looks, charm, and that golden hair, with a perfectly trimmed moustache and beard, looks almost regal. I really shouldn't be thinking like this, my darling Thomas only twelve months in his grave… '

He had been such a brave man, bold and daring. Thomas had served as a major in the 3rd Dragoon Guards. When Queen Victoria sent his regiment to Abyssinia to challenge the Emperor, Thomas was more than ready to lead his men into battle. All of Lord Napier's men fought well, soundly defeating the enemy at the Battle of Magdala. No British troops were killed, but twenty were wounded, of whom Thomas was one. The wound wasn't serious but blood poisoning set in and he died on the voyage home. He and Jessica had been married just two years and had looked forward to raising a family, but that wasn't to be. Since Thomas's death, Jessica had remained at Berg House and looked after her father. Her mama had died five years ago; she would have adored Thomas. Now Jessica was the only one to care for Papa, as she had no siblings. Papa's health was failing, he coughed frequently and Jessica was sure she had seen specks of blood in his kerchief. He would not speak about it, but Jessica knew it was serious. It seemed as though she might lose another man she loved. Jessica suddenly felt very lonely, coldness came over her and she shuddered.

'Are you all right, my dear?' asked her father. 'Are you cold?'

'No, thank you, Papa, it was nothing.'

Back at Berg House, Jessica asked, 'Do you really think the Harcourts might buy Barm House? It is in such disrepair.'

'My dear, when I tell them that by purchasing Barm House they will have a seat in the county, I doubt if they will be too worried about the condition of the property.'

'But Mr Harcourt is a businessman, Papa, and from what little I know of northerners I know that they are careful with their money.'

'Yes, so they are, but when it comes to status I am sure the condition of the property will take second place.'

'So, eventually Mr Theo Harcourt will have the seat?' asked Jessica.

'So it would seem.'

Since Thomas had died, Papa had become very protective and to Jessica it seemed as if, in her father's eyes, all men were a threat to her. Maybe because she had said to her father that she thought the Harcourts an interesting family, she had made him wary of them. Jessica would inherit Berg House, a property of some considerable size. Many a young man would find Jessica attractive, which she was, if only to lay claim to her property. It seemed to her as though Papa was protecting her by suggesting a seat for the Harcourts at Barm House, thus diverting any attention from the much superior Berg House.

*

5

William Gilman's father had passed on to him the family tea business. William was a respected tea broker and formed a pairing with a company in Ceylon. This had given him considerable power through connections with governments, banks and contacts around the world. He recalled how he and his beloved wife Emily, 'Em' as he had called her, had hosted grand parties at Berg House for retired brokers, current brokers, officials from the government of Ceylon and bankers. In those days, William and Em had a butler, lady's maid, coachman, page, cook, housemaid and kitchen maid. A happy band they were, always willing and hard working. Cook produced some wonderful meals and never seemed flustered; all the staff were prepared to lend a hand at these busy times and the parties always went smoothly.

His great sadness was that he had no son to pass the business on to. When Em died, he carried on and when Jessica married, he had hopes that her husband, although a professional soldier, would become a partner and carry on the brokerage. With Jessica, they would have made such a happy union. But Thomas was cut down in the prime of life, so William sold the business and devoted his time to Berg House. When he died, it would all be Jessica's. 'I just hope that one day she will find love again,' thought William, 'and will not be taken in by someone who merely wants the house.'

He found it increasingly difficult to walk as far as he used to; he felt short of breath at times and he had seen specks of blood when he coughed. He hoped Jessica hadn't noticed, but she was, he knew, highly observant.

Tea at Berg House

Theo brushed his jacket; it was new, the latest style. He was very proud of his appearance, some said vain, but Theo's father had always encouraged him to dress as a gentleman, in the hope that one day he might become one. The double-breasted grey waistcoat matched the grey frock coat, which he set off with a paisley ascot tie. Theo's mother smiled. 'You look a true gentleman,' she said.

Theo thought of Jessica's face; a sad face, but so beautiful. 'Her father called her Mrs Warner, so perhaps she is a widow – which may be the cause of the sadness. We shall see,' he pondered.

Theo joined his parents who were waiting in their hired carriage for the short journey to Berg House.

On arrival, they were met by the butler, a muscular man of about fifty. They were ushered into the entrance hall where Mr Gilman and Jessica came to greet them. He showed them into the drawing room, bright and spacious with windows over-looking the garden to the front of the house. Mr and Mrs Harcourt took a seat together while Theo sat on a single chair in half shadow at the end of the room.

'So pleased you could come,' said Mr Gilman. 'I hope your journey was comfortable.'

'Yes, indeed,' replied Mr Harcourt. 'The lanes here are much smoother than where we live! It was a very pleasant drive.'

'Mrs K, our cook, has been busy making some rather special cakes for our tea,' said Mr Gilman. 'Mrs K was married to a Polish man whose name had more consonants than necessary, so we simply call her Mrs K. She loves it when we entertain; it gives her an opportunity to show her prowess. Before I sold my tea brokerage we entertained frequently, now it is not so often.'

'That is a matter we need to discuss, my dear,' said Mr Harcourt to his wife. 'If we buy property here, we will need staff.'

'Oh, don't worry yourselves about that,' said Mr Gilman. 'There are many people in the nearby villages who would be glad of work. I am sure Jessica will be able to advise you.'

Theo looked across at Jessica. She glanced at him and he detected a smile.

'Now to business!' said Mr Gilman. 'Barm House is an interesting property. It has been vacant for a while, came up for auction but there was no interest, mainly because it is difficult to get to, but with the railway likely to come this way soon it would make an ideal purchase.'

'Are you sure about the railway?' said Theo's father, who had already heard rumours about a branch line.

'Oh yes, I have it on very good authority that it's not *if* it will come, but *when*.'

'Mr Gilman should know, dear,' said Mrs Harcourt. 'He does after all have business connections and I am sure we can rely on his knowledge and advice.'

'Well then, I think a viewing of Barm House should be arranged! Can you do that for us, Mr Gilman?'

'Yes, of course! Now shall we have some refreshment?'

Mr Gilman rang for Mrs K who, a few minutes later, brought in a sumptuous tea.

'Is this some of your tea, Mr Gilman?' asked Mrs Harcourt.

'Yes, I hope you enjoy it! When I studied tea brokerage I also learned tasting and how to blend – this is a blend of mine. The cakes contain the finely-ground leaves of a Ceylon green tea – they won't overpower the taste but you will experience their fragrance. It's a recipe I brought back from India and Mrs K has adapted it for our palates... now it is our favourite!'

'Delicious!' pronounced Mrs Harcourt. 'Perhaps we can have the recipe?'

'Oh, I don't know!' said Mr Gilman, smiling. 'You will have to ask Mrs K, it is her recipe and I expect there is a "secret" ingredient!'

Theo glanced at Jessica again. 'I wonder what happened to her husband, if indeed there was a husband,' he thought. 'Such beauty should not be wasted, and she is still young.'

Jessica's thoughts were with Thomas. He used to sit in this room with her and her father, taking tea and talking about all manner of things. She looked at Theo and for a moment

8

thought she saw Thomas; the way he sat, that golden hair. The shadow across the end of the room where Theo sat was now complete, as the sun had moved across the afternoon sky.

'Are you a military man by any chance, Mr Harcourt?' said Jessica.

'Yes, I am,' said Theo.

'What is your regiment?'

'I am a captain in the Royal Lancashire Militia,' said Theo.

'Militia… ' said Mr Gilman. 'That is a volunteer force, is it not?'

There was silence for a few moments. The Harcourts sensed a hint of scorn in Mr Gilman's voice.

Jessica looked embarrassed. 'Do have some more cake, Mrs Harcourt – and perhaps some more tea?'

Jessica thought a move out of the drawing room might relieve the atmosphere.

'We have a lovely garden – perhaps you would care to have a walk around it? The day is so fine, it would be a shame not to take advantage of it.'

'Excellent suggestion, my dear,' said Mr Gilman. 'Let's do that and perhaps we can also discuss Barm House.'

Berg House stood in grounds of 30 acres, which stretched down to the river running along its western boundary. It was mostly lawns and copses, largely designed by the American landscape gardener and writer Andrew Downing when he toured Europe some fifteen years earlier. Downing loved Berg House and advised William Gilman when he stayed with him how he could best maximise the acreage he had by use of trees and lawned areas, setting off the property to its 'magnificent best'.

Nearest to the house were the fruit and kitchen gardens, and an orangery for peaches, grapes, flowers and foliage plants. Previous owners had also kept pigs, cattle and poultry, but Mr Gilman did not have the inclination to keep such creatures.

The lawns were exquisitely manicured. Mr Gilman was

fortunate to have the services of local gardeners who were well skilled in looking after such gardens; most of them also worked on the larger estates in the county and brought with them the skills learned there. Mr Gilman's standing in the county meant that it was easy to find staff that felt privileged to work for such a gentleman and they were well rewarded for their skill and loyalty.

Beyond the lawns there were copses, accessed along tree-lined pathways. On the north side was the Breach Copse, and to the south was Gulley Copse.

Mr Gilman started coughing. Mrs Harcourt, concerned, suggested perhaps 'the young people' should go on ahead. 'Excellent idea,' said Mr Gilman. 'I am afraid I find walking brings on a cough, nothing of concern, but it will delay you, so please my dear, take Mr Harcourt on ahead of us.'

Theo and Jessica walked towards Gulley Copse. 'Is your father all right?' said Theo. 'Oh yes,' said Jessica. 'It's nothing serious... Papa will soon recover.' Jessica seemed slightly upset and was quick to dismiss her father's indisposition, but Theo thought now was not the time to pursue this.

'Your gardens are beautifully kept,' said Theo.

'Yes, Papa has devoted his time and energy to Berg House and is rightly proud of all he has achieved.'

'Do you have any brothers or sisters to help run this property?'

'No, Mama was ill after my birth and was unable to have more children. Sadly she died five years ago and since then I have looked after Papa.'

'Forgive my boldness, but I recall your papa introducing you as Mrs Warner... you have been widowed?'

'That is quite all right, Mr Harcourt. My husband Thomas, a fine young man, was a major in the 3rd Dragoon Guards. He was one of the two soldiers who died after the Battle of Magdala. His wounds were slight but he contracted blood poisoning and by the time he reached home, it was too late to save him. I do not talk about this with Papa now… he loved Thomas as if he was his own son and there is no purpose in upsetting him.'

'My dear young lady, what a sad, sad event… but thankfully you still have your dear papa, who must be a constant comfort to you.'

'Yes, but I do not know for how much longer. You have witnessed his illness, a fit of coughing, he does not know that I have seen the specks of blood in his kerchief and I fear there is something serious.'

'Will he see a doctor?' asked Theo.

'I have not mentioned it – he does not know that I have seen the blood and I would implore you not to mention this to anyone, or that I have told you about Thomas.'

'Of course I will not, but please let me help if I can.'

'Thank you, Mr Harcourt, I trust you with these confidences.'

'Perhaps you would call me Theo?'

'Yes, indeed, and you must call me Jessica, but only when there are the two of us, otherwise Papa might think it presumptuous of me, as might your mama and papa!'

'It shall be our secret!' laughed Theo. Jessica laughed too and for the first time, Theo saw happiness in her face. 'Progress,' he thought.

Gulley Copse was in its spring splendour; wild growing crocuses and daffodils were in profusion. Theo and Jessica walked through the copse, admiring the scenery and enjoying the fresh air. The river was visible along the border of the garden and it flowed gently along, its water crystal clear. 'So unlike the murky streams of Lancashire,' thought Theo. 'Maybe it will not be too difficult to become a southerner after all.'

Theo and Jessica saw Mr Gilman and the Harcourts making their way towards them. Theo told his parents how much he had enjoyed the walk. 'Bit different from Lancashire, I don't doubt!' said Mr Gilman.

'It's so clean and fresh,' Theo replied, 'but of course there is no industry here to make smoke and discolour the houses and to tinge the countryside. The water in the river, too, is the brightest I have seen.'

'Everything has its price,' said Mr Gilman. 'Without the industry there would be no trade and wealth, and without that we would not be able to move forward and make more discoveries that will in turn produce more wealth for this fine country. Yes, the industrial countryside will suffer and look, shall we say, less appealing than the landscape here, but in the south we do not work with our hands, but with our brains, and that is our contribution, so that together we make a formidable force which has made the British Empire as great as it is!'

'You should have been a politician, Mr Gilman,' said Mr Harcourt.

'Goodness, no,' said Mr Gilman. 'I had more important things to do!'

They all laughed and began to stroll back to Berg House.

'Perhaps you would call on us next Thursday?' said Mr Gilman. 'By then I shall be able to obtain the necessary information about Barm House, and arrange a visit.'

'That would be ideal!' said Mr Harcourt. 'We look forward to seeing you then.'

Once they had climbed into their carriage, Mrs Harcourt remarked, 'Mrs Warner seems a charming young lady.'

'Yes, she does indeed,' said Theo, who had decided for now to keep his knowledge about Jessica and her father to himself.

Theo's mother smiled, thinking to herself – as she had often done – that it was time for Theo to settle, marry and have children. He seemed so wild, but at the age of twenty-eight he really should put down some roots and take life a little more seriously. Maybe this was the opportunity; he didn't seem to want to talk about Mrs Warner, and perhaps that was a good sign, she really didn't know. Over the last few years Theo had become very difficult to understand. He was a man of moods and extremes; sometimes she felt she didn't know him at all. He spent so much time with his friends in the militia, drinking, gambling and goodness knows what else. 'I suppose that's just growing up,' she thought, 'and when he has his own family, he will find his true self.'

Barm House

As their carriage followed Mr Gilman's along the shrub-lined driveway to Barm House, the Harcourts had a splendid view of the property, although sadly it was clearly in need of an owner. The vendor, a Mr Owen, had bought the property on impulse and after five years had immigrated to America, leaving the house in the hands of agents who had unsuccessfully tried to sell it. Even at auction, it failed to attract any interest. The agents had not advertised the property after the auction and it was only local people who knew it was still available, or indeed even knew of its existence. The shrubs were overgrown although could be pruned to their correct height and spread by a knowledgeable gardener. Luckily there were few large trees and although there was an air of neglect about the grounds, closer examination revealed that all could quite easily be restored.

The house itself, with a grand entrance hall almost wide enough to drive the carriages through, was also in need of care and attention. It was of solid build and had withstood the emptiness of five years well. It was similar in appearance to Berg House, having been built around the same time in the early nineteenth century, but it was smaller, with grounds of about 20 acres.

Mrs Harcourt drew a quick breath. 'Not quite what you expected, my dear?' enquired her husband.

'It looks as if it needs much work, but let us see it closer before we say anything to Mr Gilman,' she replied.

Both carriages stopped and everyone alighted. Mr Gilman, expecting an adverse reaction from Mrs Harcourt, was quick to open the conversation. 'Berg House looked much the same as this when I bought it, but it is surprising how quickly I transformed it into what you see today, and this once beautiful residence can also be restored to its former glory in very little time. Of course, that will be reflected in the asking price which is most reasonable, and I am sure you can discuss the price with the agents and come to an agreement if you decide to purchase it.'

Berg House had not actually been in such a state, but he was determined that the Harcourts should not be put off Barm House by first appearances.

Mr Harcourt liked the sound of 'discussion with the agents'. Being a canny businessman, he was used to negotiating and rarely paid the asking price for anything he bought. He would enjoy bargaining with the agents if his wife and Theo agreed to go ahead. It also seemed as if they would be getting a bargain and, more importantly, that coveted country seat.

'Shall we all go into the house and have a look around?' said Mr Gilman, taking Jessica on his arm.

Theo thought Jessica looked radiant. It seemed as if a ray of sunshine had descended on her, brightening her appearance. She was wearing a suit in a pale green colour. The jacket had the fashionable three-quarter length sleeves of the day, under which she wore a pure white blouse. The skirt was not hooped, allowing easy movement. Since Thomas's death, Jessica had mainly dressed in darker colours, but now she felt it was the time to bring out her lighter clothes. Her father was always most generous with her allowance and she was able to buy the latest fashions. Hoops and tight corseting were becoming less popular, unless the occasion was formal, and Jessica was glad of the freedom it allowed her. She glanced at Theo and they smiled; a secret smile that was not seen by the others.

They walked into the large entrance hall. The floor was laid with stone tiles from a local quarry works, very popular at the time. In spite of the leaves which had accumulated in the corners, the neat tiling added a geometric quality and accentuated the size of the hall. A glazed door led into the reception hall, the floor of which was also made of geometric design quarry tiles. In the hall was a mahogany staircase leading to the first floor landing. They moved into the drawing room off the entrance hall and admired the attractive stone fireplace. One side led out into an orangery; the other on to a secluded garden.

'An orangery!' said Jessica. 'How delightful!'

Mr Gilman looked pleased. His daughter, he thought, would influence the Harcourts by her remarks, and this was a good start.

The Harcourts and Theo looked a little embarrassed, and said nothing but nodded as in assent. The truth was that they didn't know what an orangery was, or what it was for. Not wanting to appear unintelligent, they kept quiet.

Mr Gilman sensed this and said laughingly, 'Silly name that, orangery, makes one think that you grow oranges in it! Mind you, that was the original use, lemons as well, so I am told.'

Jessica, guessing that her contribution would be appreciated, said, 'I think orangeries are wonderful! You can grow wonderful plants and flowers as well as fruit, and, oh look, there's a stove, how marvellous! All-year-round warmth. I love the orangery at Berg House, I can sit there on the coolest days and feel as if I am on a tropical island.'

An orangery attached to a property was a sign of wealth and status; something that Mr Gilman knew would appeal to the Harcourts.

'I imagine one would need a very experienced gardener to look after such a building and its plants,' said Mr Harcourt.

'Yes, of course,' said Mr Gilman. 'There are several

15

gardeners locally quite capable of such horticulture – they can easily be contacted through their employers. Most of them tend more than one orangery. Should you go ahead and buy Barm House, I could put you in touch with a suitable person.'

Mr Gilman felt that he had made his point about the status brought by having such an extension to the property and employing a special horticulturalist. At least, he hoped that he had.

Mrs Harcourt looked thoughtful and said, 'I am beginning to grow more fond of this property – shall we continue our inspection?'

Mr Gilman quietly breathed a sigh of relief. 'So far, so good.'

'Shall we move on into the sitting room and dining room?' he said. 'I understand there is a magnificent fireplace in the sitting room.'

Mr Gilman suggested they stopped for a while in the sitting room and admired the view of the gardens to the front of the house.

Theo had been unable to keep his eyes off Jessica from the moment they had met at Barm House. She looked almost like a painting. 'I must have her,' he thought.

Jessica looked out across the gardens; she sensed that Theo was looking at her although she didn't return his gaze. It was as if a current was passing between them, creating sparks that were irresistible. She felt warm, strangely excited, as if something was going to happen, but she didn't know what. It was a feeling she had felt before, some years ago.

Along a corridor were the kitchens, two large rooms with remnants of habitation. Some pans still hung from hooks above the fireplace and although in need of cleaning, everything was in good condition. Mr Owen had not entertained much and the kitchens were underused, as Mrs Harcourt noticed. 'Not too much needs doing in here, apart from a good cleaning,' she said.

Mr Gilman breathed another sigh of relief. 'Still going well,' he thought.

Back into the drawing room, Theo saw another glazed door and asked where it led.

'That leads to a secluded garden,' said Mr Gilman.

'Oh, how entrancing!' said Mrs Harcourt. 'Do let us have a look.'

Mr Gilman opened the door on to an overgrown but perfectly formed small garden. It was hedged all round and divided into three small 'rooms'. In each room was a feature; one had a statue, one a specimen tree and the other, a pond with a fountain. There was no water in the pond but an imaginative eye could see how it would look.

'I can well see the water spraying gently out from that fountain,' said Mrs Harcourt. 'This is... oh dear, I just can't think of the word to describe it.'

'How about "divine"?' asked Jessica.

'I think that describes it perfectly,' said Theo, thinking that 'divine' also described the way Jessica looked today.

'What is upstairs?' asked Mr Harcourt.

'Let's find out, shall we?' replied Mr Gilman, leading them back towards the staircase. 'There should be a library, all country seats must have a library and I think we will find it off this landing.'

And so they did. A long room, one that could also be used for dining – particularly with 'special' guests, as Mr Gilman pointed out.

Although the Harcourts were not quite sure who 'special guests' would be, they nodded in agreement.

There were six large bedrooms, all of which had imposing fireplaces. 'I think you will find this perfectly adequate for your needs,' said Mr Gilman. 'It is also a property of some standing in the county.'

Jessica sensed that her father was almost anxious in his efforts to encourage the Harcourts to take an interest in Barm

House, although she wasn't sure why.

'Well, I am most impressed with this property!' said Theo. 'In spite of the work that needs to be done, it has character, and I think we should talk to the agents without delay, Father.'

'Good,' said Mr Harcourt, relieved that his son was so positive, but slightly puzzled as Theo usually let others make the decisions and rarely took the initiative. 'Never mind,' he thought, 'whatever the reason, the result is what I've been seeking.'

Mrs Harcourt smiled. 'That's the quickest business decision we have ever made, my dear, but you know it all depends on the price.'

'You need not be concerned about that, my dear, you know you can rely on me to get the best deal.'

'Yes,' said Mrs Harcourt, hoping that all would end happily. She had a feeling there was something not quite right, but she didn't know what it was.

'Well, I think we should all go back to Berg House, I warned Mrs K that we might be in for tea! Would you like to sample more of her delicious baking?'

'We would be delighted to accept your kind offer. You have been so generous with your time today, we are most grateful,' smiled Mrs Harcourt.

It was late afternoon when they all arrived back at Berg House; the butler greeted them and they all proceeded to the drawing room, where Mr Gilman rang for Mrs K.

Mrs K had indeed been busy baking. She knew something important was going on, it seemed more than the usual entertaining – a business deal perhaps.

'I think if we buy Barm House we shall steal Mrs K!' laughed Mr Harcourt.

'You would have to steal her because she certainly isn't for sale,' laughed Mr Gilman, 'but I am sure Mrs K knows some good cooks who would suit you well at Barm House.'

Mrs K had left the room slowly and heard the last remark. 'So that's what it is all about,' she thought. 'Fancy buying that old dump! Still, some people have more money than sense.'

'This is a large house, Mr Gilman,' said Mr Harcourt. 'How many rooms do you have?'

'Just a few more bedrooms than Barm House,' said Mr Gilman, 'although we don't use them, so really they are wasted. Barm House is a much more sensible size.'

'I think I saw a billiard room,' asked Theo.

'Yes, indeed, it is a very popular game nowadays. Have you played, Mr Harcourt?'

'Yes,' said Theo. 'I play the game with my friends in the militia, we have a club we regularly go to.'

Mr Harcourt deliberately steered the subject away from billiards. 'I have a feeling my wife would like to see your orangery, wouldn't you my dear?' His wife understood the look he gave her as he said this. Theo did go to the militia club regularly, and there was a billiards room, but Theo spent most of his time there gambling and drinking and Mr Harcourt had no wish to bring that subject into the open.

'I would love to see it!' said Mrs Harcourt, rising from her chair. 'Which way?'

Mr Gilman took her arm and led her to the large orangery, over 30 feet long and 20 feet in width.

'Oh!' Mrs Harcourt drew in a breath. 'My word, it is vast, and such lovely plants, your gardener must be excellent.'

'Yes, he is,' said Mr Gilman, 'and if you buy Barm House I am sure the orangery can in time look like this, with the help of such an experienced man.'

Mr Gilman had realised that the orangery had become very important to the Harcourts, as he had intended, and he was taking every opportunity to stress its value as part of a house and the effect it would have on the owner's status. It seemed his plan was working well.

19

Jessica stood behind them, quietly, listening. 'Papa seems determined that the Harcourts shall buy Barm House,' she thought. 'But I wonder why?'

Discussions and deals

'What do you think, my dear?' said Mr Harcourt.

'I think we should see the agents and make an offer – we will be in a good position to pay a price we want to pay if you can arrange to draw up a list of what needs to be done and the cost,' replied his wife.

'Good, I will find out what the previous price and the auction price were. I know it was several years ago but it will give us a starting point for bargaining. What do you think, Theo?'

'Whatever you say, Father. I think the property has potential and we are the people to change it from what it is to an imposing country seat!'

Mr and Mrs Harcourt were surprised by Theo's response; normally he showed little interest in anything other than his bachelor pursuits. Maybe it was a sign of a more responsible attitude.

'I shall speak again with Mr Gilman, tell him of our intentions and arrange to meet the agents as soon as possible,' said Mr Harcourt.

Mr Gilman took a deep breath, a breath of relief. The Harcourts wanted to buy Barm House. 'That will protect my dear Jessica,' he thought.

He coughed and quickly put his kerchief to his face; he had taken to using coloured cloths so that the specks of blood were not obvious. Mrs K must know, the maid who did the washing would have noticed and mentioned it. Mrs K had never said anything but sometimes Mr Gilman caught her looking at him as if she wanted to say something, but knew she must keep her knowledge to herself. She was a loyal servant and Mr Gilman rewarded her well. She earned more than most cooks because Mr Gilman had given her extra responsibilities. He could have taken on a housekeeper but he knew that would be unthinkable for Mrs K and he didn't want to lose her. Jessica he must protect at all costs; she had already suffered so much through losing her dear Thomas and her mama. 'If only, if only,' thought Mr Gilman. Now he must make sure Berg House would remain hers when he was no longer there. At times, he wished they had never met the Harcourts that day in Lebritan. 'But our destinies are already determined,' he mused, 'and what will be, will be.'

Mr Gilman had contacted the land agents. Mr Stearman was calling this afternoon to meet the Harcourts and discuss the price of Barm House. Mr Gilman had suggested to Mr Stearman that he started at a higher price than the property was worth so that he could be 'persuaded' to reduce it and allow the Harcourts to feel they had not only had a successful deal, but had got the better of a southerner. Mr Stearman had understood this; he had been an agent for many years and knew all the intricacies of business. As long as he was paid what he wanted, that would be all right.

'Congratulations, Mr Harcourt!' said Mr Stearman to Theo, shaking him by the hand. 'Here are the deeds of Barm House, of which you are now the owner.'

The deal had gone through and Mr Stearman had attended to all the necessary paperwork. He was pleased, very pleased. Mr Harcourt had paid more than he thought the property would ever realise, and Mr Harcourt was certain he had 'beaten him down', which of course Mr Stearman had allowed him to think. All in all, everybody was happy. Almost everybody.

21

Mr Gilman, who had hosted the meeting with Mr Stearman at Berg House, also congratulated the Harcourts with a handshake.

He addressed Theo. 'So now we will be neighbours, Mr Harcourt?'

'Yes, I intend to stay at Barm House and supervise the renovation and decoration work. Part of Barm House is, I understand, already habitable, and it will be convenient for me to be at the property to ensure all goes smoothly. I have left Mr Stearman in charge of hiring staff for the renovation and I shall be hearing from him when work starts so that I can return here.'

'I hope you will be comfortable there with such commotion going on, Mr Harcourt,' said Jessica. 'Perhaps you will find some time to call on us occasionally, and let us know of the progress?'

'Yes, of course Mrs Warner,' said Theo.

Their eyes met, briefly; a look of understanding flickered between them.

'Well, that is wonderful!' said Mrs Harcourt. 'Now we must make plans to return to Lancashire.'

Mr Harcourt looked somewhat bemused. He was seeing a new Theo, someone who actually wanted to work, or at least do something useful. Whatever the reason, and he suspected what that reason was, he hoped it would last and that Theo would now become a responsible person.

Mr Gilman waved them farewell. 'My dear Jessica and Berg House should be safe now,' he thought.

It was late afternoon and the shadows covered the lawns, spring flowers were dying leaving a floral 'gap'; everywhere looked as if it was waiting for summer to emerge.

Jessica, before retiring, recorded the past week's events, as she always did. She was not one for writing wordy diaries, just matters that were important to her. She put her diary into the box her father had given her, his initials WJG were on it in gold leaf. A business friend in Ceylon gave the satinwood box to her father; her father had given it to Jessica. It was one of her treasures.

2

Work at Barm House progressed well. There were no structural problems and once the rubbish had been cleared it was mainly a case of repairing, reglazing and preparing the house for decoration.

Theo had taken residence in part of the house and enjoyed walking around giving orders, although it was doubtful if any of the workers took much notice. They were courteous but it was clear they regarded him with some disdain.

'He's trade, like us,' said the foreman. 'Struts about as if he's gentry, never will be.'

'Why's that?' said one of his workers, a young apprentice just fourteen years of age.

'You have to be born gentry, that's why,' said the foreman. 'Dressing up in fancy clothes and trying to talk posh doesn't change your birth.'

'Oh,' said the apprentice, 'so I can never be gentry?'

'No, you can't, and be glad of it.'

'Why should I be glad when they have more money than I have, nice big houses and ladies in lovely dresses?'

'That may be, but they get bored because they have nothing to do.'

'Well, I wouldn't mind having nothing to do.'

'Yes, you would, after a few weeks of doing nothing you would be bored! Now come on, get on with your work, we have another job after this one, over at Lebritan.'

'What's that, then?'

'There's to be a new branch railway line and we have a station to build.'

'That's good, so we certainly won't be bored for quite a while!'

Foreman and apprentice worked industriously, as always taking pride in their work. Little wonder the railway contract had been awarded to their company.

Mr Gilman sat in the garden looking towards the copses and river. Now in full leaf, the trees were a mass of different hues of green. The garden sloped gently towards the river, giving a wonderful vista of the copses on each side.

The sun warmed him, he felt content. He knew that work at Barm House would soon be finished, Theo had kept him and Jessica informed as promised.

A carriage approached Berg House; it was Theo's, making his report on progress as usual. He called to Jessica that Theo had arrived. She appeared several minutes later, not in a hurry to greet Theo. 'Strange,' he thought, 'they seem almost disinterested in each other; maybe Jessica has lost interest in Theo and Barm House.' He hoped that was the case.

'How goes the work?' asked Mr Gilman.

'Very well,' replied Theo. 'Another two months and I think all will be complete. I hope so, I would like it finished before winter.'

'That's grand,' said Mr Gilman. 'Let's have coffee outside today, shall we? You can tell us more then.'

They sat around the table on the lawn. Mrs K brought out the coffee and a plate of her cakes.

'Ah, Mrs K, thank you,' said Mr Gilman, and turning towards Theo said, 'Now what are your plans for the interior of Barm House?'

'Well, I have some patterns for the floor and wall coverings, there are some very colourful new designs available now.'

Jessica gazed at Theo; he wore a fashionable lounge suit in olive green, the daywear that was gradually replacing the more formal frock coat for gentlemen. His hat was a low-crowned bowler. He was tall and this suited him well.

'What designs in particular do you have in mind for Barm House, Mr Harcourt?' asked Jessica.

'I have been reading about Mr Morris and his textile designs, he has a new wallpaper design called "Fruit" which I find interesting. Also there are some similarly patterned floor rugs, maybe I shall look at those.'

'You mean Mr William Morris?' said Mr Gilman.

'Yes', said Theo. 'Have you heard of him?'

'But yes, I understand he has some very innovative designs. He is friendly with Rossetti, they have a summer retreat not far from here, I believe.'

'What do you think of his designs, Mrs Warner?' asked Theo.

'They are very bold, I prefer lighter, plainer designs, but I am sure that Mr Morris's work will be popular for many years to come.'

'I shall call again in two weeks' time, if that is convenient, Mr Gilman. By then there should be more to report,' said Theo.

'Thank you, that is most considerate of you.'

'I have much to thank you for Mr Gilman, without you I wouldn't have found Barm House, and certainly not at the price for which my father was able to buy it. I am indebted to you.'

Theo raised his hat to Mr Gilman and Jessica and made his way to his carriage.

'All goes well!' thought Theo. 'Mr Gilman has no idea what is happening, I think he believes that Jessica and I have no interest in each other.'

*

Jessica got up. 'I must talk with Mrs K about the lunch and dinner,' she said, 'and then I have some letters to write.'

'Very well, my dear,' said her father, glad that she was so settled. She had taken the place of Em so well and the household ran smoothly. 'I do hope she finds happiness when I am gone,' he thought. 'She shouldn't be alone.'

Jessica went to discuss the day's menus in the kitchen, where Mrs K was already busy with preparation.

She was very fond of Mrs K. When dear Mama died, Mrs K had been a tower of strength to her and Papa and she regarded her as an aunt rather than a servant. Servant was never a word she liked; both she and Papa thought of their staff as part of their family, such that was left of it.

Jessica went to her room; soon Theo would come to her. Nowadays Mr Gilman took a long nap after lunch and this left Jessica free to do as she wished without his knowledge. She had been meeting Theo secretly twice a week for some time now. He left his carriage along the lane and walked along the drive so as not to be seen or heard.

Jessica's heart started to race at the thought of Theo; her thoughts were constantly with him, she had become a good actress in not showing these emotions. When he touched her, caressed her, she felt a tingling running through her body and a feeling of longing.

Last time he had visited her, they had stopped talking and suddenly Theo had started caressing her breasts, then her thighs... the sensation was unbelievably wonderful. She felt a gentle throbbing inside her and as Theo pressed his body closer to hers she felt that she would melt. He had carefully taken off her undergarments and slowly and gently entered her. His rhythmic movements made the throbbing more intense and then she felt as if there was an explosion, Theo too gave a gasp and then both fell quiet.

She had little experience of men, there had only been Thomas before Theo and their marriage had been cut short. Thomas had loved her but he hadn't the gentleness of Theo. With Theo she felt like a real woman – she was fulfilled.

There was a gentle tap on the door; Jessica quickly let him in.

'You are becoming an excellent actress my dear,' said Theo.

'Yes, I am!' laughed Jessica.

'You are sure your papa and the servants have no idea of our meetings?'

'Absolutely none at all,' said Jessica. 'We are safe.'

Theo held her close, kissed her, then stood back. 'I think I am in love with you, my dear Jessica,' he said.

'Oh Theo, I never thought I could love again, but I feel the same.'

'That is wonderful, my darling.'

Theo embraced Jessica again and then moved her towards her bed. He laid her down gently and undressed her. She loved him doing this, and she knew the delights to come.

This time it was different. Jessica felt special somehow; the throbbing was more intense and after she reached the climax the throbbing continued. Usually it subsided but this time it grew faster; she knew she would have another climax, she knew she wanted another one.

'More, more!' she said.

Theo could feel her pulsating muscles around him, squeezing him; he again became hard, very hard, and moved inside her with a passion he had not felt before. Jessica groaned with delight enjoying the sensations and then they both felt as if they had fused in an explosion of ecstasy.

They lay quietly on the bed, Theo put out his hand and Jessica held it, there was nothing to say, nothing could add to that moment. Jessica felt as if something wonderful had happened.

*

The days passed. It was a warm, balmy summer.

Gradually the leaves turned from their verdant green to the gold, brown and red of autumn.

Mr Gilman felt at ease with the world. Barm House was complete and as far as he was concerned, that was the last they would see of Theo. Jessica appeared to take little interest in him and was attending to matters at Berg House as usual. There was there a different air about her, he wasn't sure what. 'If only Em were here,' he thought, 'she needs a woman's company.' There were few women of Jessica's age in the area, and most were young women with families whose husbands worked on the estates, living in Morton Terrace, a row of cottages in East Leah. There was a small school there, which their children attended.

'But,' he thought, 'Jessica seems content with her life; she has been a good daughter and will be well rewarded when I am no longer alive.'

He coughed suddenly and quickly put his kerchief to his face. The specks of blood were becoming more frequent and he also felt discomfort in his chest. He knew it was not a passing ailment and guessed it was more serious. There was little doctors could do for such an illness; it would have to take its course. How much longer that would be he did not know, but he knew, deep down, that he was unlikely to see another summer at Berg House.

They dined together, his appetite was not as good as it used to be – 'as you get older, so the stomach gets smaller,' he told Jessica and Mrs K, who showed concern at the small amounts he ate.

Jessica had a healthy appetite; her father thought it seemed to be increasing. She seemed to be filling out. He was pleased, as she had lost some considerable weight when Thomas died and it was a long time before she regained her appetite.

It had been a long, warm summer. Mr Gilman spent many days

sitting in the garden, he watched the leaves gradually turn to their autumnal colours, but still it was warm. His cough seemed less frequent, which he put down to the mild weather.

'Jessica looks happy,' he thought, 'but I do wish she would mix more. However if she is happy how she is, then so am I. I hope that I live long enough to see her married again.'

Jessica and Theo had continued to meet, sometimes as much as three times a week.

Jessica knew that one day this would have to cease. It was important that she married again for the future of Berg House, but Theo was not eligible for her. She could only marry within her social class, Theo was trade and therefore marriage between them was not possible. But, she was enjoying the thrill and the physical pleasure of it and would continue to do so until there was a suitor. Without her mother, it was difficult to find an eligible bachelor and she would have to rely on her friends in the county. She hoped that this would happen while her dear papa was alive; he seemed better lately. Maybe her worries were unfounded.

The days were getting shorter. It was too cool for Mr Gilman to sit outside and he spent most of his days indoors, taking a nap after meals. His cough had returned and at times was violent. He felt very tired after an attack of coughing and some days did not rise until late in the morning.

Jessica became concerned and asked her father if she could call for the doctor. Mr Gilman this time agreed; he was getting weaker and didn't have the strength to argue any more.

The doctor gave him a thorough examination. 'You need a tonic, Mr Gilman,' he said. 'Take this each morning.' He handed Jessica the bottle.

The doctor made his farewell to Mr Gilman and he and Jessica walked down the stairs into the entrance hall.

'Tell me the truth, Doctor,' said Jessica. 'I know it is serious, I have seen the blood in his kerchief when he coughs.'

'Yes, it is serious, and I am sorry but there is nothing I can do. Your father has consumption and it is only a matter of time. Make him comfortable, keep him warm, that is all I can advise.'

'Thank you, Doctor,' whispered Jessica.

'I know Mrs Gilman died some years ago – do you have anyone here to help, a female friend perhaps?' asked the doctor.

'Yes, Mrs K our cook will help, she is as an aunt to me since Mama died.'

'That's good,' said the doctor sympathetically. 'Please call me if Mr Gilman deteriorates. I will come straightaway.'

Jessica stood at the entrance and watched the doctor drive away. She felt sad, very sad. She also felt strange. She wasn't sure what it was, perhaps worry about Papa.

'Are you all right, my darling?' asked Theo. 'You look pale.'

Theo was making one of his calls; he and Jessica had made love and were sitting gazing on to the garden.

Jessica told Theo about her father.

'Oh, I'm so sorry,' said Theo. 'It is little wonder you look pale. Is there anything I can do to help?'

'No, what will be, will be, I just hope that Papa doesn't suffer.'

'I am sure he won't.'

Theo was not really that concerned about Mr Gilman. In fact, his death would clear the way for Theo's plans. He was thinking about his next move; with no opposition from Mr Gilman he could marry Jessica and then Berg House would be his. A woman became the property of her husband on marriage, as did all her assets. But now was not the time – he must be patient.

'Until next week, then, my darling,' he said.

Jessica kissed him goodbye, then returned to her window seat. She still felt a little strange.

Winter 1869

The mourners filed out of the church at East Leah, led by Jessica. Mrs K was by her side at Jessica's request; both women walked slowly and respectfully, each glad of the other's support. Theo and his parents followed some way back. Mr and Mrs Harcourt had been most upset to hear of Mr Gilman's death and insisted on making the journey for the funeral. Barm House was now complete, so they were staying with Theo.

The wake was a small gathering; Jessica dutifully spoke with the mourners. Theo and his parents stood in a corner of the drawing room, quietly talking. Mrs K, as always, was there, knowing what to do and what to say, and what not to say. 'She is my rock,' thought Jessica.

The Harcourts approached Jessica; they had already expressed their sadness at her father's death. They had respected Mr Gilman and although they were acquaintances rather than friends, were still moved by his demise.

'Thank goodness you have Mrs K, my dear,' said Mrs Harcourt to Jessica.

'Yes, she is like a mother to me.'

Mrs Harcourt wanted so much to know what Jessica's plans for the future were, but now was too early to ask.

Sensing this, Jessica said, 'There is much to do here at Berg House. I must discuss this with Mrs K and the staff so that we can make plans for the future.'

'Oh please, do let us know if we can assist,' said Mr Harcourt. 'I know we are far away but Theo I am sure will be pleased to act on our behalf.'

Theo looked at Jessica, interested to see her reaction.

Jessica smiled and thanked Mr Harcourt.

'You look tired, my dear,' said Mrs Harcourt. 'It must have been such a wearying time for you, you must take plenty of rest.'

'Yes, thank you,' said Jessica.

She moved away from them and took Mrs K's arm.

'I am very tired – can we bring this to a close without appearing discourteous?'

'Yes, Miss Jessica, leave it to me.'

Mrs K went quietly but purposefully around the room and gradually the mourners left, leaving her and Jessica alone.

'Thank you, I think I will lie down for a while.'

Jessica left and went to her room. Before she went to lie down she took out her diary and, as usual, made some notes. At the end she wrote, 'The second month and still no sign.' She put the diary back into her satinwood box, lay on the bed and fell asleep.

Spring 1870

'You are tense, my darling,' said Theo. 'Are you unwell?'

'No, not unwell,' said Jessica, and then hesitatingly she told Theo that she was expecting his child.

'Well, that is wonderful!' said Theo. 'Now we shall be married as soon as possible.'

'No!' said Jessica, quite firmly.

'No?' questioned Theo. 'Why not? You have told me that you love me, you carry my child, why should we not marry?'

'Oh Theo, do you not know the rules? I can never marry you, we are not the same.'

'What do you mean, not the same?'

'You know what I mean, Theo.'

'No, I do not, what I do know is that we love each other and that surely is "the same"?'

'Have you learned nothing since you have lived here?' asked Jessica. 'I must marry within my society, I cannot marry into trade.'

Theo was stunned into silence for a few moments.

'You love me, you carry my child but I am not good enough for you?'

'If that's how you want to put it,' said Jessica.

'And just what do you intend to do, find some lord or baronet that will accept you and a child conceived out of wedlock?'

'Theo, I cannot and will not marry you. My dear papa would never have allowed such a marriage.'

Theo realised that his plans for owning Berg House were slipping away, but what was he to do?

'I shall go away soon and stay with some friends on the east coast. I shall have the baby and then return here. We cannot see each other again. On no account must anyone ever know that you are the baby's father.'

Theo was becoming angry, but he knew that anger would not change Jessica's way of thinking. Maybe he should try another approach.

He put his arms around her. 'My dearest darling, I do understand, but I can't live without you, we can't end our wonderful love that we have both so enjoyed.'

'Yes, we can, and we must.'

'But how will you explain the baby?'

'I have some cousins in the east. I shall say it is their child who was orphaned after they were killed in an accident. They don't come here so no one will know that it is not the truth.'

'And you will bring up our baby alone?'

'I hope not, I shall find a husband from within the county. There are many who would be pleased to have Berg House as their seat.'

'As indeed would I,' thought Theo.

'Please go now Theo, I am tired.'

Theo took a deep breath and walked away. 'This cannot happen,' he thought. 'If she won't have me, I will make sure I have Berg House.'

Summer and Autumn 1870

'It may be summer but it is certainly cooler here than in East Leah in the spring,' thought Jessica. 'The wind always seems to be easterly, no wonder the locals wear thicker clothes than we do at home.'

Luckily for Jessica, the seaside town of Aldwell on the east coast had a small business that made stylish knitwear, most of it being sold in London, and so she was able to add to her wardrobe not only to keep warm, but also to keep fashionable.

She was staying with some old friends of her papa, Mr and Mrs Ross, who had retired to Aldwell some years ago. Mr Ross had worked with Mr Gilman as one of his chief tea tasters and he and his wife had always been very fond of young Jessica. When she had written to them and told them of her predicament they were very willing to help. Mr Gilman had been a business colleague and a respected friend; they had attended his funeral and suggested then that Jessica might stay with them, not knowing how quickly she would accept this offer. They welcomed her with great warmth and promised that they would never tell a soul about her baby's parentage. Together they would invent a story about cousins who had been killed in a tragic accident, leaving their baby without parents. This in time would satisfy Jessica's county acquaintances and any prospective suitor. Her secret was safe with them.

Jessica liked Aldwell; it was a small, rather quaint fishing town where everybody seemed to know everybody else.

Mr and Mrs Ross had a house on the cliff overlooking the sea; the view was wonderful. Mr Ross had told her about the sea battle against the Dutch some 200 years earlier when there was massive loss of life on both sides. Sadly, it ended in stalemate. 'All those lives lost for nothing,' thought Jessica. He said that the battle would have been clearly visible from the house they now lived in.

Jessica was very fond of Mr and Mrs Ross and they spent many hours talking and walking. Mr Ross was very interested in local history; he was able to show Jessica all the interesting features of this small town.

Mrs Ross used to help at the town's school, and Alice, one of the young girls at the school, would sometimes call in on a Sunday after church. Alice was a quiet girl and Mrs Ross had encouraged her, and all the other girls, to read as much as they could. Alice's family could not always afford books so Mrs Ross would lend her theirs. Alice's father was one of the many Aldwell fishermen. When the catches were good there was plenty of money, but when the catches were low there was only money for the essentials. 'I expect she will eventually marry a fisherman,' thought Mrs Ross; there was little choice for the young girls in the town as fishing was the only living for men. Most of the girls went to work in the knitwear business; it was better pay and conditions than working in service and they were taught a trade. There were two very big houses in Aldwell where the owners employed several servants, including lady's maids, but their owners also had London homes and all their servants came from the city. No chance of a local girl getting a job in one of those houses.

Jessica too liked Alice and used to read to her. Alice was told that Jessica was a cousin and she never asked any questions, she was pleased to have found a new friend.

The weeks passed and Jessica knew her time was very near. It had been arranged to have her baby at Mr and Mrs Ross's home; giving birth in hospital was not for women of Jessica's social standing. Mrs Ross knew well how to assist at a birth and had prepared their spare room for the event.

Jessica had not thought much about Theo during her stay in Aldwell. She knew she would never see him again and now she would have the baby to care for. The 'orphaned child' story had been learned and well rehearsed; nothing could go wrong.

'Just once more, my dear,' said Mrs Ross.
    'Oh!' screamed Jessica. 'I can't!'
    'Yes, you can, you are nearly there – just one more push!'
    Jessica gave what seemed to her like a body-splitting push and then after a few moments, she heard the sound. A cry.
    'You have a lovely son, my dear,' said Mrs Ross.
    Jessica, exhausted, asked for the child and held him close to her. He had wisps of golden hair and a rather long face.
    'He's a handsome fellow,' said Mrs Ross. 'What will you call him?'
    'I thought "Culbert",' said Jessica.
    'That's an unusual name, is it in your family?'
    'Not exactly… but it is the name of a friend of Papa's. He always spoke warmly of him, so that shall be my son's name.'
    'Very well, my dear, we shall have to have him registered. Shall he have your surname?'
    'Yes, he shall be Culbert Warner,' said Jessica, who, completely exhausted, fell asleep.
    Mrs Ross removed Culbert from her arms and placed him in the crib, then left the room as Jessica slept quietly and peacefully.

In the weeks that followed, Jessica and her baby son became a familiar sight walking along the Aldwell promenade. There were other young mothers with their children and Jessica enjoyed their company. No one asked questions, they just accepted her and her baby; there was a great bond between new mothers, irrespective of class, in this part of England.
    A long track led to the harbour where the fishermen brought in their catches and this was one of Jessica's favourite walks. The fishermen always raised their caps and spoke to her. She

noticed that Alice was there, chatting with them, in particular with a young lad who helped his father unload the catch. It wasn't heavy work; they mainly caught herring, shrimps and small fish they called dabs, all easy for a young lad to handle. The fishermen were always keen to talk about their catches; they were hard working men, their skin weathered by many days at sea.

'Hello, Alice.'

'Hello, Mrs Warner.'

'Have your friends caught a lot of fish today?'

'Yes, Mrs Warner, come and have a look!'

Jessica wheeled her pram over to where Alice and the young lad were pulling baskets along.

'This is my friend, Ben,' said Alice.

'Ben, this is Mrs Warner – she's teaching me reading.'

Ben stood up and looked towards Jessica. He was a tall lad and like most of the youngsters in Aldwell, lean and muscular, even at his age. His skin was already taking on the swarthy look of a fisherman.

'I'm very pleased to meet you, Ben.'

Ben looked down shyly.

'Come on Ben,' said Alice, 'Mrs Warner is a nice lady, there's no need to be shy.'

Ben smiled. 'I'm very pleased to meet you, Ma'am,' he said.

Jessica smiled and said, 'I'll see you on Sunday afternoon, Alice – you can bring Ben if you like.'

'Oh, thank you, Mrs Warner.'

Ben looked as if he wasn't sure about this as he carried on unloading the baskets of shrimps.

Jessica walked back along the harbour path. On the way she passed a long cottage with a large garden; this was the home of Mr and Mrs Ross's son and daughter-in-law. Jessica had been introduced to them recently. Mr Ross was away on business often and he and his wife travelled extensively, so they were not often resident in Aldwell.

Jessica knew she should soon return to Berg House, where Mrs K and the other staff had been looking after the house awaiting Jessica's return. Jessica had confided in Mrs K about the baby, sure that her secret would be safe with her. She also knew that she wouldn't have fooled Mrs K with the cousin story; Mrs K was far too canny for that.

Jessica thought that Aldwell was so tranquil she could stay forever, but knew that her duty lay at Berg House and the longer she stayed, the more difficult it would be to return.

She couldn't help but wonder whether Theo was still there. She couldn't ask anyone, as it would arouse suspicions. By now her feelings towards Theo were mixed; she had loved him, or had she? Maybe it was just passion, after all she was young and had all the feelings young women have. Months away from him had not caused her distress so it must just have been natural emotions, which would have happened whoever it had been. Perhaps she was even slightly afraid of Theo now – but why should she be, what could he do?

'I think the time has come for me to return to Berg House,' said Jessica to Mrs Ross.

'Yes, my dear, I suppose you're right. We have so loved you and little Culbert being here... but I know you must go back.'

Jessica was pleased Mrs Ross had said this; it strengthened her resolve.

'I shall take the Aldwell train to Haletown. There I can board the train to London and then on to East Leah.'

Since Jessica arrived a new line had been opened connecting Aldwell to Haletown, which meant that there was no need to travel ten miles on the bumpy road for the last part of the journey. It was a pleasant journey and travelled through the marshy countryside, crossing the river and then on to

Haletown, passing farms and wooded areas. Rail travel was becoming more popular and certainly reduced travelling times. Without these trains, Jessica's journey would have taken several days instead of just one.

Mr and Mrs Ross stood on the station platform at Aldwell, waving goodbye to Jessica and Culbert.

'Maybe one day we will see Jessica again,' said Mrs Ross, sadly.

'I do hope so,' said Mr Ross, 'and also young Culbert – it will be interesting to see what sort of chap he becomes.'

'I hope his father won't be difficult,' said Mrs Ross.

'Why should he be? He must learn respect for young ladies such as Jessica. There was never a possibility of marriage between them, he must have known that.'

'Apparently not,' said Mrs Ross. 'I think we may hear more about this business.'

Back home, Mr Ross carefully noted in his 'train diary' the time of the train on which Jessica and Culbert had left Aldwell.

'Why are you doing that?' asked his wife.

'It's just an interest. I think that one day, people will want to know who went where and when on trains – maybe someone will find this useful. I shall keep a record of all the journeys we make and all people we meet and say farewell to.'

His wife laughed, but thought that he could indeed be right; one never knows what people will find useful in years to come.

Berg House, 1871

'Oh, he's a little darling,' said Mrs K, fussing around Culbert. 'Such lovely fair curly hair, he will be a handsome one when he grows up, that's for sure!'

'Yes, I'm sure he will,' said Jessica placing him in the crib.

'Now, you must expect some expressions of condolences

from the staff, I have told them that your cousins died in the Newark rail crash. It was in all the papers, I showed it to them.'

'Thank you Mrs K, you are wonderful. How lucky I am to have you!'

Jessica sat in her room. It was late evening as she completed her diary notes for the day and put the book in her satinwood box.

She was exhausted; it had been a long, long day but now she was back at Berg House and life must return to normality. She got into bed and fell asleep almost immediately.

The weeks passed. Culbert grew quickly; he was a healthy baby. Jessica took him out each day walking around East Leah. The story of her cousins' accident had soon spread and the local people praised her for taking on a young child. As time went by, there was no hint of anyone believing anything other than the tale that they had been told. Jessica felt safe.

It was the autumn. Culbert was now one year old; he was a big baby and tall for his age. All the staff loved him and Mrs K had been both delighted and honoured when she was asked to be one of his godparents. It was very unusual for a member of staff to have such a role, but the circumstances were unusual and Jessica only wanted what was best for Culbert. Jessica had also asked Mr and Mrs Ross to be godparents; she had chosen those who knew Culbert's parentage, as a safeguard.

It was the season of thunderstorms, loud spectacular thunderstorms. In this part of England a storm became 'trapped' between the hills and seemed to go on forever. Jessica liked storms; her papa had taught her to have no fear of them and had taken her outside during storms to watch. She still liked to do this, and thought it sensible to bring up Culbert in a similar way.

It was very loud this evening. No rain at present, just the huge flashes of light and crashes of thunder. Jessica stood in the garden; Culbert was in his pram with his eyes open wide.

Gradually the noise lessened, the flashes were less frequent. Jessica heard a noise. A carriage was approaching along the drive.

A man in a tall hat and dark clothes alighted. Jessica couldn't see too well; the light was fading rapidly.

'Hello Jessica, how are you, and how is my son?'

Jessica froze.

The man stood in front of her. He smiled and looked at Culbert.

'My, you have a fine boy – or should I say *we* have a fine boy?'

'Theo, what are you doing here?' Jessica trembled as she spoke, which did not go unnoticed by Theo.

'I have come to see my son of course, why should I not?'

'But you know what we agreed!'

'Agreed? I agreed nothing – you told me we could not continue our relationship and that no one must know I am the father of your baby. Telling me is one thing; my agreement to it is another. I repeat, I agreed to nothing.'

Jessica couldn't believe this was happening, she didn't know what to say.

'By the way, what is his name?'

Jessica stood silently.

'I asked, what is his name?' Theo's tone was now almost aggressive, not like the Theo that Jessica remembered.

'It's Culbert.'

'Culbert? What an odd name, why ever do you call him that?'

'It is after a friend of Papa's.'

'Of course, it would be.'

The rain had started to fall and grew heavier.

'I must take Culbert inside, we shall be soaked.'

Theo turned towards his carriage. He looked back at Jessica. 'I will come again next Monday, we have matters to discuss.'

Jessica went back quickly in the house, closed and bolted the door.

Mrs K heard the door close and came into the entrance hall. 'Whatever is wrong, Mistress Jessica? You look as if you've seen a ghost!'

'Worse than that!' said Jessica. 'A ghost isn't real, Theo is.'

'Oh no, I thought he had gone back up north!'

'Seems not.'

'What does he want?'

'I don't know, he's coming to talk to me on Monday. Oh dear Mrs K, just when things were going so well!'

'Come on my dear, I'll make you some cocoa and fetch some warm milk for Master Culbert.'

Nothing could have prepared Jessica her for what Theo had to say.

'I want us to be married.'

Jessica studied Theo's face. She seemed to have slipped into some sort of nightmare.

'I can't marry you! We are not of the same class. I would be ruined! No one would speak to me.'

'That is so important to you, isn't it? Social standing is all that matters to you.'

'No, many things matter... Culbert matters.'

'And I do not?'

Jessica said nothing.

'I shall let it be known I am Culbert's father, then there is nothing to stop us being married – in fact it will be necessary.'

'No, no, no! I will never marry you!'

'Then I shall ruin you by telling all.'

'Why do you say this? Why can you not just leave us to live our lives?'

'Because, my dear, you were willing to take me to your bed,

which you seemed to find a most satisfactory arrangement, and in my "social circle", that means marriage if a child is the result.'

'No, I will not marry you!'

'That is your final word?'

'Yes, it is.'

'Very well, then. I shall make it known in the county about us and our child.'

'No, you cannot! What can I do to prevent you doing this?' Then came the fatal strike.

'I want Berg House.'

'What? You can't... you mustn't... It was Papa's, then mine – you cannot have it!'

'I can, and indeed I will. If you do not marry me, you will assign Berg House to me as a gift, I will have a legal document drawn up.'

'And what will become of me and Culbert?'

'You can stay here until the boy is old enough to travel, then you and he must leave. I know you have money from your father's will.'

'What about Mrs K and the staff?'

'When you go, they go, I want nothing of you here after that. It is a reasonable offer, I could make you leave straight-away but I won't do that, besides I have business to attend to at Barm House and in the area. I have been living at Barm House since you left and shall be there permanently from now on.'

Jessica felt drained of strength and emotion but pulled herself upright. 'Very well, you can have Berg House. Culbert is more important to me, but I too make a condition – which is that you must never try to contact Culbert.'

'My dear, when you assign Berg House to me I shall have no reason to contact either of you. You will both be nothing to me.'

The truth was at last becoming apparent to Jessica; it was Berg House he had wanted all along, not her. He probably had other women, but none with a property like Berg House. She couldn't believe how easily she'd been taken in, but she had and now she must suffer the terrible consequence.

'I shall contact you when the solicitor has drawn up the deed of assignment.'

Theo left Jessica sitting very still, sobbing into her handkerchief.

Theo thought his plan had gone very smoothly indeed. He had expected Jessica to put up more of a fight for Berg House and was puzzled by her lack of resistance.

'What's wrong, Mistress Jessica – what's happened?' asked Mrs K, who had come into the drawing room when she saw Theo leave.

'He wants Berg House. If he doesn't get it, he will disclose that he is Culbert's father.'

'Oh, the awful rogue! Whatever will you do?'

'I shall have to agree, I cannot let it be known that I was taken in by such a man.'

'My dear, you must do what is right.'

'He said we can stay here until Culbert is old enough to travel, then we must leave – you and all the staff as well.'

'Well, I wouldn't want to stay with him as master, that's for sure, neither would any of the others.'

'Oh, Mrs K, what have I done?'

'What's done is done, no point in worrying about what can't be changed. Now, time you had a rest.'

Today's diary entry was one that Jessica never thought she would write, but write it she had to. 'One day, someone will read the truth of all this,' she thought as she carefully locked her diary in the satinwood box.

Theo was back at Barm House; he was pleased by the interest shown in it by the local people.

He had bought new furniture. The house was adorned with brightly coloured chairs, tables and had all the latest fittings. He only occasionally returned to visit his parents and seemed to have settled into his new way of life. He had met some young men in the local militia and carried on in their company much as he did back in his native Lancashire. There were many evenings of drinking and card playing. Theo had also become interested in various activities in the area, presuming that he and Jessica would be married. Now everything had changed.

He paced up and down the room; he was furious. How dare she refuse him? He had given her a son, was that not enough?

He didn't love her; he never had, although he had told her so. Berg House was his love and all he wanted. Now he would have it. He couldn't have Culbert, that would break their agreement. For a moment he felt a tinge of sadness, but only for a moment.

Some visitors had arrived in East Leah; they too were seeking a property to buy. The couple and their unmarried daughter Sara were from Yorkshire and like Theo, wanted to own a status-giving property in the south.

Sara was an attractive young woman, vivacious and clearly self-willed. Yet there was a kindness about her when she spoke with local people, in whom she seemed to have a genuine interest.

Until this point, Theo had only admired from a distance. He had more pressing matters to attend to.

3

Culbert was now two years old; his golden curly hair gave him an angelic appearance. Jessica took him out for walks most days and had many admiring looks and words from the local people.

'A fine young lad, your cousins' boy – he must be a comfort to you after your papa's demise,' said one young mother that Jessica often met.

'Indeed. Culbert is a sweet child, such a shame my cousins never lived to enjoy him.'

'Yes, it was a terrible crash… I don't trust these trains, always thought someone would be killed, now several have.'

'At least we can get to places quicker than by carriage. '

'As long as we get there alive!' said her friend.

Jessica had almost come to believe the 'cousins' story, having told it so many times. Mr and Mrs Ross wrote to her frequently and took a great interest in Culbert. Mrs Ross still thought the name odd, but Jessica said that he could always change it when he was older if he wanted to. They had asked Jessica to send a photograph of Culbert; he was changing in appearance so rapidly, as young ones do.

Jessica had arranged to have Culbert's photo taken at a photographer's in Port Hamon. Now that the Lebritan branch line was open it was easy to reach and, as she had told her friend, much quicker and more comfortable than going by carriage. Culbert liked the train and would sit looking out of the carriage window, gurgling away with delight.

They arrived at Port Hamon and made their way to the photographer's studio. Mr Strutt was a kindly man, who had a gentle way with young children. Culbert was dressed in his best clothes, his golden hair gleaming.

'Oh, what a charming little boy!' said Mr Strutt. 'What is his name?'

'Culbert.'

'Culbert... hmm, that is unusual. Is it a family name, my dear?'

'In a way, yes,' said Jessica.

Mr Strutt had a small chair, which he placed so that Culbert could stand and half turn towards him. It was a classic pose for young children and suited Culbert well.

The photographs were taken and Mr Strutt complimented Jessica on how well Culbert behaved.

'Thank you, he has a good disposition,' said Jessica.

They walked back to the railway station where they boarded the Lebritan train. It was now late afternoon and the days were growing shorter. The aromas of autumn filled the air.

The Assignment

'I will ask you one more time. Will you marry me?'

'No, Theo, no! There is no more to be said about it.'

'Very well, then you know what must happen. I will return in one week from today with my solicitor and the deed of assignment.'

'Do what you must,' said Jessica in a resigned tone.

Mr Strang, the solicitor, stood with his hands in his waistcoat pockets and looked thoughtful. He had jet-black hair and an equally black beard. He was young but well qualified, speaking in measured tones with the manner of a much older man.

He laid out the document on the table in the drawing room and read through the pages. Theo had left nothing out; Berg House was to be his and Jessica would give up all rights to it, as would Culbert and any issue he produced. It was final.

Jessica hesitated and looked up at Theo.

'You can still change your mind, my dear.'

Jessica picked up the quill and signed where Mr Strang indicated.

'There, it is done,' she said.

Theo signed and Mr Strang signed as witness. He then carefully poured some hot sealing wax under the signatures, placing his ring in the wax. He asked Theo and Jessica to put their hands on to the seal and declared the document delivered.

He handed the document to Theo. 'So Mr Harcourt, you are now the owner of Berg House. You are a lucky man.'

Theo took the document, looked at Jessica and then said to the solicitor, 'Our business here is finished, thank you, Mr Strang.'

Mr Strang left the drawing room with Theo and Jessica standing in silence, watching him.

'When do you want us to leave?'

'There is no urgency; you must prepare a story for your staff and friends. Have you thought of going abroad?'

'Where?'

'France perhaps? I understand it is a very interesting country.'

Jessica felt as though she and Culbert were being exiled, but she had little choice. She had already considered a move to France.

'Yes, very well, I shall make plans for Culbert and I to travel to France. I have to arrange for Mrs K and the staff to find positions elsewhere, I cannot just walk out on them.'

'I understand. Perhaps you will let me know when you intend to leave, I too need to make plans.'

'What sort of plans?'

'Oh, I have ideas for Berg House! There are some innovative architects around now, I have a fancy for the Italianate look.'

Jessica didn't know what to say or think, but then what she thought didn't matter. She wouldn't be there to see the changes, so Theo might as well do whatever he wished. What she didn't know was that Theo also had ideas regarding Sara and although the document was signed, he would feel safer if Jessica and Culbert were far away, which was why he had suggested they should go to France. He knew too that Jessica had spent some time in France when younger and was familiar with the language and customs. It all was falling into place.

Mrs K and the rest of the staff lined up in the drawing room. Mrs K knew what Jessica had to say but the staff had not been informed as yet. They knew, however, that since Mr Gilman's death things had not been right at Berg House. They had accepted the 'cousins' story – some wondered if it was true, but they were all loyal to Jessica, as they had been to her father.

'I am sorry to tell you all that I have decided to leave Berg House and take Culbert to live in France.'

There was a gasp from the line of staff.

'I have arranged the sale of the house and shall be leaving some time next year when I have made the necessary arrangements – not only for myself, but also for all of you. I shall find you all employment elsewhere in the county. Mr Gilman was highly respected and anyone who has worked for him will easily find a position, especially with my help.'

Jessica paused, waiting for the reaction.

Mrs K led the way. 'Oh, Mistress Jessica! We are so sorry, but we do understand, and you have young Culbert to think about, you must do the best for him.'

'Yes, Mrs K, a French education will be excellent and he will be able to speak the language, which may well be useful for him when he is older. I also have family friends in France that I stayed with when younger, who I hope will welcome us there.'

'Do you know when you will leave?' asked Mrs K.

'Not exactly, but you will all know as soon as I do, be assured of that.'

Mrs K shepherded the staff out of the drawing room, back to their duties.

Jessica sat down; she felt emotionally drained. How could this have happened? Oh, if only she had never met Theo! She remembered her father's warning, a warning she had not taken seriously. If only she had.

That evening before retiring, Jessica completed her diary and put it back in the satinwood box. She lay on the bed and wept silently before falling asleep with exhaustion.

The Photograph

The doorbell rang. It was the postman with a package; Mrs K took it and thanked him.

It was addressed to Jessica and had a Port Hamon post-mark.

'It must be Culbert's photographs! Mrs K, come and look.'

'Oh, what a beautiful picture!' said Mrs K. 'Doesn't he look a little angel!'

'Not for much longer, I think,' laughed Jessica. 'I have promised one for Mr and Mrs Ross and I must now tell them about Berg House... I haven't had the courage to do it before.'

'They are good friends.'

'Yes, they are like you Mrs K, honest and loyal. Maybe I will stay with them for a while before we leave for France.'

Jessica sat at the table and wrote the letter. It was difficult, so difficult. She was full of emotion when she recounted the events, but wasn't sure what her emotions were. She was sad to leave Berg House, she felt she had let her father down, and Theo, she didn't know what she thought about Theo. 'If I had married him he would still have ownership of Berg House and of me. Papa would have turned in his grave at the thought. I have done the right thing, I know I have.'

With the letter, she sent a photograph of Culbert. It was small, about 4 inches high and 2 inches wide, and was hand coloured. 'Yes he does look angelic; he also looks like Theo,' thought Jessica.

Jessica asked Mr and Mrs Ross if she could come and stay for a few weeks. She knew that after she finally left Berg House she might not see them for some time, if ever. Suddenly everything seemed so final.

A reply came a week later, the postal deliveries were much quicker now that the rail link had been established at Lebritan. Mr and Mrs Ross extended an invitation to Jessica and Culbert to come whenever and for as long as they liked. They asked no questions; they knew Jessica would tell them when she came.

Spring 1873

Now three years old, Culbert was growing fast. It seemed he would be a tall boy.

Christmas had come and gone and the wintry weather was fast moving away to make room for spring once again.

Jessica had arranged to visit Mr and Mrs Ross in April. She had been in Aldwell in the spring two years ago and she didn't suppose much would have changed. It was comforting to go to such good friends and other people she had come to know; she hoped they would remember her.

Mr and Mrs Ross were waiting at Aldwell station, hugging

Jessica warmly as soon as she alighted the train.

'My, young Culbert is growing into a tall young man!' said Mr Ross. 'Come along, let's go home and have some tea – not as good as your dear papa's, but very acceptable I think!'

Aldwell, as Jessica had thought, was exactly the same as before, a busy fishing town but with other industries that made it prosperous. It was also becoming popular with visitors; the rail station had made it possible to travel from London in just a day. On the cliff top was The Grand Hotel, a name that suited not only its size but also the guests. It was luxurious; the nobility and other high-ranking ladies and gentlemen staying there would regularly promenade along the sea front when the weather was fair. A theatre had opened on the pier nearby and some of the actors and actresses from London performed there. It was considered very select and plays by T.W. Robertson were very popular – this season his *Society* was being performed.

'I could stay here with Culbert,' thought Jessica. 'But no, it is too narrow for him, too limited in opportunities. I shall stay a while, though, and let us both enjoy all the town has to offer.'

Culbert by now was walking quite well. The sea air seemed to suit him and he played with some of the young children who lived nearby. There was a small grassy hill near Mr and Mrs Ross's son and daughter-in-law's home, and local children spent many a happy hour rolling down the short slope, racing each other to the bottom. Across from the hill was a large common. It was dotted with broom shrubs, their yellow flowers gleaming in the spring sun; the children loved them and ran in and out of the bushes playing hide-and-seek. Being taller than other children of his age, Culbert was able to play with the older children and had plenty of company.

In the afternoons after his nap, Jessica would read to Culbert before he had his tea. He enjoyed these times and always listened intently.

Mrs Ross hadn't pressed Jessica to tell them the purpose of her visit. They enjoyed her company and loved having young Culbert around, but they knew that something momentous had happened.

Mr and Mrs Ross sat in stunned silence.

Jessica had told them everything, leaving nothing for them to imagine. She had thought it best.

'But why go to France?'

'I think Theo would rather we were as far away as possible, but it suits me – Papa's friends Monsieur and Madame Julien will welcome us. I shall write to them and tell them what has happened and arrange to go to them next year, if I may stay with you until then.'

'Of course you can, my dear. In fact, you could stay with us forever if you wished but we understand your wish to move away and start afresh with young Culbert.'

'I would love to live here, in Aldwell, but I think Culbert needs somewhere where he will be able to have more choice in his future. Aldwell is wonderful, but for young men I think is rather limited. I really can't see Culbert being a fisherman!'

They all laughed; the idea of this angelic-looking young boy spending days at sea with all the dangers it brought was unthinkable.

'You are right, my dear. Culbert will be able to speak two languages – it is so much easier when you are young. He will not have to learn another language; he will speak it naturally. Why, he may even become a Frenchman!'

'Who knows?' said Jessica.

Culbert, sleeping in his room, was unaware that his future was being discussed.

During the winter, the tides were high. From her bedroom window up on the cliff, Jessica could see the waves pounding on the beach, some crashing over the promenade. Most of the fishermen kept their boats along the river estuary and were able to pull them back, well away from the rising river. The harbour had a treacherous entrance; it was narrow, and the undercurrents, or rip tides as the locals called them, could pull a boat under. Aldwell fishermen had grown up understanding the tides and currents, so there had never been an accident. They were too careful. The young lads learning would first be taught these important matters before they could venture out alone. The fishing boats were passed on to son from father generation after generation and each year were checked, repaired and painted with loving care.

'Jessica!' called Mrs Ross.

'Yes, what is it?'

'Alice is here to see you.'

Alice, a girl when Jessica last saw her, had quickly matured into a young woman, although only fourteen. She had left school and found a job at The Grand Hotel.

'How lovely to see you Alice, come and tell me what has been happening since I last saw you!'

Alice told Jessica about her job at the hotel, she was a maid and being young, did all the menial tasks. She was a hard worker and didn't mind, it paid quite well and she was able to give her parents some money each week.

'What about Ben?' asked Jessica.

Alice blushed a little. 'We are walking out together.'

'Oh how marvellous! He is such a nice young man.'

'Yes, he's working all the time with his father now on his boat. One day the boat will be his.'

'You must bring him round for tea, Alice, I would love to see him.'

'Thank you Mrs Warner, we would like that very much. How is Master Culbert?'

'Like you, grown taller!' said Jessica.

At that moment, Culbert ran into the room with his

spinning top. He stopped and looked at Alice; he didn't remember her, he was too young. Jessica told him that Alice was a dear friend and Culbert held out his hand to her. They shook hands slowly and Alice looked at Culbert. 'My, he is tall and very good-looking! One day he will have all the young ladies wanting to walk out with him!'

Alice made her way back home. She was pleased to have seen Mrs Warner and Culbert, she had missed them and had wondered if she would ever see them again but knew now that they would be staying for a while.

Alice lived with her parents in a small corner cottage that was about five minutes' walk away from Mr and Mrs Ross's house. Very near, but very different. Alice's home had a sitting room with a tiny kitchen off it; upstairs were two small bedrooms. Water was from a well in the backyard and there was a shed with an earth closet. Very few houses in Aldwell had sanitation or piped water, just the big ones on the hill and cliff. One of the reasons why Alice enjoyed working at The Grand Hotel was because there were bathrooms – one that staff could use once a week.

'Will you be here for Christmas?' asked Alice.

'Yes, we will,' said Jessica, 'Culbert is old enough to understand it now, so I think it will be quite a noisy time!'

'Are you going to live with Mr and Mrs Ross always?'

Alice was full of questions today, thought Jessica.

'No, Alice, we shall go to France to live next year.'

'France? Why?'

'Because that is the country where young men can be educated and learn many things, then they can marry and have children and a very happy life.'

Jessica wasn't really sure what to say, but what she said was true. France was considered to be the country to study art and literature. England was full of opportunities for those wishing to make their way in engineering and associated industries, but the Continent – France in particular – was the place for more gentle study.

'But how will you get there? Where will you live? What will you do?' Alice's questions came in a fast stream.

Jessica laughed. 'We will get there by boat, Alice, then when we are there we shall stay with my friends Monsieur and Madame Julien who live in a small town, about the size of Aldwell in the north of France. It is called Chateauneuf St Vincent.'

'How do you know these people?'

'My dear papa was a friend of theirs and when I was your age, I used to stay with them; that was when I learned to speak French.'

'Do they have a big house?'

Alice couldn't contain her amazement at all this, she had never been away from Aldwell. She knew where France was, but that was all. The thought of actually going there filled her with excitement.

'Yes, Alice, they have a big house and they have a son Armand and a daughter Janette – oh, and they also have a dog whose name is Jacko.'

'Goodness,' said Alice, 'it must be a big house!'

'Monsieur Julien is mayor of the town and a very important man, but he is also very nice and kind and everyone loves him.'

'Oh, well then I needn't worry about you and Culbert!'

Jessica laughed and gave Alice a hug. 'No my dear, you needn't! It is so kind of you to be concerned for both of us.'

'What a gem is Alice,' thought Jessica, 'so young, yet so mature.' She may not have the learning of girls she knew in East Leah but she had an old head on those young shoulders and a heart full of kindness. Ben was a lucky boy.

Ben had sat quietly during this exchange. He liked Mrs Ross's cakes and took the opportunity while the ladies talked to enjoy as many as possible.

'Ben, we are neglecting you!' said Jessica.

'No, you aren't Mrs Warner, I am enjoying my tea and listening to your news.'

'How is the fishing?'

'Pretty good, the cold weather now is good for the fish, they come inshore to feed.'

Ben was doing most of the fishing now. He was a tall lad and strong, his father went out occasionally but was gradually passing on the work to Ben. Fishing takes a hard toll and Ben's father was lucky to have a son to take over, for Ben would provide for his parents when they could no longer work. Couples with no children or savings faced life in the local workhouse when they were no longer able to earn a living. The word Bolham sent a shudder of fear and dread around those who might have to face the end of their lives there.

Bolham was a large, long, severe-looking building standing high above the river and marshes between Aldwell and the hamlet of Blywell. Such was its reputation that there were those who preferred to gradually waste away from starvation rather than live within its grim prison-like walls. Mr Charles Dickens had documented life in a workhouse in his novel *Oliver Twist*, particularly life as it was for children. Some local people had heard of this story and knew that all that was said of the terrible conditions for the poor was true.

Mr and Mrs Richard Ross

'Our son and his wife will be coming here for Christmas. I know they live just along the road but we do like them to stay over the festive period! Please will you and Culbert stay also?' asked Mrs Ross.

'We will be delighted, but I do feel we are imposing on you, we have been here several months now.'

'Not at all, my dear, we love having you here, you both bring the house alive.'

Jessica wondered if she was right to go to France or whether she should stay there. No, it could be difficult, one day people might discover Culbert's true parentage. At present only Mr and Mrs Ross knew, they had not told their son and daughter-in-law and the 'cousins' story still held. Anyway there was so much more opportunity for both her and Culbert in France. 'A new start... Yes, we must make a new start!'

Culbert was beginning to get excited, festive trimmings were hanging around the rooms and Jessica explained to him the reason for the celebration. Alice and Ben continued to call in and helped make the paper chains. Mrs Ross had invited them to visit on Christmas morning for mince pies before returning to their homes for Christmas dinner. Culbert asked if they would be staying with them, but Jessica explained that they had their own mamas and papas to be with. Culbert had become used to Ben and Alice being around, now regarding them as his family.

It was a cold, crisp morning, Mr Ross had lit the fire early and the logs were glowing red.

There was a knock on the door and there stood Ben and Alice, rosy-cheeked from the cold, salty air.

'Happy Christmas!' they called out as Mrs Ross ushered them into their house.

Jessica and Culbert were looking at some books amid the wrapping paper strewn on the floor.

Jessica handed a small parcel each to Ben and Alice, who graciously received them. Jessica had bought them both a book, which she knew they would treasure. Their reading had greatly improved over the months because of Jessica's tuition.

Mrs Ross came in with a plate of mince pies and offered them to Alice, then Ben. They both loved Mrs Ross's baking and were very grateful recipients. Alice's mother tried hard but her kitchen was cramped and the range had very small ovens, which limited what she was able to cook.

Mr Richard Ross and his wife Adelaide were there, having walked along from their home earlier. Richard was away a lot, Jessica was not quite sure what he did, something to do with publishing she thought, Adelaide also went away, not with her husband, but to stay with friends. They were a quiet couple.

Ben and Alice chatted with everyone and then after about an hour, left for Alice's home. Jessica knew that their Christmas lunch wouldn't compare with hers but Ben and Alice's place was with their parents, where they felt comfortable.

The day went well. Culbert played with his new toys and spent much time with his new books.

When all the celebrating was over, Jessica sat with Mr and Mrs Ross quietly, each with their own thoughts.

Jessica's thoughts were with Berg House.

'I must make plans to leave for France,' she thought, 'but first I have to return to Berg House one more time to see Mrs K and the staff and arrange for their employment elsewhere.' She had already made enquiries and knew they could all be accommodated; it was now a question of when. It would then be final.

'After the New Year I shall return to Berg House,' said Jessica to Mr and Mrs Ross. 'I need to ensure my staff are looked after and also have to collect a few items.'

Mrs Ross looked at Jessica and saw the sadness in her eyes.

'Yes, my dear, it has to be done, but you know you and Culbert can stay as long as you wish.'

'You are both so kind, but we must go soon. The longer we leave it, the more difficult it will be.'

Later in her room, Jessica recorded the day's events in her diary. She wrote of Christmas day with Mr and Mrs Ross, Mr and Mrs Richard Ross, Ben and Alice and then, as an afterthought, she recorded the addresses of them all. She put the diary back into her satinwood box and went to bed.

Spring 1874

Berg House looked the same as ever when Jessica arrived late afternoon at the end of April. Culbert was now walking and running and was the first to meet Mrs K.

'Well, young Master Culbert, the sea air has made you grow!'

Mrs K met Jessica and threw her arms around her. She knew Jessica wouldn't mind and wouldn't consider it out of place; they had known each other for many years. They both knew that this would be their last few days together.

Mrs K wiped tears from her eyes. 'Come along Miss Jessica, you must be worn out.'

'Oh, not so much, it was a beautiful train journey and Culbert loved it – he was so good!'

'Well, that's a blessing! Now, let's go and see about your tea. I expect you're both hungry and thirsty.'

'Culbert can eat with me, he's a big boy now.'

'That's lovely, I won't be a minute, and you two sit yourselves down.'

Mrs K returned a few minutes later with a tray of tea and cakes that she knew Jessica would enjoy.

'Any news, Mrs K?'

'You mean about HIM?'

'Yes, I mean about Theo,' said Jessica, laughing at the way that Mrs K referred to him. She had never liked Theo from the very start. Although she had not said anything much on the subject to Jessica, now she felt she could say what she thought.

'Well, he's been prancing about round here measuring things, and then, Miss Jessica, he brought a young lady with him.'

'Really, who?'

'Her name is Sara someone or other, her parents are buying property round here, seems like the whole county will be owned by foreigners soon.'

61

'Foreigners?'

'Well, northerners… they're foreign to me!'

Jessica laughed. 'Yes, I know what you mean.'

Jessica, for a moment, felt a pang of envy, but this was quickly followed by annoyance.

'I think he might have waited until I left before he came here, especially bringing someone else. Did the staff say anything?'

'No, they didn't see them, thankfully.'

'Good. Well the most important thing now is for me to contact my friends at the other houses and arrange your employment there. There are two houses that need staff and will take you, perhaps you can talk to the others and decide who would like to go where and with whom?'

Mrs K looked down. She felt this was the end of an era. 'I mustn't show my unhappiness, that wouldn't do,' she thought.

'Yes, Miss Jessica. We are all so grateful for all you have done, you know we shall miss you very much.'

'But we can write to each other, can't we?'

'Yes, of course we can, and we will!'

'Come on Culbert, it's a lovely morning. Let's go into the garden and look at all the flowers.'

They walked down towards the Gulley Copse, which was always a picture this time of the year with wild narcissi filling the spaces the snowdrops had left vacant. Then a cloud passed in front of the sun, the light dimmed slightly and the air took on a cooler feel.

Suddenly a figure appeared from near some trees. Jessica jumped and grabbed Culbert.

'My, my, you are nervous, my dear,' said Theo.

'Theo, what are you doing here? What do you want?'

'I wondered when you will leave permanently, my dear. I don't think that is an unreasonable request, after all you are living in my property, as are all your staff.'

'Culbert and I will leave for France as soon as Mrs K and the staff are settled in new positions. That should be next month, then you will be rid of us.'

'Good, and how is young Cuthbert?'

'Culbert, his name is Culbert, not Cuthbert, and he is very well.'

'So, you still insist on calling him by that strange name. When he is older he will probably realise how peculiar it sounds.'

'Well, then he can call himself something else if he wants to when he comes of age, that is his right.'

'I know you couldn't name him after me, but you might at least have consulted with me about his name instead of choosing the one you did.'

'Why are you so bothered about his name? It won't matter to you, we won't be here and you will never see us again.'

'I just feel sorry for the lad, he will have enough to put up with without being burdened with a name like that.'

'You dislike it because you know it came from my father's side of the family. You didn't like my father, did you?'

'I think it more correct, my dear, to say that your father didn't like me – he thought I wasn't good enough for you because I am trade. Well, Miss Sara's father doesn't have the same high ideas, and both he and she find me most acceptable.'

'Oh yes, I have heard about Miss Sara.'

'I knew Mrs K would have told you. Miss Sara and I will soon become engaged to be married and when we are, we will live at Berg House, it shall be our seat.'

Theo knew that this would hurt Jessica – not the marriage, but being able to call Berg House his seat.

'I wish you and Miss Sara every happiness Theo. Now come, Culbert, let's go and look at the flowers.'

Jessica would not rise to the bait; she was too well brought up to lose her temper although she was very angry. She knew that Theo was trying to provoke her; she took Culbert's hand

and they slowly walked towards Gulley Copse, as though they had just been talking with a passer-by of no importance to them.

Theo stood, looking at them as they walked away. 'Well, that's it,' he thought, 'she still could have changed things, even now... ' But it was the end and he must make plans for his betrothal with Sara.

The Betrothal

'I am so happy for you, my dears,' said Mrs Baillie, hugging her daughter Sara and beaming at Theo.

'Let's toast the happy couple and wish them many years of married bliss!' said Mr Baillie.

It was a small gathering to celebrate the betrothal of Theo to Sara. They had decided to do it as they would have done in the north, both families having originated from that part of the country.

'I understand you have great plans for Berg House, Theo.'

'Yes, I favour the Italianate style as does Sara and we thought we would have work start as soon as possible. After we are married next year, we shall live at Barm House until Berg House is ready.'

'Why don't you two live at Barm House? It is a lovely building and you have done so much to it.'

Mr Baillie was puzzled that Theo insisted on he and Sara living at Berg House, he could see so little difference in the two properties.

'Berg House is special, it is a superior building and will make a fitting home for Sara and me, and, I hope, our children.'

'Oh, how wonderful!' said Mrs Baillie, whose one desire now was to have grandchildren.

'Sara, my dearest, you prefer Berg House, do you not?' asked Theo.

'I just love it, Theo, and your idea to create an Italianate look. Mama, we have seen the plans of Her Majesty's residence on the Isle of Wight that is in the Italianate style and I would love Berg House to look like that!'

'Well, you can't go wrong with having the same taste as our Queen,' said Mr Baillie.

'No, indeed not, although I cannot understand why Prince Albert dislikes it so,' said Mrs Baillie.

'I can tell you why!' said Theo. 'It is because he is German and he finds the Italianate style too fussy. We all have different tastes.'

'It's just as well he is not redesigning Berg House otherwise we might have an imposing German castle in the countryside!'

Theo looked and smiled at Sara. 'How wonderful she is,' he thought, 'and we have so much in common – her parents are also in business in the north, they don't call me "trade".'

The Baillies, like the Harcourts, had a family textile business that was very profitable and had allowed them to invest in property in the south. They also had met with scorn from some of the locals, who seemed to find them inferior. But that didn't matter now, they thought. This is a perfect match, Theo is a handsome young man, who seems to have 'penetrated' the local society, and has two large properties. Not many locals can say the same, so let them do as they please. It is probably because they are jealous.

They knew nothing of Jessica and what had happened before Theo met Sara. They had been told that an elderly gentleman and his daughter lived at Berg House and when he had died, his daughter was so distraught she went to live with some relatives abroad. Theo had never disclosed what he paid for Berg House, which surprised Mr Baillie. Northerners were very keen to boast of what they had paid for anything including property, especially if it had been bought at what might be considered a bargain price. Mr Baillie thought that perhaps Theo had been in the south for so long, he now felt it was not good taste to talk about money.

Sara was happier than she had ever felt in her life; she was to marry a wonderful man and be the mistress of two houses. How perfect! She thought of their wedding, it would be in the north in their hometown of Gothmer and soon the date would definitely be fixed. Her friends would be so envious! How lucky she had been to meet Theo.

Wedding Preparations

'You look so beautiful, just like a princess!' Mrs Baillie looked admiringly at her daughter, who was having the final alterations made to her wedding dress.

Sara had chosen ivory satin. It was trimmed with Honiton lace, which had become very popular with those who could afford it because it had been the choice of Queen Victoria for her wedding dress. Sara did not much like the now-favoured white for wedding gowns, her dark brown hair and medium complexion was better suited to ivory, but the lace trim was a pure snowy white.

Sara was of average height and build, unlike the willowy ladies of the southern counties. She and her mother had carefully chosen her dress to accentuate her features and complement those of her taller groom.

'Well, that seems to be just perfect,' said the seamstress. 'I shall have the dress ready next week.'

The date had been fixed for the wedding and Theo and Sara had visited the church, St Mary's in Gothmer, where they were to be married.

Theo was to stay with his parents until their wedding day, when he and Sara would travel to East Leah to take up residence at Barm House, prior to their move to Berg House.

'Theo is calling tomorrow, last time he can see you before the wedding!' laughed Mrs Baillie.

Sara couldn't conceal her excitement. It was all so wonderful, her parents had arranged a splendid wedding supper and all their friends and relatives were coming. Her father's family originated in Ireland and several were making the long journey. Sara felt privileged to have so much attention poured on her. She had met Theo's parents and some of their friends who had all fallen for her happy, vivacious nature and natural beauty.

'Well my dearest, this is the last time I will address you as Mistress Baillie.'

'Oh yes, Theo, isn't it wonderful? Soon we shall be Mr and Mrs Harcourt! My family are so happy for me, even my cousins from Ireland are coming to our wedding and there is one in particular I haven't seen in years, cousin Culbert.'

Theo's face turned ashen.

'Cousin Culbert?' he spluttered as he said it.

'Yes, whatever is the matter Theo? You have gone quite pale, are you ill?'

'No, no, of course not, just seems a strange name.'

'What, Culbert? It may seem strange here, but it's an old Irish name and I think there are plenty of Culberts there!' laughed Sara. 'Why, even that prim widow daughter of Mr Gilman at Berg House has a relative called Culbert, a cousin or some relative on her late mother's side, I believe.'

'How did you know that, my dear?'

'Oh, local gossip I heard from the young women in Morton Terrace when we were looking for property – seems there are so few visitors here that one with an unusual name is remembered. He came to see Mr Gilman when he was unwell they said, and was asking directions to Berg House.'

'What sort of chap was he?'

'They said he was a real handsome one; tall, fair hair and a lovely way of talking, like the Irish have, you know, that's probably why the local girls remembered him!'

'Really? I didn't know there were any relatives, he must have been the same age as Mr Gilman.'

'Younger probably, otherwise the young ladies wouldn't have taken such an interest!'

Theo felt as if he had been struck. He sat down.

'Are you sure you're all right, my dearest?' asked Sara.

'Yes, I'll be all right, I'm just a little tired.'

'Of course, you have been busy with arrangements and travelling back and forth to East Leah, you must be exhausted.'

'Theo looked very pale, is he all right?' asked Mrs Baillie.

'I hope so,' said Sara. 'I think he is just tired.'

'What caused him to go pale so suddenly, what were you doing?'

'Mama, really, we were just talking and I mentioned that cousin Culbert from Ireland would be coming to our wedding. It was something about the name Culbert, though goodness knows why or what.'

'Maybe it brought back an unpleasant experience.'

'I don't think so, he just said it was a strange name.'

'Hmm, seems odd that should upset him so.'

'Never mind, he's all right now and he will be splendid on the day!'

Farewells

It was always going to be a sad day. Mrs K had been dreading the moment but she knew it had to come. All bags were packed and the carriages had arrived to take Jessica, Culbert and all their belongings to Port Hamon. There, they would board the boat bound for France and a new life for them both.

Jessica looked up at Berg House; she tried not to show her

sadness but it was there for all to see. Mrs K had lined up the staff and told them not to be weepy. 'It won't do Mistress Jessica any good to see us all mopping our eyes and blowing our noses.'

Jessica threw her arms around Mrs K. 'I will never forget you. I shall write very often.'

'I know you will Mistress Jessica, and I know that you and young Master Culbert will have a wonderful life in France. Be happy for all our sakes.'

Jessica went along the line of staff and shook their hands, bidding them all farewell and thanking them for their service over the years. She had left gifts for them all with Mrs K, which she would distribute once she and Culbert had left.

'Come along Culbert, we are going for a big boat ride.'

'Oh Mama! I love boat rides.'

It was all a game to Culbert, thought Jessica. Thank goodness she had made the move while he was still young and hadn't any ties in East Leah.

Mrs K and the staff waved until they could no longer see the carriages. They walked slowly back into Berg House to start the removal procedure. From now on, this would no longer be Jessica's seat.

4

France 1875

Chateauneuf St Vincent was just as Jessica remembered; it was over ten years since she and her father last spent one of many pleasant and happy stays with their great friends, Charles and Etta Julien.

Charles and Etta's house was large, very large, and the last building in the Rue Hubertus. Charles had inherited it from his father who had been a successful businessman, travelling throughout Europe and occasionally in America. His success and business acumen had meant that Charles had also inherited a considerable amount of money. Charles, though, was not idle and neither did he boast of his wealth. He worked quietly in the town, using the knowledge he acquired from years of study about varied subjects to help and encourage the local businesses. He was now the mayor. France was in precarious times politically, but nevertheless interesting times. The air of change, not only in France but also across Europe, had seen an emergence of free thinkers, philosophers, and political analysers, all anxious to propound their views and theories. Charles read the words of these people and although he had no aspirations to national politics, felt that he could, in a small way, help to mould and shape his local community.

Etta, Charles' wife, was of French-Algerian origin. They had met while Charles was visiting Rabat and Etta's beauty had

70

captivated him. She had the Mediterranean skin colouring so prevalent in the North African countries, which had drawn Charles like a magnet. The instant attraction however had turned into deep love, equally given and received. After two years of marriage Armand was born; he too had the olive complexion of his mother and now, aged fifteen, was a handsome young man, admired by many young ladies. Like his father, he craved knowledge and read avidly. He enjoyed helping his father in his work in the town and although university had been suggested, Armand did not want to leave the beautiful countryside of his home and exchange that for life in Paris or Strasbourg. Both universities were undergoing troubles, which suited Armand and gave him a good excuse for remaining in Chateauneuf St Vincent. Etta, of course, was delighted as she had no wish for their son to be so far away from them; he was a quiet, gentle boy and she feared that his manner would not fit in well with the extrovert behaviour of other students that she had heard of.

Their daughter Janette was just two years younger than Armand and was in most ways the opposite in character. Very outward going, Janette would make friends with anyone and everyone. Etta sometimes worried for her, but she was a loving daughter. 'As the years go by she will quieten a little,' thought Etta.

'Well, well – and who have we here?' asked Charles, looking straight at Culbert.

Culbert, now five years old but tall for his age, politely offered his hand to Charles and said, 'I am Culbert sir, I am five, and very pleased to meet you.'

Charles laughed. 'You have a lovely son Jessica, and his manners are so very French – he will do well here. Now come you two, you must be exhausted. The annexe is ready for you, but first you must have some refreshment after such a long journey.'

Charles ushered Jessica and Culbert into their large kitchen, where Etta was waiting for them with a large jug of home-made lemonade and some slices of cake.

Culbert's eyes went straight to the cake. Etta laughed. 'Come along Culbert, have some of my special rum cake, you will love it!'

It was a recipe that had been handed down for several generations and was a favourite in the Julien household. Charles' mother, affectionately known as Grand Mere to most people in the town, had taught Etta how to make it.

Jessica sipped the lemonade slowly; she was tired, but happy. 'At last,' she thought, 'we can start living our lives, away from Berg House and all its memories. Here we will be safe, no one can hurt us any more.'

'Now then,' said Charles, 'we must let you two unpack and rest, there will be plenty of time for talking and reminiscing tomorrow and the day after, and the day after!'

He led Jessica and Culbert through to the annexe, which was on the forest side of the house.

'This is lovely, Mama,' said Culbert. 'Look, trees everywhere, it's better than at home!'

Jessica laughed; a laugh of relief at the immediate happy reaction from Culbert. 'Yes,' she thought, 'it will be better than home, no doubt about that.'

News From Home

'What is that you are reading, Mama?'

'It is a letter from Mrs K, my dear friend in England,' replied Jessica.

'She looked after us, didn't she Mama?'

'Yes, she looked after us very well.'

When Jessica and Culbert left England, Mrs K was offered a post with one of Jessica's friends, but she felt it was time to retire so went to live with her sister in Port Hamon. She never forgot Jessica and young Culbert, and promised to write; she missed them both dearly and often wished they would return to England.

Times are changing here, as with you I expect. We now have Mr Disraeli back as prime minister, he and Mr Gladstone seem to be taking turns at running the country!

Lots of new laws are being passed, particularly with children in mind, which must be good. He is going to stop those poor little lads being sent up chimneys, he certainly took notice of what that Mr Dickens said and wrote about.

I can't imagine young Culbert climbing up a chimney, what a dreadful thought! How is the young man? Five years old now, I expect he is growing taller by the day and soon he will be going to school. You must tell me how he does, especially speaking French.

My sister and I went to East Leah last week, HE has been changing Berg House, you wouldn't recognise it. It looks so much bigger and all Italian looking. I suppose he thinks it will look like a royal palace, always had ideas above his station. No one speaks to him much; he keeps buying things for the village, new meeting hall, new musical instruments for the band. I suppose he thinks that money can buy him friends.

The letter continued with news of Mrs K's sister and their life in Port Hamon; Jessica read the entire letter then carefully put it into her satinwood box. 'Dear Mrs K,' she thought, 'it could all have been so different.'

St Paul's School

Dear Madame Warner,

I am very sorry to have to write this letter to you but events of the past two weeks make it necessary.

Culbert, your son, is behaving in a manner that does not fit in with the standards of this school.

I am sad to say that he has been showing a side of his nature that is unpleasant, and indeed at times frightening to the other scholars.

Culbert must learn to control his aggression. I understand that boys of his age tend to be boisterous but Culbert's behaviour goes beyond that. He has hit other scholars when they say something with which he disagrees and as a result is becoming a disruptive influence.

I ask you, therefore, to speak with him about this matter, and I hope to see an immediate improvement. If there is not, we will have to consider Culbert's position in this school.

You will understand that I must consider the good of all scholars in this matter.

Yours sincerely,
Mme D Levois
Head Mistress

Jessica felt shaken. 'What has happened to my son, my lovely boy?' she thought. 'Can this really be?' Mme Levois had welcomed Culbert into the local school, St Paul's, just five years ago, and until now had given Jessica no reason to doubt that he was a fine scholar in all ways.

'It's just growing up,' thought Jessica, 'after all he is ten years old now, an English boy in a French school. He has had to learn two languages at the same time; it must have been a struggle for him to keep up with the others. He is just asserting himself, yes, that is all it is. I shall write to Mme Levois and tell her that Culbert is going through a passing phase and there will be no further problem with him. But I must speak with him, he won't realise that his behaviour is upsetting the other scholars.'

'I was only standing up for myself, Mama,' said Culbert. 'They laugh at the way I talk sometimes, because they say I am not French. They also say that my eyes are crooked.'

'They are just jealous, my darling, they cannot speak two languages.'

'Well, it makes me very cross sometimes.'

'You must try not to show that you are cross, and you must not fight with them, otherwise Mme Levois will not let you attend St Paul's.'

'Very well Mama, I shall be good.'

Jessica sighed with relief. 'Well, that's all it was,' she thought. 'Strange that Mme Levois should react in such a way.'

The summer of 1885 was long and hot. Jessica enjoyed walks in the forest where there was shade from the ever-present sun. Armand and Janette, Charles and Etta's son and daughter, were home for two weeks and Jessica was happy in their company. Armand, who had qualified as an architect, was working with a friend of Charles in Curveux. This had pleased Charles because he had thought that Armand would stay in his hometown and when the opportunity had arisen for him to study, Armand had gladly accepted. Janette lived in the south of France; she had met Louis, a man some fifteen years her senior and they lived in a villa near Nice. Charles did not approve of Janette's choice but there was nothing he could do, she was a headstrong character and nothing he or Etta said made any difference. They were just thankful that she kept contact with them and visited when she could.

Culbert, now fifteen years old, had finished his schooling and was considering his future. He had made several friends in the town and seemed to have settled down in spite of his earlier behaviour problem. No more had been said about the matter so Jessica assumed all was well. Culbert certainly seemed a perfectly behaved young man and gave her no cause for concern.

'And here is *mon petit* Culbert!' said Janette. She pronounced Culbert in the French style, to which Culbert had become accustomed. They embraced and walked into the garden chatting to each other.

Armand looked thoughtful. 'Armand, how goes your work?' asked Jessica.

'Very well, very well indeed,' replied Armand. 'I enjoy designing most of all, there is so much scope now for architects, especially those with a sense of history, and detail.'

'It sounds as if we shall hear more of you in years to come,' said Jessica.

'Well, I hope so,' laughed Armand. 'I would like to be known, and remembered, for good things and those that will last.'

He looked outside. 'It looks just as good as always in the garden.'

'Yes, I expect you remember happy days playing with Janette and later, also with Culbert.'

'Hmm,' said Armand.

He turned away. 'I must talk with Papa, he likes to hear all the news about the business, and I will see you at dinner.'

'So, Culbert, what do you think you will do now that school is finished?' asked Armand.

'I am not sure,' replied Culbert. 'I like Chateauneuf St Vincent but there is not much to do here, but I do not want to leave Mama, she has been so good to me.'

'You must think of yourself now,' said Jessica. 'You cannot stay here forever. Why not go to Paris, all young men go to Paris! Is that not so, Charles?'

Charles laughed. 'Yes, indeed, it does broaden a young man's horizons. Why not, Culbert? I could arrange for you to work with a friend of mine. It would be clerical work, it would pay a small salary and give you the opportunity to look around and see how other French people live!'

'What a wonderful offer,' said Jessica. 'What do you say, Culbert?'

'I am most grateful, but I think I will wait a year, if that is agreeable to you Monsieur Julien. I would like to get some experience of working. The father of one of my school friends owns the café in town and has asked if I would help them, because they are very busy.'

'I think that sounds an excellent idea,' said Charles. 'Work for a year for your friend, then we will see about a move to Paris.'

'That sounds perfect,' said Jessica. 'We will all be happy!'

Armand looked across at his sister. 'What are your plans, Janette?'

'Oh, I shall return to Louis in a couple of weeks, he is on business in Switzerland at present.'

'Are you happy?' asked Armand.

'Of course I am, why do you ask? Do I not look happy?'

'Yes, no reason,' replied Armand.

There was a short silence, broken by Etta. 'Let's move into the garden and drink our coffee there, shall we?'

'Armand seems troubled.'

'Do you think so, my dear?' said Charles.

'Yes, there is something on his mind.'

'I expect he is thinking about his new designs. He is very conscientious, you know.'

'No, it's not that,' said Etta.

'Well then, what?'

'I am not sure, but he seems to be worried about Janette.'

'Goodness, my dear, Janette is twenty-three years old; she's not a child. Armand has never approved of Louis, and you know that.'

'No, it's not Louis.'

'Well, what is it, if it isn't Louis?'

'I'm not sure.'

'You have said that twice, my dear,' laughed Charles. 'If it isn't his work, and it isn't Louis, than there isn't much left, is there?'

'Perhaps there is, perhaps there is,' said Etta. 'Come, let us go inside, it is becoming cool out here.'

They all returned to the house. Charles and Armand relaxed with glasses of brandy while Jessica, Etta and Janette helped clear the dishes away. Grand Mere, who had always cleared the table, washed and dried the dishes, had died three years ago. She was missed, not only for all the help around the house, but because of her wisdom.

'Do you still miss Grand Mere?' asked Armand.

'Yes, we do,' said Charles. 'She was a wise woman.'

'How did she like Culbert?' asked Armand.

'I think she liked him well enough, she didn't spend so much time with him as she did with you and Janette, of course, but she treated him as one of the family. Why do you ask?'

'No special reason.'

Charles, Etta, Jessica and Culbert stood in Rue Hubertus outside their house, waving as Armand and Janette left to return to their respective homes.

'I wonder when we will next see them both,' said Etta.

'Yes, indeed,' replied Charles. 'They both have busy lives, we must not expect them to keep visiting old parents!'

'You have two wonderful children, although not children now,' said Jessica. 'They are a credit to you both.'

'Thank you,' said Etta. 'You bring up your children to know right from wrong and to behave as responsible citizens, and you hope that when they are no longer children they will continue to develop with the same principles and pass them on to their children. Now, of course, they are adults and what will be, will be, but I think Armand and Janette will always do what is right.'

'Yes, I'm sure they will,' said Jessica.

She looked at Culbert, who was gazing down the road. 'Now Culbert, we must talk about you starting work.'

'Of course, Mama, I look forward to it!'

Café Marc et Louise

'This is your section, Culbert,' said Louise. 'You must look after the customers at these tables, take their orders, bring their meals, make sure they have everything they need and make them feel happy.'

'Happy?' questioned Culbert.

'Yes, happy. People come here to enjoy good food, to talk with their companions, and above all to be happy – it is our duty to make sure that all happens. Of course, when it does, we are more likely to get good tips!'

Culbert and Louise both laughed, but Louise knew the importance of satisfied customers; they had worked hard to build a good business in their small and successful restaurant by concentrating on these three factors. Many customers had recommended them to influential friends and acquaintances and their reputation had spread.

Louise had trained Culbert in the style of their business and now she felt he was ready to work with the customers. He wore the 'Marc et Louise' uniform which Louise had designed and which had become well recognised, not only in Chateauneuf St Vincent but also further afield.

Culbert, with his golden hair and athletic physique, was a handsome young man: one of the reasons Louise had employed him. She felt that his presence would attract new customers, particularly ladies, who were now starting to dine out in small groups without the company of their husbands. His ability to speak both French and English fluently was an added attraction; he looked older than his years and had a confidence that matched. Several English visitors touring Europe had found time to visit their restaurant on their travels.

'That was a long, long day,' said Culbert, collapsing into one of the comfortable armchairs in the private room behind the dining area.

'Yes, we are doing very well!' said Louise. 'You must be very tired, it has been busy like this for the past six months, and you have worked very hard.'

'I love it, Louise, meeting all the people, sharing their experiences, and, making them happy!'

'You have certainly done that, and Marc and I are well pleased with you.'

'Tell me Louise, do my eyes look crooked?'

'Crooked?'

'Yes, when I was at school some of the boys used to say that my eyes were crooked. Now when I am tired, I find that things do not seem quite clear.'

'Let me look,' said Louise. 'Mmm... I see what they meant, although they were unkind to say it, I think you may have what is called a "turn" in your eye, but I expect they called it by other names.'

'Yes they did, but what does it mean?'

'It means that the eye muscle doesn't work as well as it should so that when you look at something, one eye looks straight at it but the other looks slightly to one side. I only know this because a friend of mine has an eye like that. It can be an inherited condition. Does your mother or father have such a condition?'

'My mother doesn't... my father died when I was very young. I never knew him.'

'Oh how sad, what happened to him?'

'Mama told me that he was a soldier, an officer who was killed in a battle in Abyssinia. He was a very brave but a very unlucky man – he was wounded and died later from blood poisoning.'

'Well, whatever the cause I think that you can have some treatment. You would need to see an eye specialist.'

'Hmm, maybe, it seems to only affect me when I am tired.'

'Yes, but you should find out if it will affect your eyesight as the years go on. There's an eye specialist, a Monsieur Arlt, who visits Chantes once a year and treats people with eye problems without any charge. I think he is due there in two months' time.'

'What an excellent idea! Why does he not charge?'

'He is what is called a philanthropist, Culbert, he thinks it is wrong that only rich people should have treatment and he gives his services free once a year in a clinic for people who are not wealthy. When he was young and studying, some friends of his family who lived in Chantes let him stay with them and they helped him during his studies. He is Austrian, but has never forgotten his French friends.'

'Well he is a true friend of France. I shall tell Mama, then find out when he is coming and go to see him,' said Culbert.

Culbert looked in the mirror that evening. 'I wonder what my father looked like,' he thought. 'Mama always says I look like him; she must have been very sad when he died.'

The streets of Chantes were narrow, with tall buildings seeming to vanish into the sky. Culbert and Jessica walked slowly along, feeling as if the walls on each side of the street would fall on them and they would disappear beneath their weight.

'It is very dark here Mama, I wouldn't want to live in this town.'

'Oh, there are better areas,' said Jessica. 'When you have finished with your eye examination, we shall walk along the boulevards which are outside the town centre. There, it is beautiful.'

'Have you been here before, Mama?'

'Yes, indeed, I spent some of my childhood here. My papa travelled the world and we stopped in many interesting places.'

'What about your mama? You have never mentioned her.'

'No, Culbert, I never knew her well, she died when I was young and she and Papa were always so busy that I was unable to spend much time with her. I had a governess for my education and our housekeeper was as a mother to me. My father entertained many important business and government people and my mother had to play her part, that was their priority.'

'Oh, it is sad you didn't know your mama very well, do you regret that?'

'No, that was the way life was then, I accepted it, I had a good life as a child and had much to be thankful for. There were many children where we lived who had little to eat or wear so I really cannot complain about the lack of my mother's company in my childhood,' replied Jessica. 'Now, we must find the room where Monsieur Arlt consults, it is along here near the church.'

Chantes church towered above the other tall buildings of the narrow streets with a spire almost in the clouds. At the end of the adjacent road was a long, sombre building.

'There, that is it,' said Jessica.

'What sort of building is that?' asked Culbert.

'Well, it's an asylum for people who have illnesses of their minds.'

'Why is Monsieur Arlt in there? I thought he was an eye doctor.'

'Yes, he is, but it is not easy to find somewhere to hold his clinic. There are other eye doctors in the town, charging very large fees, who will not allow him to use their premises or be near to them. This was the only building he could find with a large enough room to hold his clinic. The other eye doctors think that he will find it so distasteful, he won't come back. But they're wrong, it makes him more determined to help those who cannot afford the big fees.'

Culbert laughed. 'I like the sound of Monsieur Arlt,' he said.

'Look straight at my light,' said Monsieur Arlt. 'That is good, now with the other eye.'

Culbert sat absolutely still while Monsieur Arlt carried out various tests on his eyes, reading letters and looking at colours.

'You have what is called strabismus.'

'Oh, my friend said it might be called a turn of the eye.'

'Yes, that is the same, I just give it the real name!'

'But what can I do about it?'

'I shall give you some eye exercises to do, also you must wear some spectacles, these will make your "lazy eye" work harder and the muscle will become stronger. It takes time and you must persevere, otherwise when you get older it will be more difficult to correct and your eyesight may not be so good. After about a year, providing you have done the exercises, you will be able to stop wearing the spectacles.'

'I will do as you say Monsieur Arlt. I am very grateful to you.'

Monsieur Arlt looked across at Jessica. 'Tell me Madame, did your husband have such a condition in either of his eyes? This is an hereditary condition.'

'No, Monsieur, he did not.'

'Maybe his father? It often misses a generation.'

'I wouldn't know Monsieur, my husband's father was not alive when we married and there were no photographs.'

Monsieur Arlt looked at Culbert. 'I am sure, young man, that you understand what I mean about this condition being hereditary?'

'Oh yes, Monsieur,' said Culbert.

'It may be that when you are older and marry and have

children this will show again, but don't worry, you know it can be corrected.'

'I will make sure if that should happen, it will be corrected. I was taunted at school because of my eyes.'

'Well, that is how young people are,' Monsieur Arlt smiled, 'and I don't suppose it will change!'

'My, my, you look very distinguished!' said Louise. Culbert laughed. 'Monsieur Arlt is a good man, and I am fortunate that you, Louise, knew about this eye condition and also about his clinic. Now I must go back to work and see if the young ladies like my new appearance!'

The young ladies did indeed like his appearance, and thought he looked not only attractive but also academic. Business at Marc et Louise flourished.

Family Gathering, 1890

'How wonderful, we are together, all of us healthy and happy,' laughed Charles.

'Yes, let us raise our glasses and be thankful that we are one happy family,' replied Etta.

Charles, Etta, Armand, Janette, Jessica and Culbert sat around the large table in the garden in the warmth of the June evening. Charles and Etta, now both in their sixties, felt content with their lives. Armand was a successful architect, Janette had married Louis, much to their surprise but also delight, and their friends Jessica and Culbert gave them much pleasure by their company. France too was in a more settled phase politically and provided a welcome for all with new ideas and talents from countries throughout Europe.

'My goodness, Culbert, how you have grown!' said Janette. 'How old are you now?'

'Twenty years now, Janette,' replied Culbert. 'Time here

moves at a pace I enjoy – not too fast, not too slow, gives me time to enjoy myself as well as work.'

'So, what are your plans?'

'Well, I have finished my restaurant training here in Chateauneuf St Vincent. I have had excellent tuition in all aspects of the business so now I will be able to work as a manager in Paris, and then who knows, perhaps I will open my own restaurant!'

'That is wonderful!' said Janette. 'You have worked hard and deserve to do well.'

'When are you moving to Paris, Culbert?' asked Armande.

'Oh, quite soon, I shall start in Restaurant Phillipe in Paris next month, and I hope that after gaining more experience I shall find a manager's position in a café or restaurant near the Place du Tertre.'

'You will miss him, Jessica,' said Charles.

'Of course I will, but he is a man now and it is time he made his own way. I cannot be with him forever,' laughed Jessica.

'Well, let's all drink to that, shall we?' Charles raised his glass and they all joined him wishing Culbert success.

'I am afraid I must return to my office,' said Armand. 'It has been a wonderful time but I have so much work, it cannot be left any longer.'

'We understand,' said Charles. 'We are grateful that you were with us as long as you were, and we mustn't get in the way of your work.'

'I shall be back in a few months,' said Armand.

They waved goodbye as the carriage took Armand along the road towards Curveux.

'I'm so proud of him,' said Etta. 'You must be just as proud of Culbert, Jessica – our sons have turned out so well.'

'Yes, indeed, Culbert has achieved far more than I ever hoped for!'

Jessica turned away and walked into the house. 'How well everything has evolved,' she thought. 'After all my troubles, life seems to smile on me.'

'What a glorious afternoon!' said Janette. 'Come Culbert, let us go for a stroll in the forest. I have two more days before I return, we can walk and talk as we did all those years ago.'

Culbert and Janette ambled along through the dense forest; leaves were at their greenest and thickest and formed a roof, allowing little light through.

Culbert put his arm around Janette's shoulder. 'You are a very attractive lady, Madame Janette!'

'Oh Monsieur, you are so forward!' Janette laughed and ran in front of Culbert.

Culbert caught up with her and when they stopped, he held her close. She looked up at him but did not pull away.

'As I said, you are a very attractive lady.'

Culbert held her more tightly and closer until she could feel his warm breath; still she did not resist.

Culbert kissed her, a full kiss on the lips. His tongue searched for hers, and Janette felt that she was melting into his body.

His hands moved across her breasts feeling their fullness, their tongues entwined and a sensuous thrill ran through their bodies.

Culbert could feel himself hardening; he stroked Janette's thighs and moved his hand upwards, now feeling the moistness where her legs met.

He placed Janette gently on the forest floor, slowly removing her underwear so that he could admire her bronzed skin and slender body. The dappled light through the trees created stripes of light and dark tan along her legs and across her firm stomach.

Janette groaned softly. 'I am ready for you, Culbert.'

'Yes, I know. I want you very much, I always have.'

He slowly entered her, moving rhythmically, feeling the soft sensation of her body. 'Make it last,' whispered Janette. 'It is just perfect, make it last!'

'I will, my love, I will.'

Culbert moved more slowly but each time penetrated further. It was heaven.

'Now!' Janette's voice was distorted by the urgency of her passion.

They lay locked, quiet, with just a few sounds from the forest above them.

'You are quite a lover Culbert... I expect the young ladies of Chateauneuf St Vincent have enjoyed your talents!'

'A few, yes, but not like that, it was different, special.'

'Is it better with a married woman?' Janette laughed.

'It is better with you,' said Culbert.

'Come, let us continue with our walk,' said Janette. 'We still have a way to go before we return to the main path and then home.'

'Armand, what has happened?' asked Charles.

'We were just half a kilometre along the road from here and one of the horses went lame. There was no fresh horse available, so I must wait until tomorrow.'

'Never mind, Curveux's loss is our gain, if only for a day. Come Armand, we can sit in the garden and enjoy the rest of the afternoon.'

'Armand, what are you doing here?' Janette spluttered the question, completely taken aback by Armand's presence.

'Well, that is a nice greeting from my sister! My goodness you look flustered, what is the matter?'

Culbert walked into the garden, saw Armand and stopped, unable to move. He stifled a gasp.

'What is wrong with you two?' said Charles. 'If I didn't know better I would have thought you were up to something you shouldn't be!' He laughed.

Culbert and Janette looked uncomfortable, not knowing what to say. Armand's presence had taken them by surprise.

'Armand is to stay one more night with us, one of the horses went lame and he must wait until tomorrow before he can return to Curveux.' Charles sensed there was an atmosphere and thought it best to state a fact, rather than ask questions.

'Oh, that is good!' said Culbert. 'I am sure Janette is pleased, aren't you Janette?'

'Yes, yes, of course, I'm sorry Armand, I thought maybe there had been some sort of accident... which was why I reacted as I did.'

'Well, that's all right then! Come everyone, we can carry on where we left off earlier today!' Charles poured wine for everyone and all seemed calm again.

'Culbert, Janette is eight years older than you, and she is a married woman. I know you think us French are liberal in our ways but I don't want my sister hurt – not by you especially, you are almost family!'

'What do you mean Armand? Janette and I are good friends, I don't see her that often and I enjoy her company when I do.'

'Oh, stop it Culbert! I know what's going on, I have seen the way you look at Janette. You always have, even when you were younger.'

'So, what are you accusing me of?'

'Tell me what you have done, then I will know what to accuse you of.'

'I have done nothing wrong.'

'You are lovers, aren't you? You and Janette are lovers.'

'All right, so we are... but it only happened once. She was willing – I didn't force her. She wanted it as much as me.'

'Culbert, there are plenty of young women in this town, and there will be plenty in Paris. Find one your own age, and preferably not married.'

'You are very reserved and traditional, Armand. Don't you ever live dangerously?'

'No, I don't, because there is no future in it. If you continue like this you will eventually be alone; no one will want you. You may enjoy your affairs with married women but in the end they return to their husbands and you will not find a wife with that sort of record. I suppose you and Louise at the café are also lovers… is that why you've stayed here so long?'

'Oh, Armand, you can be so boring. I am only twenty, let me live a little.'

'Well, it's time you started to settle, that's all.'

Armand walked away, leaving Culbert standing in the now almost dark garden.

'Culbert, Culbert… what are you doing out there? Come in, we're having a nightcap.'

'Coming, Mama.'

Culbert walked in to the house with a confident air. 'No one is going to tell me how to run my life,' he thought.

Jessica rubbed her eyes; they were tired. 'Enough,' she thought, 'I must rest now and continue studying tomorrow.'

Grand Mere had been a seamstress in her younger days and knew the skill of invisible mending. She had shown Jessica her work and had started to demonstrate the art, but her hands were swollen with arthritis and she found it difficult to sew. She had, though, made notes and now Jessica was able to study the skills. Jessica knew that Culbert would at some time leave and she would need something to occupy herself, and of course the payment for such work would be substantial. Grand Mere had told her that she had a natural talent and that, in her words, 'it is important for France that this skill is perpetuated.' Jessica had laughed at the time but now realised that Grand Mere was right and so for the last two years, she had studied, practised and completed some mending for clients in Chateauneuf St Vincent who had been long-standing customers of Grand Mere. They were delighted that 'the English lady' had continued Grand Mere's work and Jessica had a small but steady flow of commissions.

The main invisible mending company was in Paris but Jessica had heard that a seamstress called Isobella had a business in Enville, which was not too far away. Perhaps she might learn more there, and one day have her own business.

Etta was delighted that Jessica had taken such an interest and had introduced her to Grand Mere's clients.

'I could never work with a needle as Grand Mere and you can,' said Etta. 'I think my fingers are the wrong shape!'

'Your fingers are very shapely, but it isn't an easy skill. I learned to sew when I was a child.'

'Who taught you?'

'We had a wonderful housekeeper, Mrs K, who was as a mother to me. She taught me.'

'Ah yes, Mrs K, the lady you write to in England.'

'Yes, that's right. She is a true friend.'

'Well, she will be very pleased to know of your progress with this skill.'

'Indeed, I have told her that I am learning and she has been most encouraging, she says I should go to Isobella in Enville and learn more.'

'I am impressed that Mrs K knows of Isobella!'

'Mrs K is a needlewoman of some repute and she knows about others in the same field. She said that Isobella has a fine reputation in England, especially with the aristocracy who go shooting and often snag their tweed jackets and trousers. Invisible mending is much cheaper than a new suit and men prefer to wear the same clothes – unlike us ladies who like to buy new ones each year!' Jessica laughed but also experienced a moment of sadness, knowing that she would probably never see England again.

'What a splendid idea, why don't we both go to see Isobella and spend some time there? It's a beautiful city.'

'Oh Etta, how wonderful! Yes, I would love that.'
'Good, then it is settled, I will arrange for a carriage and we shall go next week.'

Enville

It was just over thirty years since Enville had been developed. There were now many streets and squares, a new *préfecture* and an arts museum rivalled only by The Louvre in Paris. The citizens of Enville had good reason to be proud of their city and were delighted to welcome visitors who strolled their boulevards and enjoyed the cafés and restaurants.

Etta and Jessica marvelled at the splendour of it all. Chateauneuf St Vincent was so small by comparison; they felt overwhelmed by the enormous buildings and open spaces. Yet there was a beauty, the traditions of the city's past remained, especially in the imposing statue of The Goddess standing proudly in the city centre, commemorating the citizens' resistance to the Austrian siege of 1792. A proud city indeed, thought Jessica, maybe important people, leaders, would rise from this place in decades to come.

They found Isobella in Rue Masurel, a narrow street that formed an incomplete circle attached to the larger boulevard running through the city. All the buildings were three storeys high with large windows, although little light could enter due to the nearness of the buildings opposite. An architect's idea of beauty, perhaps, thought Jessica, but the reality left the street beautiful only on a plan. However, it was a fashionable street to be in and an address sought by those who were skilled in various crafts.

'Come on up,' said Mme Isobella. 'My work area is on the top floor, there is good light there – downstairs is for living and storage!'

Jessica remarked about the lack of light. 'We must sacrifice something for a good address,' said Isobella. 'If I had an address in any other part of the city I wouldn't get the business. It doesn't make sense, I know, but that is how it is.

'I knew of your Grand Mere,' said Isobella. 'She was a skilled lady and her reputation spread afar. I am so pleased that you knew her and have learned from her.'

'Where did you learn this skill, Madame?' asked Etta.

'Mama and Grand Mama were also needlewomen. It is inherited I think and good things that are inherited should be used, do you not agree?'

'Oh, yes indeed!' said Jessica, 'I am pleased I am able to do this work, but I didn't inherit the skill, I was taught.'

'Well then, perhaps you will pass on your skill to your children.'

'No, I don't think so,' said Jessica. 'I have but one son, and he is in the restaurant business.'

'That is good too! France is becoming famous for its cafés and restaurants. Between you and your son, you should do very well!'

Etta and Jessica strolled back towards where they had arranged to meet their carriage, Jessica carrying a parcel of books that Isobella had given her.

'You'll be very busy now,' said Etta.

'With Culbert gone to Paris, I must do something with my time. Maybe I will expand Grand Mere's list of customers in Chateauneuf St Vincent.'

'Yes, I think you will!'

The carriage rolled along gently through the countryside. Jessica had enjoyed her day and was full of ideas.

'Jessica, is everything all right between Culbert and Armand?'

Jessica was surprised. 'What do you mean, Etta?'

'Well, I thought I heard them shouting... The day Armand

came back unexpectedly, they seemed to be arguing.'

'I don't know, Culbert didn't say anything.'

'Maybe it was nothing important.'

'Oh, I'm sure it wasn't, what on earth could they have to argue about? They rarely see each other.'

'It seemed to be something to do with Janette.'

'Really? I am sorry Etta but I have no idea, Culbert only talks to me about the café and his work.'

'Did you two ladies enjoy your day?' asked Charles.

'Yes, we did,' said Etta. 'Jessica has books from Isobella which she hopes to learn from and extend her business.'

'That is wonderful, a family tradition carried on by our "English family"!'

Jessica smiled. 'You have been so kind to us, I am glad that I can make a contribution in this way.'

'Come, let us have a glass of wine to celebrate,' said Charles. 'Then I expect you two will want a rest before we have dinner.'

Jessica carefully recorded the events of the day in her diary; she was delighted with Isobella's books and put them carefully in her desk. As she wrote, she pondered what Culbert and Armand could have been arguing about. 'What has Janette got to do with it? Oh no, I hope Culbert hasn't done something he shouldn't have.'

There had been gossip in Chateauneuf St Vincent about Culbert and young women. 'Just normal growing up,' Jessica had thought. 'Of course he's bound to be the subject of gossip because he is English. There is nothing I can do or say, he is twenty now, a man, I have no control over him, what he does is his responsibility. But I hope that he hasn't done anything to damage the good names of Charles and Etta; they have been so wonderful, never judging, and always ready to help.'

Jessica closed her diary and placed it in the satinwood box. She was tired, very tired; a long day but a good one, apart from the question about Culbert.

5

1892

Jessica coughed a little as she read Mrs K's letter. Spring had
arrived after a cold winter, but there was still a chill in the air.

> I am so pleased that Mr Culbert is doing so well, twenty-
> two years now, my, how the time has flown since we were
> all at Berg House!
> I don't suppose you are interested any more but I shall
> tell you anyhow, my cousin in East Leah tells me that HIS
> two sons are now at university and will join the army
> when they have finished their studies. I hope it is the
> proper army, not the volunteers HE was in! Thank good-
> ness Mr Culbert is doing something useful with his life.

And so Jessica read on; now it all seemed so far away, another
life, another time. Dear Mrs K.

Jessica coughed again, this time there was a slight rasp,
she put her handkerchief to her mouth and to her horror there
were specks of blood. 'Oh no,' she thought, 'this is what
happened to Papa!' She walked to the kitchen and poured
herself a glass of water.

Etta appeared in the doorway. 'Are you all right, Jessica?'

'Yes, I'm fine thank you, Etta, just a cough, must be the cold
wet weather.'

'Hmm... ' said Etta. 'You've been coughing for some time

now, I think you should see the doctor.'

'No, it's nothing, it'll go when it is warmer.'

'Well, you know how you feel,' said Etta. 'But promise me you will see a doctor if it doesn't go soon!'

'Yes, yes Etta, I will of course!'

Jessica went back to the annexe; it seemed much bigger now that Culbert wasn't there. Two years had passed since he moved to Paris and now he was manager of a large café in the Place du Tertre. He had always been fascinated by this part of Paris and loved walking among the artists, admiring their work and chatting with them. His café was now a fashionable place to visit and attracted many European visitors, especially those on the European Tour. He had promised to visit Jessica again when he could get away; she hoped that he wouldn't leave it too long.

Summer 1892

'This is the café everyone talks about,' said Mary.

'Mmm, I can see why,' said her sister Melvina.

'We must try it, come on Mel!'

They walked into Café Benedict. It was large and airy, unlike many of the Parisian establishments, and it had an air of difference; an air of modernity.

Culbert was walking across the main floor of the café to check on a table when he saw Mary. He stopped abruptly.

'Monsieur, may we have a table please?'

Culbert said nothing.

'Monsieur, may we have a table please?'

Culbert stuttered slightly. 'Yes, yes, of course, please follow me.'

'Are you English, Monsieur? If not then your English is excellent, for a Frenchman that is!' Mary and Melvina laughed.

'I am English, Madame, but I have lived in France since I was a child.'

'Mademoiselle, please,' said Mary smiling.

'Oh, pardon Mademoiselle, and your companion?'

'Yes, we are both Mademoiselles,' laughed Mary. 'This is my sister.'

Culbert stared at Mary. He had never seen such beauty in a woman; everything about her was perfect; her figure, her skin, and her hair.

'Are you all right, Monsieur?' asked Melvina.

'Yes, yes, indeed... Now what can I get for you ladies?'

'Whatever you recommend, Monsieur.'

Culbert went back to the kitchen and called to Franc to make some special coffee for the ladies. He steadied himself on the table. 'What is happening to me?' he thought, 'I'm behaving as if I'm a love-struck swain.' He pulled himself up straight and took the coffee from Franc. 'I will serve the ladies.'

'What brings you to Paris, Mademoiselles?' asked Culbert.

'We are travelling through Europe to see as many sights as we can, before we have to settle into marriage,' laughed Mary.

'Do you have an intended?'

'Oh, what a quaint way to ask,' laughed Melvina. 'Mary has, sort of, but nothing fixed, she's too independent to let someone else tell her what to do.'

'I don't blame her,' said Culbert. 'Everyone should be able to marry who they wish.'

'Well said, Monsieur,' said Mary.

'Enjoy your coffee, Mademoiselles.'

Culbert backed away and left Mary and Melvina sipping their drinks.

'He seems a charming young man,' said Melvina. 'So handsome, with those blond curls.'

'Yes, he has an air about him I like,' replied Mary.

'Oh, that sounds interesting!'

'Well, it could be… ' The two ladies laughed and finished their coffee.

That evening, Culbert sat in the comfortable chair in the flat he lived in above the café. 'She shall be mine,' he thought. 'I will have her.'

'Shall we go into Café Benedict again, Mary?'

'I think we shall.'

Culbert was waiting; he had been waiting since Mary and Melvina left the café the previous day. He knew they would come back.

'Good morning ladies, what an honour to see you again.'

'Oh Monsieur, you flatter!'

'And why not?'

Mary and Melvina sat near the window; Culbert pulled a chair alongside them.

'Have you visited the Artists Quarter and seen them at work?'

'No, we haven't.'

'Then I shall take you! We shall stroll around there this morning, then have lunch together.'

'You are very forward, Monsieur,' said Mary.

'Don't you like being forward?'

'I think I do.'

'Good, then that is settled.'

Culbert, Mary and Melvina walked around the Place du Tertre. The warm, sunny day had brought many artists into the small square, all busy working at their easels.

'Do you paint, Monsieur?'

'No, but I enjoy looking at paintings,' said Culbert. 'Please will you call me Culbert?'

'Culbert?' said Mary. 'That's unusual, is it a family name?'

'I think so, my father died when I was a baby so I don't know about him or his family.'

'I think it's Irish, isn't it?' said Melvina.

'Well whatever it is, it's your name so we shall call you by it,' laughed Mary.

They wandered for two hours talking with the artists, laughing and enjoying the warm morning.

Culbert took them to a small restaurant near the river; they sat watching the boats while they had lunch.

'Have you been to the Palace of Versailles?'

'No, not yet,' answered Mary.

'Good, then I will be delighted to take you both. It is an experience that must not be missed!'

'You are knowledgeable about France, Culbert – do you ever visit England?'

Mary looked quizzically at Culbert, wondering how such a handsome young man was as yet unattached.

'I haven't been back to England since we came here when I was five years of age. France is my home, although I will always be an Englishman.'

'I think that you can be both. Our countries have not always agreed in the past but I think that they do allow dual nationality,' said Melvina.

'Well, that will indeed be useful I suppose, if and when I consider going to England. Where in England do you two delightful ladies come from?'

'We live in London, in one of the south-west suburbs.'

'And is that where your intended is?' Culbert turned towards Mary.

'Oh really, you mustn't take anything Mel says seriously! A friend of Papa's calls to see me, he's a boring banker but Papa thinks he's suitable for me!'

'And is he?' asked Culbert.

'Probably, but he will still be boring!'

'And you Monsieur Culbert, do you have a young lady?'

'No one special.'

'But you must have some family somewhere – you said your

father died when you were a baby, what about your mother?'

'Mama is in Chateauneuf St Vincent; she lives with some friends, in an annexe of their house. We both lived there until I moved here to Paris.'

'Do you see her often?'

'Occasionally, when I can, she understands how busy I am. In fact, I shall visit her soon, I think the winter has not been kind to her health.'

'Oh, sorry to hear that, I hope she'll soon be better.'

Mary, Melvina and Culbert strolled along the promenade by the Seine, enjoying the rest of the afternoon.

'Sunday, if you ladies are both free, is a good day to visit the Palace of Versailles.'

'We shall be delighted! Shall we call at your café at ten o'clock?'

'Excellent,' said Culbert. 'Until then.'

'*A bientôt*, as the French say!' laughed Melvina.

Culbert had spent more time thinking in recent days than he had for a long time. 'Mary is such a beauty, and her sister Melvina, what fun she is! I'm not sure which one I like the best... '

'I must visit Mama,' he mused, 'her health is not good from what Etta tells me. I will write and tell her I am coming next week.'

Versailles

The train journey was brief; partly due to the rail link, Versailles was fast becoming part of Paris in shared culture as well as in proximity.

The day could not have been better. The sun shone as it had not shone for several months, the air smelled of the greenery of spring growth.

Mary looked absolutely radiant, thought Culbert, her fair hair and complexion seemed to reflect the sun. Melvina with her darker hair and skin had a coquettish look about her, which made Culbert smile inwardly.

'Today you will absorb the culture of a golden era in the history of France. The Palace of the Sun King and the beautiful gardens designed mainly by Le Notre, these are all matters that English gentleladies should know of and be able to discuss when in England.'

Melvina laughed. 'Oh dear, are we to have an examination?'

'No, just a guided tour by your humble escort, Monsieur Culbert Montaigne.'

'Indeed, then we must listen,' said Mary.

Since becoming manager of Café Benedict, Culbert had used the surname Montaigne. He had not told his mother this yet, but knew she would understand that Warner was not a surname that a manager of a French café would have. Mary and Melvina, of course, were not aware that Montaigne wasn't his real name.

The Palace of Versailles, or *Château de Versailles* as the French called it, gleamed in the morning sun. Culbert, Mary and Melvina gasped at the panoramic view of the palace; it seemed endless.

'But there is so much more to see,' said Culbert. 'You must have heard of the Hall of Mirrors, but I want to also show you my favourite area, we call it the Queen's House.'

He led the ladies through the palace into the garden and turned towards the wooded area on the north side.

'Oh!' gasped Mary. 'It's wonderful!'

The Queen's House, built for Marie Antoinette, stood beside a lake and its mirror image appeared in the glassy water.

'The Queen had an eye for beauty. She chose this place for her house and was instrumental in much of the planning and design of the palace,' remarked Culbert.

'Didn't the King have many lovers?' asked Melvina.

'Of course, the aristocracy were expected to have lovers but remain married to secure the bloodline. The same happens in England and probably throughout the world.'

'And do you agree with those morals, Monsieur Culbert?' Melvina looked straight at him as she asked the question.

'I'm not aristocracy, just an ordinary businessman, Mademoiselle Melvina. Those standards do not concern me.'

Mary smiled. 'Monsieur Culbert, now you must take us to the Hall of Mirrors. We have heard so much about it!'

'Yes, let's go there now – you may be surprised at what you see! The pictures of it make it appear a very large hall, but you may find it is not as big as you think.'

They wandered back into the main building and entered the Hall of Mirrors.

'I see what you mean,' said Mary. 'The mirrors give an illusion of size, but really it's not as large as I had expected.'

'But it's still so very beautiful,' added Melvina.

'I can imagine the kings and queens walking through here, the statesmen standing here... what a wonderful sight it must have been,' said Mary.

'Now we too can admire it,' replied Culbert.

The train moved out of the station at Versailles on its way to Paris. It had been a day to remember for all three visitors.

'You look serious,' said Mary.

'We have had such a wonderful day but I cannot help thinking of my mama, I must visit her soon. She has been coughing for some time – I think her father also suffered from a persistent cough, I hope it's not serious.'

'What happened to her papa?'

'Sadly, he died from consumption – though I'm not sure what that means.'

'I think it describes any problems with the lungs,' said Mary. 'Maybe she will be better now we have warmer weather.'

'Yes, I hope so. I shall go next weekend. Will you ladies be staying in Paris for some time?'

'I think we will,' said Mary looking at Melvina and smiling.

'Good, then we can meet again, perhaps?'

'Of course, and we would like to know how your mama is.'

Chateauneuf St Vincent, Late Summer 1892

Jessica sat under the large, sprawling branches of the ancient maple tree. The wide finger-shaped leaves shaded her from the intensity of the sun. A hot summer had followed a cold, cold winter and now the warmth seemed to penetrate her skin, giving her a feeling of peacefulness.

Etta came to sit with her. 'How wonderful! Culbert is coming on the next train. We shall be so pleased to see him again – how well he is doing in Paris!'

'Yes, I'm so pleased for him, I was never sure how it would all turn out for us both... at least he has a good chance now,' said Jessica.

'That sounds a little morbid Jessica, the doctor said that as long as you rest and have plenty of fresh air and sun, he sees no reason why you should not recover well from this recent illness.'

'My papa had trouble with his lungs, I fear it may be inherited.'

'Maybe, but it also may be the weather that is inherited.'

Jessica laughed. 'You could be right, perhaps the French air may serve me better.'

Culbert appeared at the end of the garden. He ran to Jessica and Etta, embracing his mother.

'Careful Culbert, you will squeeze the life from me!' said Jessica, laughing.

'Oh, that's not possible, Mama! You have so much life in you, I could never do that, you will live forever!'

'I hope not!' said Jessica. 'I think I will be happy with my allotted span, eternity is not for me, at least not on this earth.'

They all laughed and sat and talked together until the sun gradually lost its strength and the air cooled.

'Mama, I have met a wonderful woman. Mary is her name. She is delightful, beautiful, charming... I think I'm in love!'

'Oh my goodness Culbert, how marvellous! Who is she?'

'Would you believe, Mama, she is English? She and her sister live in London and are doing the European tour. They're staying in Paris rather longer than planned, I am pleased to say.'

'You are twenty-two years of age now Culbert – perhaps you should think of settling, even marrying?'

'I'm not sure, Mama, but I cannot stop thinking of Mary. She is in my thoughts every minute of my waking hours.'

'Oh goodness, you are love struck!'

'Is that bad, Mama?'

'No, it is not, but for a relationship to last there must be more than infatuation because that will soon fade.'

'How will I know if Mary is my true, real love and not just a passing infatuation?'

'You must not see her for several weeks, then if you still feel the same, it is real. If not, you will have already met someone else.'

'Very well, but I don't like the thought of telling Mary that.'

'If she loves you, she will be pleased to do what you suggest. If she is infatuated, she will go away and you won't see her again.'

'You are very wise, Mama.'

'Culbert, at my age I have time to sit and think, there is little else to do.'

'Are you not feeling better, Mama?'

'Yes, I'm feeling better and I hope that I will live long enough to see you happy, in whatever direction your life takes.'

'Oh Mama, of course you will!'

Culbert spent four happy days with Jessica, Etta and

Charles, but then it was time to return to Paris. Culbert thought constantly of Mary – and also of Melvina. 'What a beautiful pair they are,' he reflected, 'but it's Mary I want, and Mary I shall have.'

'We have enjoyed your stay so much!' Etta embraced Culbert as he stood on the station platform waiting for the Paris train. 'Your dear mama seems so much better each time you stay.'

'Yes, I know, I'm thinking of asking her to move to Paris with me. I realise her home is with you but I think that we must be together, I know her health is failing.'

'You are so astute Culbert. We love having Jessica with us but you are right, she misses you and if you are together, perhaps life will be better for her.'

'I will write when I have arranged something. It won't be long, I hope.'

Etta waved as the train pulled away from the platform. 'Such a kind young man,' she thought.

Café Benedict, Autumn 1892

'Come on Mary, it's about time you saw my apartment. So far all you have seen is where I work, now you must see where I relax.'

'And how do you relax, Culbert?'

'I read a lot. Often I am very tired so relaxing is just that, doing nothing and then sleeping!'

They climbed the narrow staircase to Culbert's apartment above the café; it was surprisingly large, the outside appearance belying its inner vastness. The buildings in the streets around the Place du Tertre were tall and narrow, but they were very deep and much space lay behind the small facades.

'This is amazing!' said Mary. 'It's vast, how wonderful!'

'I am glad you like it; it suits me well. It is too large, but that is better than too small, I think!'

Culbert took Mary into his bedroom. She looked apprehensive. 'Don't worry,' Culbert laughed. 'Here you have the best view over the streets and squares and can see for a long way because we are so high. This is the room with the best view, which is why I chose it for my bedroom.'

Culbert turned to Mary and put his arms around her. Mary pulled back slightly. 'Culbert, what are you doing?'

'You know what I am doing, I want you... I have wanted you from the moment I set eyes on you. You want me too, I know you do.'

'Oh, so what makes you think that?'

'Well, you are in my bedroom aren't you?'

Culbert had an urgency about him. He took Mary's blouse off and removed her bodice. Her breasts were small and firm, the nipples pert, upright. Culbert felt his pulse pounding. He cupped her breasts in his hands, then leaned forward, kissing her nipples. Mary did not resist, but moaned softly and held him in the embrace. Culbert continued to undress Mary, all the time becoming harder and harder. He felt Mary's thighs, her abdomen and then her soft pubic hair. Mary groaned again but still held him tight. He lifted her swiftly on to his bed, removed his trousers and underpants to reveal a hard upright organ throbbing with desire. Mary looked at him and then pulled him on to her. He entered her easily and then rhythmically moved inside her. 'Oh Mary, I can't wait much longer... ' Mary was moving with the same rhythm. Culbert could feel the muscles inside her gripping him, then relaxing. She was in full orgasm, then the climax came for them both, together; it lasted and lasted. Mary went into another orgasm even more intense. Culbert felt as if he was in heaven. When they were both spent, they lay together in silence.

'How is your mother?' asked Mary after they had rested and regained their breath.

'She's not in good health. I think I will bring her here to Paris – it isn't fair for Charles and Etta to look after her anymore.'

'I agree, she is all you have. It's your duty to look after her.'

'Will you meet her, Mary?'

'Of course, if you want me to.'

'How long will you stay in Paris?'

'We have no definite plans, perhaps I may stay here forever!'

'That's a very good idea,' said Culbert, looking into her eyes. 'What about Melvina?'

'She can decide for herself, I am not her keeper... but she likes Paris better than London, so maybe she will stay too.'

'Excellent, then we will all be happy.'

'You've been with him, haven't you?' Melvina looked quizzically at Mary.

'And what if I have?'

'Do you love him?'

'I don't know... he is a very good lover.'

'Did you get pleasure as well as him?'

'Oh yes, very much so!'

'So, are we staying in Paris for a while then?'

'I think so. What about you, Melvina?'

'Well, I would rather be here than London... Yes, I shall stay if you will, we have the apartment for as long as we want.'

'Good, then that's settled, I shall tell Culbert. By the way, he's going to ask his mama to come and live with him, her health is poor and he needs to look after her.'

'Of course, that's good. Perhaps we can also be company for her.'

'Yes, I'm sure we can. I'll ask Culbert what we can do to help.'

Melvina put down her book; her eyes were tired. 'What a day!' she thought. 'Now I have something to look forward to.

Maybe I'm not Culbert's first choice… but I think he may be a man to enjoy a little diversion occasionally. We shall see.'

'Mama, this is Mary, and this is her sister, Melvina.'

Jessica moved slowly towards the sisters.

'We are delighted to meet you, Madame,' said Mary. 'Please come and sit by the window, you can see the river from there.'

Mary and Melvina's apartment was in a large building along the Quai de Valmay. It belonged to their father, a diplomat, who used it when his duties necessitated a stay in Paris. When he had no need for it, Mary and Melvina would stay there. To them it was a second home. Culbert had been very impressed when he first visited it, realising then that the sisters had wealth as well as beauty.

'So, you are coming to live in Paris with Culbert, Madame?'

'Yes, and please call me Jessica, we're not formal in the country!'

They all laughed and the atmosphere was relaxed and happy. Mary and Melvina told Jessica about their home in London and how their father worked for the British Government. Jessica listened with a contented air. 'Culbert has chosen well,' she thought.

'We shall have such fun,' said Melvina. 'We can go out for day trips and enjoy ourselves all the time.'

'I think you have forgotten that I work!' laughed Culbert.

'No, of course not, anyway we can take Jessica out with us when you are working, then she won't be alone.'

'That will be perfect,' said Culbert. 'Don't you think, Mama?'

'Yes, Culbert, but you young people must remember that I am slow now and cannot keep up with everything you do!'

'I am sure we will all be happy,' said Mary. 'Paris is not for rushing, it's for enjoying slowly!'

Back at Culbert's apartment, Jessica smiled and looked at

Culbert. 'Which one do you like the best?'

'Mama, really, it is Mary that I love and I shall ask her to marry me soon.'

'Are you sure?'

'Yes, why do you ask?'

'I saw the way that you look at Melvina. I think, Culbert, that you like both young ladies.'

'Like yes, but I love only one, Mama.'

'Well, make sure that is so, just make sure.'

'Has your mama seen the Eiffel Tower?'

'No, she hasn't, this is her first stay in Paris.'

'Do you think she would like to see it? Mel and I could take her when you are at work.'

'Excellent idea, if she agrees,' said Culbert.

Jessica and Mary strolled along the avenue towards the tower; the trees lined the roadway almost making an arch. Jessica was enthralled by the scenery and stopped frequently to gaze back along the avenue, to appreciate the splendour of it.

Mary wore the latest style of walking suit, much as Jessica had worn all those years ago when in England but with a shorter skirt and 'leg o'mutton' sleeves, the current fashion. Jessica admired her outfit. 'Thank you, Jessica. I understand that you're a skilled needlewoman?'

'Yes, I suppose so, I studied invisible mending with Grand Mere in Chateauneuf St Vincent, then with Isobella in Enville. After that I had a small business, which was very successful.'

'You don't work now, then?'

'No, my eyes are tired when I work for too long. It's a skill for someone younger.'

What Jessica didn't tell Mary was that she had made a considerable amount and had given much of this to Culbert to pay for his living expenses in Paris. Jessica didn't need the money now and she knew that Culbert would work hard. He had not disappointed her; she was proud that he was so successful. 'Now he is possibly approaching marriage,' she thought, 'let's hope that life will run smoothly for him.'

They approached the tower; a small group was gathered, waiting for the lift.

'First stage, I think, Jessica?'

'Yes, Mary, that will do well.'

'You can see the boundaries of Paris from the first stage, higher it is difficult to see anything clearly, and much more expensive!'

Jessica and Mary enjoyed each other's company. Melvina had decided not to come with them; she wasn't happy with high places, they made her dizzy, she said, and she didn't want to spoil the day for Jessica and Mary.

The lift travelled slowly up the angled leg of the tower to the first stage, where Jessica and Mary alighted. The view, as Mary said, was magnificent; the entire city was there and the green fields beyond its boundaries were clearly visible. They walked around the four sides of the stage enjoying the fresh air, free from the aromas of the city at this height.

'What a shame that your sister does not like heights! This is so beautiful.'

'She will have to enjoy the view from our description!' replied Mary.

'So, you are afraid of heights?'

'Oh yes, very afraid,' laughed Melvina.

'And you, Monsieur Culbert, are so busy that you cannot leave your café today!'

'Oh yes, my deputy has been called in to help because we are so busy!'

Culbert gently steered Melvina on to his bed. This was the moment he had been waiting for, and he could not believe it had happened so easily.

Melvina was two years younger than her sister. She was also

slim, but not too slim. Her auburn hair shone and complemented her tanned skin.

Culbert ran his hands through her hair. 'It is beautiful, just beautiful.'

'Are you going to marry Mary?'

'If she will have me.'

'She'll have you, but why don't you want to marry me?'

'If I marry you, Mary will go away. If I marry Mary, I can have you both.'

'Culbert, you are despicable.'

'Yes, and you would rather be my lover than my wife, wouldn't you?'

'So does that make me despicable also?'

'No, it makes us two of a kind, so we shall always be friends… that is, as long as Mary never knows.'

'Well, she won't know from me.'

'Good. Now, no more talking.'

'How was Paris from the tower?' asked Culbert.

'It was divine,' said Mary, 'and Jessica and I had such a lovely time! After the tower we went to a lovely little street café and had the most delightful fruit tarts – not as nice as those in Café Benedict, of course, but still delicious!'

The small individual fruit tarts made with seasonal fresh fruits, then glazed with a crystal clear gel encased by the lightest butter pastry, were becoming a national delicacy. Bakeries vied to make not only the best, but also the most artistic versions, some creating tarts almost impossible to eat, seemingly just to enjoy as an art form. Culbert, always with an eye for fashions, had made sure his pastry chef concentrated on tarts that stood out not only their looks, but also for the flavour of the fresh fruit.

'You have a very successful businessman for a son, Jessica,' said Melvina. 'Many of our friends now regard this café as among the top establishments of its kind in Paris.'

'Yes, I'm very proud of him,' said Jessica.

'But I couldn't have done it without you, Mama, that I know.'

They all laughed, happy in each other's company, all having enjoyed their day, but not all knowing quite how it had been spent.

'I shall ask Mary to marry me.'

Culbert stood facing his mother, as if asking permission.

Jessica laughed. 'Culbert, you need not stand to attention!'

'No, of course not,' laughed Culbert, and sat on the settee.

'However, as you are both under twenty-five years old, you need the permission of your parents before you can marry. That is French law. I give my permission of course, but what of Mary's parents?'

'Ah, I didn't know that, but I cannot see why they would refuse, can you Mama?'

'I don't know, Culbert, some parents are very protective of their daughters, and I believe you told me that Mary's father wanted her to marry a banker in England.'

'Yes, she mentioned that but she didn't seem interested in him, neither has she seen him for some time because she's been here in France, mostly with us!'

'That may not matter. The marriage, while not arranged exactly, may be expected, so be prepared for a problem.'

'So what would I do then?'

'Well, first you must ask her to marry you. We can't do anything before that, can we?'

Culbert and Mary walked along the promenade of the Seine; it was an autumn evening, still, but fresh with a hint of a chill in the air.

'Mary, it would give me the greatest honour if you would become my wife.'

Mary jumped. 'Culbert, my goodness, just like that! I really don't know what to say!'

Mary had imagined that Culbert would make a romantic proposal in an equally romantic setting and was quite unprepared for this rather blunt way of asking.

'Well, you could say yes.'

Mary laughed. 'All right, I shall say yes, but you must ask again on one knee.'

'Must I?'

'Yes, or I shall say no.'

'All right.' Culbert went on one knee and said, 'My beloved Mary, will you marry me, please?'

Some passers-by stopped, smiled and clapped. Mary looked at them, then at Culbert, 'Yes, yes I will!'

The passers-by cheered, Culbert lifted Mary in his arms. 'I am going to marry the most beautiful lady in Paris!' he announced to the small audience.

Everyone laughed and continued to clap; Culbert and Mary embraced and walked away hand in hand, leaving the spectators looking on.

'We must go to Mama,' said Culbert. 'We need her permission, although I know she will give it, then we need your parents' permission.'

'Must we have their permission?'

'It's the law. Why, will there be a problem?'

'No, I don't think so.' Mary looked a little troubled, the euphoria of the proposal now dampened by this news.

Back at Café Benedict, Culbert, Mary, Jessica and Melvina raised their glasses of champagne. 'To the happy couple!' said Melvina. They all drank the toast.

'So, you have to get our parents' permission to be married?' said Melvina.

'Yes,' said Jessica, 'there is a form to sign if the parents are not resident in France, and the justice who marries you must see that signed form.'

'Well, that won't be a problem then,' said Culbert.

'How do you know that? You don't know our parents.'

'No, and the justice won't know their signature, will he?'

'Culbert, that's against the law,' said Jessica.

'But what difference would it make?' asked Culbert.

'Well, none I suppose... but really, I don't know, let's ask Mary's parents first.'

'Once you're twenty-five it won't matter, here or in England.'

'I know Melvina, but it frightens me.'

'Oh come on Mary, Grandfather's trust is yours when you're twenty-five, that's four years away. Time goes quickly... we're so busy, you won't notice it at all!'

'But what if our parents find out?'

'What can they do? It won't affect your inheritance, or would you rather marry that boring banker Papa has lined up for you?'

'Not in a million years! Culbert is the one for me.'

'Good, then I will write the letter and we can find a justice to marry us.'

Culbert listened as this discussion went on. He knew Mary would inherit some money one day, she had hinted at it, but he didn't know how much or when. Now he was halfway to knowing.

'Culbert, will you agree to this?'

Culbert looked at the letter written by Melvina, allegedly from their father. 'It looks convincing to me and I don't think the French authorities will check. We're not French, so they won't care too much.'

'Good, than all we need to do is find a justice and then we can arrange the date!'

'Charles, whose house I lived in with Mama, is a justice – he could marry us.'

'No Culbert, we shouldn't involve someone we know.'

'But supposing, when we are married, he asks why he

couldn't have done the ceremony, what shall we say? He may be offended.'

'Oh goodness, I hadn't thought of that! We are getting involved,' said Mary.

'Maybe if Charles does marry us, then no one will question it,' said Culbert.

'Yes, of course, excellent!' said Melvina. 'Let's do that.'

'I'm not happy with this, Culbert, but I see your reasoning. I just hope that we won't have reason to regret it.'

'Thank you so much, Mama, Charles will surely be delighted to marry Mary and me if you ask him.'

'Very well, it is done, we shall see what he says.'

The Wedding, 1893

Culbert and Mary, Jessica, Melvina, Etta, Armand and Janette gathered in the small room within the *hôtel de ville* in Chateauneuf St Vincent.

Charles had been delighted when Jessica had asked him to marry Culbert and Mary; he gave the consent letter from Mary merely a cursory glance before filing it in the marriage register cabinet. Culbert told Charles that he wished to be married in the name 'Montaigne', and so it was recorded.

The ceremony was simple but solemn. Armand and Melvina were the two witnesses required and duly signed the register.

Charles and Etta had offered their home and garden as a venue for the wedding feast, which Culbert and Mary had readily accepted. The garden, where they had all spent so many happy times, was adorned with bunting and flowers, tables were laid around the lawn and the delicious buffet provided by Culbert's staff from Café Benedict was a feast for the eyes.

They drank toasts, ate, laughed and danced the afternoon away. Everyone was happy.

'So, you've tied the knot at last!' said Janette.

'Yes, I need to settle and think about our future, business, children... '

'Good, then I wish you and Mary every happiness – particularly Mary.'

'And what do you mean by that?'

'Oh come on Culbert, you are a ladies' man, you will never be happy with one woman. Mary's sister is quite a beauty too, isn't she?'

Culbert looked embarrassed. 'Shut up Janette! It's our wedding day, don't spoil it.'

'Oh, I shan't tell,' laughed Janette. 'But don't hurt her Culbert, she's too nice, probably too nice for you.'

Janette walked away, not looking back at Culbert.

'Do you have a wife, Armand?' asked Melvina.

'Yes, I do and she would have loved to have been here but she is away at present on some important business – so we had to choose who would come and I won!'

'What is this important business, or is it a secret?'

'No, goodness me, no secret, we are architects and have a very big contract. Today it's being finalised and one of us must be present to sign.'

'Oh, I see,' said Melvina. 'So you have a clever wife, Armand?'

'I doubt if she would call herself clever, we both studied and qualified. It was more difficult for a woman but she was determined and succeeded, now she is accepted on the same terms as I am.'

'It's not easy for a woman to find success in business or even to be in business at all, she has done well.'

'Yes, I'm proud of her.'

'And your friend, Culbert, he has also done well – a good business in Paris and now married to my beautiful sister.'

'Culbert has been like a younger brother, I am glad he's settled now.'

'You think he will settle?'

'What do you mean, Melvina?'

'Oh, I think you know Armand, I think you know... we are both aware of Culbert's character, are we not?'

Armand did not answer but drank the remainder of his wine. 'I must mix with the others,' he said, wandering away to join his mother and father.

'Will you join Culbert in his café business, Mary?'

'Yes, I think I will. I love mixing with all the different people. We have so many travellers from all over Europe in Paris now, it's so exciting.'

'You will be a great asset I am sure. Will you live at the café apartment?'

'We will for now, perhaps some time later we will move into the suburbs. We shall see... the business needs expanding, that must come first.'

'And what about your sister Melvina?'

'Melvina has Papa's apartment in Paris, she can be there as long as she likes, Papa and Mama are away for some time and when they return, they will live in London.'

'Such a shame they could not be here!'

Mary looked a little embarrassed. 'Yes, but they are so far away and it was just not possible... Could I have a little more wine, do you think? My throat is quite dry, I haven't talked so much for a long time!'

'Of course you can, and you must be tired. It's been a long and exciting day for you.'

'Yes, and a very happy day!'

Charles, Etta, Armand and Janette waved as Culbert, Mary, Jessica and Melvina drove away from the house in a decorated carriage. First, they would return the short distance to Paris. Melvina had agreed to stay with Jessica while Culbert and Mary went on their honeymoon to Italy.

Lake Garda

'You couldn't have chosen better, Culbert, this is delightful, and the air is so clean, so fresh.'

'Many a customer has told me about this place, so I relied on their good judgement for a honeymoon destination. I am glad you're not disappointed!'

The small town on the west side of the lake was surrounded by lemon trees and olive groves, while to the north and east rose the impressive Dolomites, part of the Alps.

'I could stay here forever,' said Mary laying back on Culbert as they sat by the lakeside.

'Me too, but I think Café Benedict wouldn't do so well here, there are not enough people.'

'Not now, but one day perhaps.'

They walked along the stony edge of the lake. Fishermen were returning from a day's work, unloading their catch at the small market. Their catches were not big but enough to make a living; most of the families in the local countryside had olive groves and from them, the living was good.

Turning into the cobbled street, they walked past the stalls selling tomatoes, lemons and vegetables, all vying for trade by claiming that theirs was the best.

The small apartment Culbert had rented from a friend in Paris was adequate for two people; it was not luxurious, but had all they wanted. There was a narrow pathway above them that led up into the hills, and tucked away was a small monastery, now a shrine for travellers. The well-tended gardens around the buildings were filled with lemon trees and tomatoes, their fruits hanging heavily on the branches.

'It's more difficult coming down than going up,' said Mary. 'It's hurting my back, it's so steep.'

'I will carry you, my darling.' Culbert lifted Mary into his arms and carried her down the remainder of the slope.

'Oh Culbert, I didn't know you were so strong!'

'For you, my darling, I have the strength to do anything.'

They laughed and continued down the slope, back to their apartment.

'One day, we must definitely live here,' said Mary.

'If only, but there would not be a living, we could not afford it.'

'But I have my inheritance Culbert, that will mean we will be able to afford it. I will have it in just under four years' time, when I am twenty-five.'

'But surely it's not enough to live on? What about our children?'

'There will be more than enough for you, me and as many children as we want!'

Culbert laughed. He was not going to ask Mary the extent of her inheritance in case she thought he was showing too much interest.

'That's settled then, when you are a rich heiress we shall live here with ten children!'

'I think three children will be sufficient, Culbert; two will argue and compete, a third brings balance, a sort of umpire.'

'Very well then, three it is.' Culbert was glad to have steered away from the subject of Mary's money; nothing must jeopardise his plans.

The days passed. Culbert and Mary, relaxed and refreshed, returned to Paris. It was time to prepare for the busy late autumn and winter season.

6

Jessica sat in the small courtyard garden at Café Benedict. It was a warm afternoon; 1895 had been a good year so far, the seasons were as they should be, and now in early summer the days were long and peaceful.

Her cough had become persistent in spite of the warmth and now flecks of blood often appeared in her handkerchief when she coughed. She had seen Etta's doctor but he could do little. She knew it was the same illness that her father had; she knew the outcome.

By her side was her satinwood box, now full with her diaries. There had been so much happening in the last few years and it all had to be recorded.

Culbert came into the garden. 'How are you, Mama?'

'I'm all right, Culbert. Don't worry about me.'

'But I do, Mama, you are not well and I want to help.'

'There is nothing you can do Culbert. What will be, will be.'

Culbert looked at the satinwood box. 'That must be full by now,' he smiled.

'Yes, and when I'm no longer here you shall have it, but you must promise me that you will not open it, but pass it on to your firstborn.'

Culbert looked taken aback. 'Why?'

'That is my wish, please do not question it.'

'Very well Mama, of course I will do what you say.'

'By the way, is Mary pregnant?'

'You are very forthright Mama! Yes she is, but only a few weeks. How did you know?'

Jessica laughed. 'A woman always knows about another woman, that is something you won't ever understand!'

'Maybe one day I might, but not now!' Culbert laughed too.

'When I die I want you to write to Mrs K. She is your godmother; she is very old now, but she will live longer than me. I don't feel that I can write to her at the moment; ask her also to tell your other godparents.'

'Yes, of course Mama, I will do whatever you say. Mrs K was a good friend to us.'

Jessica sighed. 'I will sleep a while now. Thank you for all you've done for me, I hope you will be happy! Please keep Mary happy, she will make a wonderful mother... don't ever hurt her.'

Culbert looked surprised. 'Of course I won't hurt her Mama, why should I?'

'Yes, why should you?' asked Jessica, then smiled and gave a small gasp, her head fell to the side, and it was all over.

The Funeral at Chateauneuf St Vincent

Culbert was surprised to see how many people came to the small church. As well as Charles, Etta, Armand and Janette and their respective spouses, there was quite a crowd from the town, also people Jessica had known, worked for and worked with in the time she had lived there.

The service was respectful but not unhappy; thanks were given for Jessica's life and the many contributions she had made to the community.

After the service, Jessica was laid to rest in the small cemetery on the edge of the town near the forest she loved so well.

Back at Charles and Etta's house, Culbert and Mary thanked their hosts for allowing them such wonderful hospitality.

Charles replied that it was a privilege to have known Jessica, wishing Culbert and Mary every happiness in their forthcoming event. 'One life ends, another begins,' he said. They all raised their glasses to his sentiment.

'So, your café does well, I understand,' said Armand.

'Yes, very well, I'm hoping to buy my own one day,' said Culbert.

'Well you certainly know how to run such a business! Where do you have in mind?'

'I'm not sure, maybe in Paris, or maybe we will return to England, it is a long time since I was in England... I would like to see it again.'

'Would you live there?'

'No, probably not, I would like to live six months in each country, I have dual nationality so that isn't a problem.'

'Is there anywhere in particular in England where you would open a café?'

'There is, as a matter of fact. When I was a child I lived in a town on the east coast that was always very popular with wealthy Londoners. My style of café would suit them well.'

'Hmm... sounds good. Paris-on-Sea perhaps?'

'Yes, something like that!'

Armand and Culbert laughed, but Culbert was serious; he had plans.

'Well, how is my friend Culbert?' Janette moved across the room to Culbert, who was now alone.

'All the better for seeing you,' Culbert said quietly.

'Naughty boy, you will be a father soon! Be responsible, Culbert.'

'Must I?'

'You don't change, do you?'

'No, especially when a woman as beautiful as you is near me.'

'Oh Culbert, behave yourself, this is not the time nor place, but I suppose you don't know when the right time is.'

'Maybe one day I will, but for now, perhaps not!' Culbert laughed.

Louis watched them. He turned to Armand's wife. 'Do you know Culbert?'

'No not really, Armand has told me about him but I hadn't met him until now.'

'Be wary of him, my dear, be wary.'

'Goodness me, why?'

'Just be wary.'

Louis waved to Janette; she smiled back. 'I must go to Louis, Culbert. Maybe we shall meet again some time.'

'Maybe we shall, who knows?' replied Culbert.

Dear Mr Culbert,

I was so sad to learn of the death of your dear mama and I thank you for taking the time to write to me. You were very young when you left England so we did not know each other for long, but your mama and I were dear friends for many years.

Maybe you will return to England one day, I hope so. I am old now so I doubt if we will meet again but I will always remember you.

It was a shame that you never knew your father, I expect your mama told you about him, she and I were very sad when it all happened. It was all so unfortunate but at least some good came of it in the end. But that was long ago, now you have the future and your wife to think of, maybe you will have children too, I hope so.

Thank you again for writing to me, I have written to Mr and Mrs Ross, your godparents, to tell them the sad news.

Culbert studied the letter from Mrs K and was glad that he had written to her as his mama had requested. Now for the future.

Paris 1896

'I think we should discuss our future. Now that we have Jessie, we need to think where we're going to live and work.'

Mary looked at Culbert. 'You want to start a business in Aldwell, don't you?'

'Yes, I think it would be ideal. I know the area, I know some people, at least I did, and two of my godparents live there. It's now a fashionable resort, so there would be plenty of money to make there.'

'But you also want live in Paris?'

'Of course, we could spend time here and in England!'

'Well, what business will you have here in Paris?'

'I have the option to buy Café Benedict, if I can raise the capital, and of course I will need capital to start in Aldwell, I must talk with the bank.'

'There is no need Culbert, the inheritance is mine next year, there will be enough to buy both businesses.'

'What!'

'Yes, the interest rate has been good and the amount has almost trebled, I am a "woman of means", as the saying goes!'

'But are you sure you want to spend it in such a way?'

'And what other way should I spend it?'

'I don't know really, and it is a very good business proposition.'

'Culbert, I love you, the money will be ours, we shall spend it for our good and for that of Jessie and any other children we have.'

'Mary, you are wonderful! How can I thank you?'

'Well, we could make a start on those other children!'

Culbert laughed. He held Mary in his arms and embraced her, and then gently he lifted her and took her into the bedroom.

'You're not too sore?'

'No, I'm all right... I've healed from the birth. You may find it a bit different, though!'

They made love slowly and tenderly. Mary lay back. 'Well, perhaps that's number two on the way!'

'I hope so,' said Culbert. 'Jessie's such a delight, it will be nice for her to have a brother or sister.'

Culbert couldn't believe what Mary had said, he knew her inheritance was due but he had dared not mention it. Now the money was his, he could fulfil his dream of a café in Paris and one in England. He could return to Aldwell where he had such a happy childhood and show everyone how successful he had been. Life was good, very good.

'What's this box under the bed?'

'Oh, that's Mama's box, the one I told you about. She said that I mustn't open it but must give it to our firstborn, with the key, when they're old enough.'

'Really, why on earth did she say that?'

'I don't know... maybe it's boring stuff. She probably thought I wouldn't be interested and might throw it away. She may have thought that if it was for a grandchild, I'd treasure it.'

'Mmm, a wise woman, your mama.'

'Yes, she was – I miss her, but we have our Jessie, and more to come!'

1897

Culbert couldn't speak; he read the letter, read it again and again.

'This is a fortune, Mary.'

'I told you the amount had trebled. Seems even more than that, grandfather was a clever man.'

'Very clever; he must have thought a lot of you, too.'

'Yes, thankfully he did!'

The inheritance was more than enough to buy Café Benedict, start a new business in England and have plenty left over. 'Mary, I have an idea. Do you think that Melvina would run a café in England for us?'

'I think she would be delighted, I know she wants to go back to England, it would be an ideal opportunity for her.'

'I think we should ask her straight away, then she can go and find premises. I have a list of available properties in Aldwell.'

'You haven't been idle, have you?'

'No, I haven't, we need to start a café in Aldwell before anyone else does. Property prices will soon rise when all the wealthy Londoners come there. I have a list of empty places which in a year or two will cost three times as much.'

'Well done, Culbert, always the astute businessman,' Mary laughed.

'I'm so happy, Mary, especially now that you're to have our second child. The world is wonderful!'

Culbert went back into the café; he took a deep breath. 'That went better than I thought,' he mused. Not only was Mary happy to use her money for the businesses but also it solved the problem of Melvina. She was now pregnant with Culbert's child, she didn't show yet but soon it would be obvious. She had to leave Paris. The idea that she should run the Aldwell business was an inspiration, thought Culbert, and it solved a business problem. Melvina was a shrewd woman and he knew she would be able to do all that was necessary in England. He would have to contact his friends in Aldwell to make arrangements for the birth and help with the subsequent care of their baby. He knew whom he could trust; it was vital that Mary never knew about him and Melvina or all would be lost.

Aldwell, Summer 1897

Melvina was very tired. The journey had been long and arduous and still there was the last part to complete, the train to Aldwell from Haletown. Culbert was in an excited mood. It was the first time he had been to England since he and his mother left all those years ago, but he remembered that rail journey; how he had loved it.

The train chugged along, white smoke billowing across the flat landscape. Nothing had changed: the marshes, the river, the village where the train crossed a bridge and then a wider river leading eventually to the sea.

Mr and Mrs Richard Ross were waiting on the small station platform. Culbert knew it was them as no one else was there. They greeted Culbert as if he was a long-lost friend.

'This is my sister-in-law Melvina, she is the lady I told you of who will be in charge of my Aldwell business.'

'You must be exhausted, my dear,' said Mrs Ross.

'Yes, it has been a long, long journey,' replied Melvina.

'No more talking, let us go home and then you can rest. Plenty of time in the next few days for talking business.' Mr Ross ushered them into his carriage and they drove the short distance to their cottage.

'That's where I used to play when I lived here, I used to roll down that hill!' Culbert laughed and Melvina looked towards where he pointed; she could imagine young children playing on the soft green grass.

They went indoors. It was as Culbert remembered although he only went there once, his memory of the Ross's parents' house was better.

'Your parents, are they still here?' he asked.

'Yes, they are, though elderly now and they need our help, which we are pleased to give them.'

'That's good, I would like to see them, if possible.'

'You shall,' said Richard. 'We will visit them in two days for afternoon tea, I thought you would like that.'

'I remember afternoon tea with your parents well!'

'Good, but now you must rest.'

'Culbert has told us all about your husband Melvina – how proud you must be, but such a pity he is serving where you cannot go with him.'

'Yes, Africa is such a wild country although now Benin City is safe, my husband will be out of danger.'

'But what an honour to personally guard Her Majesty's representative there!'

'It is, but it doesn't make the separation any easier.'

Culbert and Melvina had contrived a plausible story to explain Melvina's reason for coming to Aldwell with Culbert, and her pregnancy. First, of course, a husband had to be invented, and it was decided that he should be a captain in the Royal Artillery; serving in Benin City was thought a safe explanation and one unlikely to be checked. The recent Punitive Expedition had led to a consular appointment and it was known that several officers had remained to guard the consul and the offices.

Their story had been accepted and Mr and Mrs Ross were most impressed that Melvina, being pregnant, should want to be involved in Culbert's business. Melvina had said that she could not stay at home and do nothing; this was the best way to get through her pregnancy without her husband and also to help her sister and brother-in-law.

'It is unusual here for a woman to have such a position in business, especially one who is expecting a child. We have much to learn from the French!' Mr Ross, himself an astute businessman, was impressed with Melvina, her obvious business sense, her determination and tenacity. 'She will make a success of this venture for certain,' he thought.

He spread several sheets of paper on the large table. 'Here are details of empty business premises in the town, I have chosen three that I think suitable in size and position, but the final decision, of course, Culbert, is yours.'

'True, but I would like your advice, Richard; you know these premises and their history. I must be guided by you.'

'Fine, well, I think we should look at this one in Duke Street, it is narrow at the front but very deep. This gives it atmosphere and is perhaps not unlike some of your French cafés. Then there is one in Main Street which is wider at the front but not so deep; the advantage there is that you may be able to put some tables outside in the good weather – and then there's this one at the end of Main Street, also narrow but very deep… it has great potential, too.'

'Interesting, when shall we look at them?'

'We can start tomorrow, if you wish!'

'Melvina, how do you feel now?'

'Oh, I am well now, thank you Culbert. I shall look forward to viewing these properties.'

Culbert could barely contain his excitement. 'My own café here in Aldwell. How Mama would have loved this! She would have been so proud.'

'I prefer the one in Duke Street. I know there is much work to be done but I like the situation and there is a courtyard garden at the rear.'

They had looked at the three premises and Culbert was the first to show a preference.

'I thought you would have preferred the one with an option to have tables outside,' said Richard.

'Hmm… I'm not sure if England is ready for that, at least not here in Aldwell. Maybe in a city but not here – not yet. Also it's colder here, even in summer, than in Paris, there are not the tall buildings to shelter the street.'

'I agree,' said Melvina. 'I love the Duke Street property.'

'Well then, that is settled. Melvina will be there and I think her preference is as important as mine.'

'Good, then we go ahead with the purchase,' said Richard. 'I will also contact the builders and other tradesmen to do all the alterations. I will leave ordering of the furniture and fittings to you, Culbert. Shall we all go and celebrate with some wine?'

'Do you remember Ben and Alice, Culbert?' asked Richard.

'Why yes, we used to play together and Mama used to read to us all, I remember them coming on Christmas Day and we ate mince pies!'

'What a memory! You're right, and they are still here. They now have a son, Albert.'

'I would love to see them, and I must introduce them to Melvina.'

'That can be arranged, we will invite them for tea and talk about old times.'

Ben and Alice and five-year-old Albert sat in the long room at the front of Richard's cottage.

'Alice, you look very well!' said Culbert.

'Yes I am and I'm so pleased to see you again after so many years, I wondered if you would ever come back. We were so saddened to hear about the passing of your dear mama, she was so kind to us.'

Ben, his skin even more reddened by days at sea, was tall and muscular, just as Culbert had remembered him.

'Is the fishing good, Ben?'

'It comes and goes, depends upon the weather, but as long as it's cold there are plenty of fish.'

'And young Albert here, will he help you?'

'Maybe, I don't know, I won't make him, times are changing. There's more work now, there are other ways to earn money apart from catching fish. I had no choice, but I want him to be able to choose.'

'You have a daughter I hear, Culbert,' Alice said.

'Yes, we have and another child to be born later this year. We hope to have three.'

Alice looked down.

'What is it, Alice?' asked Culbert.

Alice turned away and wiped a tear from her eye.

Ben looked at Culbert. 'How about a walk around the green Culbert, to have a look at where we used to play?'

They walked along the road to the hill they used to roll down as children and looked at the broom bushes where they spent happy days, playing hide-and-seek.

'I am so sorry Ben, what did I say to upset Alice?'

'It wasn't you Culbert, please don't think that, Alice so wanted more children and when you said you would have three, it made her sad.'

'She can't have more children?'

'No, when Albert was born it was a difficult birth. He was a very large baby and she was damaged inside, she cannot have any more children.'

'Oh, I am so sorry, but Ben you have a lovely son and Alice is well, you must be thankful.'

'Of course we are, but we had hoped for more, like you – three or four.'

'Don't worry, I'm sure you will all be happy.'

Culbert realised that this might be the ideal situation for Melvina and him; it would need careful planning and thought.

'Come on Ben, let's go back, they will think we don't like them if we stay out too long!'

The builders worked long days and the café in Duke Street gradually took shape. Culbert inspected regularly and was pleased with the progress.

'I must go back to Mary. You'll be all right here, you have good friends and you are so capable.'

Melvina smiled. 'I enjoy this, playing the part of an officer's wife, running a business, what more could a young woman want!'

'Soon we'll have our child, though we must be more careful in future.'

'I was careful, Culbert, I used the douche each time... What else can I do?'

'I know, I know, but we cannot have another child, how would we explain that?'

'There's no question of that until well after I have given birth, so let's not worry about it!'

Paris, Winter 1897

'She is just beautiful my darling!' Culbert held their second daughter in his arms. 'What shall we call her?'

Mary smiled. 'I thought Brigitte.'

'Yes, I like that, Brigitte it shall be.'

'When do you go again to Aldwell, Culbert?'

'Soon I think, Melvina is so competent but I feel that I should visit to encourage her and make sure she does not feel alone. Also of course, it is my business!'

'Has Melvina found a young man yet?'

'I don't know, maybe, perhaps she will tell me when I next see her.'

'Are there any suitable young men in Aldwell?'

Culbert laughed. 'You mean other than fishermen?'

'Well, yes.'

'I really don't know, there are many visitors from London which is why I opened the café there. Maybe one of those will take her eye!'

'I have written a long letter to her. Can you take it, I don't trust the postal delivery – it seems inconsistent.'

'Of course I will, I'm sure she'll be delighted to hear all your news.'

Aldwell, Winter 1897

Melvina pushed her pram along the promenade. It was a bright winter's day and from the cliff top, she could see along the coast for miles. Christopher was just one month old. The birth had been easy, Mrs Ross Senior had not lost her midwifery skills and mother and daughter came through the event unscathed.

Alice called in often to see how they were; she had offered to look after Christopher when Melvina was in the café – an offer Melvina had gratefully accepted. Business and children didn't mix, in her opinion.

The café was going through a quiet time after its busy summer opening period. Visitors from London had been intrigued to find a Parisian-style café in Aldwell and were frequent customers. Melvina had taught one of the local women how to make the fresh fruit tarts, and they had been a great attraction. The coffee too was quite different from English-served coffee, and although visitors were the main trade, Melvina hoped that soon they could attract some locals; she knew that they needed customers all year round.

'Perhaps I should introduce some local recipes,' she thought. 'Alice might have some ideas.'

Culbert was waiting when she arrived back at the café.

'Culbert, Culbert! I am so pleased you're back! Come and meet your son.'

Culbert looked into the pram. Christopher had his golden hair; he looked a fine boy.

'Well done my darling, he looks a delight.'

'Come and tell me all your news, I know Mary had another girl. Is she all right?'

'Yes, she is well, she has written a long letter to you. She asked me to bring it as she doesn't trust the post.'

'I'm not surprised,' Melvina took the letter, 'but I can

read it later. Come, let us have some wine to celebrate your return.'

They sat and talked, Christopher gurgled a few times and Culbert held him, rubbing his back gently.

'Culbert, we must adapt to attract the locals otherwise we will have no winter business. I thought I might ask Alice if there are any local recipes we could use.'

'I agree, we can't live on summer business only – although we have plenty of money.'

'Yes but the café must stand on its own, without outside money.'

'Ah, always the businesswoman, Melvina!' laughed Culbert.

'Just as well!' Melvina smiled but Culbert's casual approach to business since Mary's inheritance had come through was beginning to annoy her.

'Oh come now, you aren't cross with me?'

'No, Culbert, but you must realise that this is a business and should be run properly.'

'Yes, you're right, I am sorry... I'm just so happy to hold my son.'

'Of course my darling, let's not talk business now, let's just be happy.'

Melvina read Mary's letter slowly and as she read, thought of life back in Paris. Although it was also winter in Paris it seemed somehow brighter and warmer than in Aldwell, which by now had few visitors. How she longed for the Paris life, but she could not return – at least not until she and Culbert had made a decision.

Melvina had always liked the mysterious role of the mistress. Being a settled wife and mother had not appealed to her, but having a child had not been part of their plan. Melvina felt tied: tied to this small backwater of a coastal town in eastern England where the easterly wind seemed to have only one direction, a straight line through the body. At times it was so cold, bitterly cold. She was glad they could afford to heat their café and home, so many people in Aldwell had poor housing. 'I suppose they're used to it,' thought Melvina, 'what you've never had, you don't miss.'

Mary's letter was a happy one, full of news about her children, the business and life in Paris. It all seemed so bright and hopeful. Mary too was a good businesswoman. 'Culbert is lucky having two such clever women,' thought Melvina. 'I wonder which one of us he will eventually spend his life with?'

Alice now was spending more time with her and Christopher; she brought their son Albert who was a lovely child, quiet, thoughtful and always making things with paper and wood. Melvina talked about Albert's future with Alice, she hoped he would not have to earn a living from the sea as had Ben and his forefathers. Alice said she hoped not, the knitwear factory was expanding and she hoped that when old enough, Albert could get a job there. He was very good with his hands, his fingers were long and thin even at such an early age and would be ideally suited for such intricate work.

Alice never questioned Melvina about her husband. She had been told about his work in Benin City and thought it was a very important position; she was full of admiration for Melvina for accepting a life with an absent husband.

'Christopher and Albert are becoming friends already!' laughed Alice.

'Yes, aren't they? Let's hope they stay friends all their lives,' responded Melvina.

Paris, 1900

'How do I look?'

Mary was wearing her new outfit, bought especially for their visit to the Paris Exposition.

Culbert looked admiringly. 'You look wonderful, as always, my dear.'

'I am looking forward to this visit so much! Aren't we lucky to live so near to this wonderful, enormous fair?'

'Yes, and enormous is correct – we shall have to spend two days at least I think if we want to properly discover all that the pavilions have to offer.'

The Paris Exposition stretched south from the Eiffel Tower, with pavilions from many countries forming the sides of the exhibition. The buildings were made of 'staff', a mixture of jute fibre, plaster of Paris and cement; temporary structures that could later be easily demolished, removed and then reused. The French government was very aware of the cost and public opinion, and had tried to ensure that this grand exhibition would raise enough money to more than pay for its construction. The French people had been told that they were privileged to be able to hold such an event. They must have trust in their government and allow them to do what was best for France.

To demonstrate the importance of the exhibition, there were many new inventions; Mr Rudolf Diesel was there to demonstrate his new engine, which he had named, naturally, the diesel engine, and there was a staircase that moved upwards while people just stood on it. Perhaps the greatest excitement was over the first talking films that were to be shown.

'I have looked at the plan and we shall ride by carriage from pavilion to pavilion,' said Culbert. 'That way the girls won't need to walk much and won't get too tired.'

'Such a good idea, it means we can enjoy it all too,' replied Mary.

Jessie and Brigitte were five and three years respectively. Both pretty girls, they were a delight to look after and had caused few problems to their parents. Mary had told Culbert that girls are always better behaved than boys, he had laughed and agreed. He knew that this was very true; his son

Christopher was prone to tantrums, possibly because there was no father there. He often found that he had to think very carefully before he spoke, remembering the story that he and Melvina had contrived and that Mary was unaware of the truth. It would have been so easy to let something slip, but so far he had not said anything to give Mary any clue as to what was happening in Aldwell.

And so the day came; Mary dressed in her new ivory outfit, Culbert with his new suit and a fashionable straw boater hat. With their two daughters, they looked the perfect family.

The carriages rode up and down alongside the pavilions all day. They made their first stop at the British Pavilion, which was a mock Elizabethan mansion designed by Sir Edwin Lutyens. Sadly they couldn't go in, it seemed to be for outside viewing only. They asked the guard and he said that the British consul was in there and that no one except consul staff could enter. Culbert and Mary, like many others, thought this strange; it seemed that the British Government did not fully understand the idea of an exhibition.

Next they saw the grand German Pavilion, a typical German-style castle with a high tower, which housed a beer hall. 'Now this is what an exhibition should be like,' thought Culbert. After viewing half the pavilions they made their way home. 'Second half another day,' said Culbert. 'No need to go straightaway, it's open until mid-November.'

'Yes, but we should go while the weather is still warm,' said Mary.

Culbert agreed and said that they should have a few days rest then complete their tour.

The summer that year was very hot, it seemed as though it would never end. The few days' rest after the visit to the exhibition had extended to several weeks. Mary did not respond well to the heat and suggested they made their second visit in the autumn.

'Armand and his wife Natalie are coming to the exhibition next Saturday, shall we meet them there?'

Mary showed the letter to Culbert who agreed it would be a good opportunity to meet them again, as they had little opportunity to talk at length at his mother's funeral.

'I remember that Natalie is very elegant and I expect very intelligent, for she is a businesswoman.'

'Yes, she is – but no more elegant and intelligent than you, my dear,' replied Culbert.

Saturday arrived and it was a perfect day, not too hot or too cool. Mary dressed in her new autumn outfit, which was in a muted green shade very popular in Paris, the children were ready and Culbert helped them into the carriage that waited for them.

They had arranged to meet Armand and Natalie at the Swedish Pavilion; this had proved to be the crowd's favourite, and its yellow and red colours were easy to find in the avenue.

Armand and Natalie stood, arms linked, waiting outside the pavilion; they saw Culbert and Mary approach and waved. Mary had to keep a tight hold on Jessie and Brigitte who wanted to run towards them. 'Wait my darlings, you must keep with us.'

Armand and Natalie embraced Culbert and Mary and all said how delighted they were to meet again. Natalie was indeed elegant; she was tall and wore what appeared to be very expensive clothes. Their business must be doing well, thought Culbert.

Armand picked up the children one by one. 'What delightful girls you have.'

Mary looked proudly at their daughters. 'Yes,' she thought, 'they are delightful!'

'Come, Armand, let's get a carriage to take us around.'

They all got into the carriage and admired the pavilions as

they trotted along; the Austrian Pavilion was very ornate with displays of lifestyles, traditions and embroidered goods. The Hungarian cupola showed mostly agricultural produce and hunting equipment while the American Pavilion was quite a disappointment to those other than American citizens. It was being used as a base for American visitors and offered little for anyone else to enjoy.

'Seems as though the British and Americans are using their exhibits as offices for their consular staff,' laughed Armand.

'Yes, they are and have been heavily criticised for doing so, but the government can't do anything because they have paid for their areas – and paid much more than most countries.'

'So we can look at the outside, but that is all?' asked Natalie.

'It seems so,' replied Culbert.

After driving along the avenues, they all decided to have some refreshments and moved along to the pavilions serving drinks and food.

Mary and Natalie sat together; Brigitte and Jessie were running around playing happily.

'We cannot have children,' Natalie said, looking thoughtful and sad.

'Oh, what a shame! But you have each other,' said Mary.

'Yes, and we have a very good business, so we are happy.'

Armand and Natalie had been married only a short time when Natalie discovered that she was unable to carry children. Armand, though disappointed, had said the same as Mary, that they had each other. Although a dedicated businesswoman, Natalie could not help her instincts and always felt a pang of sadness when she saw women with young children.

'Your business does well, I understand?'

'Yes, without a family I have the time to work, which I otherwise would not have had.'

'Then that is good.' Mary looked at Culbert, who was deep in conversation with Armand.

'So, you have settled at last then, Culbert?'

'But of course Armand, I am a married man with two daughters.'

'Well I hope that you will be very happy – and also make Mary very happy.'

'She is happy. We are also successful in business. We have two cafés now, one in Paris and another in England.'

'One in England, goodness, who looks after that?'

'Melvina, Mary's sister, she is a most capable business-woman, like your wife. Also I have friends in Aldwell where the café is, they help her.'

'So do you go to your English café to make sure all is well?'

'Of course, I have dual nationality so travelling to England is not difficult and I spend a few weeks there each time.'

'Do Mary and the children go too?'

'No, the girls are too young, and Mary is busy with Café Benedict.'

'Hmm… quite a life you have Culbert, almost like two people!'

'Yes, you could say that,' replied Culbert. 'Come, let us rejoin the ladies, it is time for us to be going; the girls will be tired by now.'

Armand and Culbert walked back to the others. 'Come on, we must be going home now,' said Culbert.

They said their goodbyes and left in their carriages.

'So what did you think of my friends?' asked Armand.

'Mary is quite charming, so are the girls, but Culbert I am still not sure about.'

'Why?'

'Didn't you see the way he looked at me? Not the sort of look I would expect from a married man! Your brother-in-law warned me to be wary of him when we were talking at Jessica's funeral – I thought that now he has children and responsi-bilities he would have become settled.'

'Yes, Culbert has always had an eye for the ladies.'

'Well, I hope he keeps his eye to himself. I would not like to see Mary and the girls hurt.'

'Me neither.'

Aldwell, 1901

'Culbert my love, how I have missed you!' Melvina threw her arms around Culbert as soon as he stepped from the train.

Christopher stood quietly by Melvina's side. Culbert went to lift him but stopped. 'No, you are too big to be lifted – I shall shake your hand.'

'He is four years now, the same as your second daughter.'

'Yes, I know, time goes very quickly.'

They drove to Duke Street and went into the café. It was spring and soon it would be full of visitors. It had been quiet during the winter, Melvina and Alice had managed to keep the business going, but they knew the busy time would soon be here.

'You have done well to keep open during the quiet months, I thought we might have to close.'

'No, it's better to keep open even if you don't have much business, otherwise people think you've gone away.'

'Good business as usual, my darling.'

'How long can you stay this time?'

'Not very long I'm afraid, but I will be back in two months when it is busy. I can explain my absence better then than now.'

'I will make the most of you while I have you!' laughed Melvina.

Paris, Summer 1901

Café Benedict was busier than ever. Culbert had taken on more staff and his reputation had spread so that people were coming from many miles away. There were now many trains into Paris from various parts of France and travelling was becoming easier. Their proximity to Versailles also made them a meeting point for visitors to the palace. Life, thought Culbert, was very good.

'I must go to Aldwell,' he told Mary. 'It's getting busy now and I want to change the style of the café in keeping with the visitors. I need to be there to see what's needed.'

'Of course,' said Mary, who by now was used to her husband's travelling. 'Give my love to Melvina.'

'I will my darling. I'll leave in the morning.'

'How long this time?'

'I'm not sure, but I'll return as soon as I finish what needs to be done.'

Aldwell, Summer 1901

Melvina was at the station as usual, with Christopher.

'Are you all right?' asked Culbert. 'You look tired.'

'Culbert, I am expecting another child.'

Melvina could not wait to tell Culbert; she had been devastated when she discovered she was expecting a child again and was not sure what Culbert's reaction would be.

'But how? Didn't you use the douche?'

'Yes, of course, but I have told you before that it doesn't always work!'

'Oh dear! Then we must think of what to do... come along, let's go to the café and have some tea and talk.'

'How far are you?'

'Only two months.'

'Good, then we can work something out.'

'What Culbert, what?'

'Well, here in Aldwell they think you have a husband. Now, if you and Christopher spent some time with him when he is on leave, then return to Aldwell and some time later, say you are expecting his child, no one will think anything of it.'

'But how can I do that? It means we will have to go somewhere for a few weeks away from here where no one will know me or suspect what we are doing!'

'Yes, that's what I need to work out.'

Richard Ross, Adelaide, Culbert and Melvina sat in the garden of Richard and Adelaide's home; the trees cast a welcome shade over where they sat.

'Melvina's husband has some leave and is coming to London for two or three weeks very soon,' said Culbert.

'Oh, how wonderful!' said Adelaide. 'You will go to him, of course?'

'Yes, I will, I'm so excited to think I'll be seeing him again and of course Christopher has not seen his papa for some time... '

Melvina and Culbert were getting so used to their contrived life that they had almost begun to believe it was real.

'I have to return to France on Saturday, so I'll accompany Melvina on the train to London,' said Culbert.

'That's good, a woman needs a companion on a long journey,' said Richard. 'But will the café function without you, Melvina?'

'Oh yes, Alice and my staff are excellent, I sometimes think I don't need to be there at all!' laughed Melvina.

The train chugged slowly out of Aldwell. Culbert, Melvina and Christopher sat side by side watching the green countryside as they passed along the riverbank.

'How did you manage to arrange this?'

'I once heard Richard's mother mention a woman in Hale-town who is not married but looks after children. They said she also takes lodgers to help with her expenses. She is quite elderly now and no longer looks after children but still has the occasional lodger, so I went to see her and asked if you and Christopher could stay for three weeks while your house is being renovated and decorated. I have paid her well and she will not think anything other than what I have told her. You're not known in Haletown, but I shouldn't talk to too many people and when you do, only pass the time of day with them.'

Annie was at the door waiting to greet Melvina and Culbert. She was a petite lady, about seventy-five years old with grey hair neatly plaited and wound around her head. Her spectacles had thick lenses, which looked like the base of a bottle. She seemed to peer at Melvina and Christopher, but her smile was very welcoming.

'This is the room, I hope it suits you and your little boy,' said Annie.

'It's lovely!' said Melvina. 'What do we call you?'

'Call me Auntie Annie, everyone does.'

Culbert left, feeling happy that part of the problem was now solved.

Annie and Melvina sat in the sitting room, drinking tea and enjoying Annie's home-made cakes. Christopher was playing in the small garden at the rear of the cottage.

'My sister Rose lives next door,' said Annie. 'These two cottages used to be just one, we lived here with our parents, then when they died we had half each.'

The cottages were up a narrow track off the main road. They looked beautiful in the summer sun and Melvina complimented Annie on how well kept they were.

'I have a man who comes to do the garden and keep the place generally tidy, I used to do it myself but I am full of arthritis now and find things difficult.'

Melvina looked at the swollen knuckles of Annie's hands. In

143

the corner of the room was a piano. 'Do you play the piano, Annie?'

'I used to, I used to teach the children that came, they loved that. Now I can't play too well because of my hands, but I haven't forgotten how to.'

'Perhaps you can play for Christopher and me sometime?' said Melvina.

'Perhaps,' said Annie.

Haletown was a small market town. The livestock market was held each Wednesday in the road opposite Annie's house. Sheep were brought from the local farms and driven through the town, chickens were brought in large baskets on carriages, and on market day there was much noise everywhere.

Melvina liked the town; she enjoyed walking along by the stream that ran through the centre and on into the countryside. She did as Culbert said and just greeted people, without getting into conversation.

Melvina had told Christopher that this was an adventure, a secret adventure, and he was to tell no one where they had been. Rather than try to invent a story for such a young boy to remember, she and Culbert had thought it best for the stay at Haletown to be forgotten as soon as possible by keeping Christopher occupied when they returned to Aldwell. As Culbert said, young children will soon forget if something else is placed in their minds soon after the event you want them to forget. They could not risk the possibility of Christopher accidentally giving them away and they knew the first few weeks back in Aldwell would be testing, but they also thought they could overcome any problems.

Evenings were spent with Annie, and often Rose would call in. They sat and talked and Melvina persuaded Annie to play the piano.

Time passed quickly and soon it was time for Melvina and

Christopher to return to Aldwell. She said goodbye to Annie and Rose and walked to the station to get the train back. 'Now,' she thought, 'the next stage begins.'

7

'Now our two countries are officially friends!' Culbert laughed as he read about the signing of the *Entente Cordiale*, which ended years of conflict between Great Britain and France. It was 1904 and Europe seemed a more settled continent. Mary was thankful that it was a good time for bringing up children. Now with two daughters and another child on the way, her marriage to Culbert was all she had hoped. The café went from strength to strength, Culbert's café in England also thrived. Her only sadness was that her marriage to Culbert had cut her off from her family; she dared not make contact with them in case the falsification of the marriage declaration was discovered. Mary knew that she and Culbert were not legally married, but maybe they could put that right one day.

'I think that Jessie will be an astronomer,' said Mary.

'Goodness, why?'

'Well, she loves to run outside when it's dark and look up at the stars.'

'I think all children like things that sparkle,' replied Culbert.

'Maybe, but not all children will go outside at night in the dark. She has no fear of it.'

'Not now perhaps, but we'll have to make sure that she's more careful when she's older.'

Jessie was a bright little girl, thoughtful and quiet, and at a young age liked looking at books; her sister Brigitte was noisier and loved to be with the café staff, enjoying their attention.

'I wonder what our third child will be like?' said Mary. 'Jessie and Brigitte are opposites, so the next one will be interesting!'

'Oh, I expect he or she will be as lovely as the other two,' replied Culbert.

Mary was pleasantly surprised at the way Culbert shared in the upbringing of their daughters, many of her friends had said that their husbands took no part in their children's lives. Mary was always pleased to tell them of Culbert's involvement.

'Melvina doesn't write so often now,' said Mary.

'Doesn't she? Well, I expect she's very busy, and the postal delivery takes so long.'

'I realise that, but I think when I have had this child we must all go to Aldwell to visit and stay for a while. I know that you go every so often so see that all is well with the business, but I would like to see my sister again soon.'

Culbert jumped slightly. 'I think we should wait until the children are older, it's a long way for little children to travel and it won't be easy for any of us.'

'But Culbert, I want Melvina to see them as they are, young and full of fun! If we leave it too long they won't be children any more.'

'Very well, then we shall do that, but not until our next child is two or three years old.'

Mary could do little but agree.

Aldwell, 1905

Christopher and Mark walked together hand in hand along the beach. Now three years old, Mark walked upright and tried to keep up with his brother. Christopher, whose golden baby hair had darkened to brown, was tall for his age and bore a strong resemblance to Melvina. Mark, with his fair hair, took after his father. Melvina smiled as she watched them. 'Who would have thought,' she mused, 'that I should have two such lovely sons, but sadly no husband. Maybe, one day... '

Just at that moment, Alice came into view with Albert.

'Wonderful news!' said Alice. 'Albert is to start work at the textile factory next week.'

'That is excellent! Thank goodness you won't have to worry about him going to sea,' replied Melvina.

'Yes, and it's a good wage with the possibility of improvement if he does well, which I'm sure he will.'

Albert, a tall, lean young man, smiled at Melvina and her two boys. 'It's good for Mama and Papa too, they won't have to worry about going to the workhouse, I shall be able to provide for them.'

The fear of the workhouse still loomed over many people in Aldwell, a fear that would remain for years, even after the workhouse had closed and become a hospital.

The textile factory had gone from strength to strength since Culbert and Jessica had first visited the town, now supplying the large London shops with their unique knitted designs. With it had come the opportunity for young people to earn a living and avoid the perils of the sea. Young women too were able to make a living, which previously they had only been able to find in service.

Albert, with his long, slender fingers, found the work easy, but hoped that one day he might progress to the office where he knew the pay was better. He knew the hardship his grandparents had faced and he didn't want his parents to have the same life. Albert had a strong sense of duty and was determined to make life as comfortable as possible for them. He often thought it would be nice to have a little brother or sister, but he had been told that could not be. Ben and Alice had not given him the details as they thought he wouldn't understand, but Albert knew that there would be no playmates for him. He enjoyed being with Christopher and Mark, they were at ease with him and Albert had begun to treat them as if they were his brothers, offering to take them to play when Melvina was busy. Melvina, seeing how happy the three were together, readily accepted Albert's help – she found running the café and looking after the two boys on her own very tiring and was glad for any help offered. Often, she wished that she did not have to live this false life, a life only made real by her two sons. 'They will never know the truth, I suppose,' she thought, 'at least not from me. Perhaps no one except Culbert and I will ever know the truth.'

Melvina looked down again at her newspaper. Mr Balfour still had problems in his Conservative Party with arguments over free trade and tariffs. It seemed very serious: there was talk of him resigning. 'Everyone seems to have their problems,' thought Melvina, 'all important and all in proportion to their lives.'

The three boys came over to her. 'Can Albert be our brother, Mama?' asked Christopher.

Melvina laughed. 'You must ask Albert that my dear, but you can only be an honorary brother, even if he says yes.'

'What's a horry rarry brother?'

Melvina laughed. Knowing Christopher couldn't pronounce the word properly she passed it off and said, 'Well, he is a brother chosen by you especially.'

'Oh good, then can we choose him especially please?'

Albert smiled. 'I would be delighted to be an honorary brother, or a horry rarry brother, whichever is best!'

'Well then, that is settled, you are all brothers together,' said Melvina.

'Now come along you three, time for tea.'

They made their way back to Melvina's café and Albert walked along a little further to his home in the town.

My dearest Melvina,
How I miss you and would so much love to see you and for you to see our three lovely children. Jessie, Brigitte,

and our latest little one, Gabrielle, are so wonderful, you will love them.

I am trying to persuade Culbert for us all to visit you but he says we must wait until they are all older. I do not want to wait. I want you to see them all so young and so beautiful.

He is very busy here but he can leave the business, the managers are very good and quite capable, I know they can be left because they run our business when Culbert comes to see you in our Aldwell café.

Perhaps you can write to him and tell him how much you want to see your nieces – maybe he will listen to you.

We all keep well, as we hope you do.

Your dearest sister,
Mary

Melvina read the letter, shaking slightly. 'What shall I do?' she thought. 'If I don't write to Culbert, Mary will think I'm hiding something or that I don't want to see her. I don't know how much longer I can keep up this subterfuge. Maybe I should just tell Mary and then Culbert and I can be together!'

Melvina sat back in her chair and gazed at the ceiling. 'Why does life have to be so complicated?'

There was a tap on the window. It was Alice; Melvina invited her in.

'There is something I want to ask you.'

'Yes, of course Alice, what is it?'

Alice looked embarrassed. 'Well, it's something Christopher said the other day. He spends a lot of time with Albert as you know and they chat a lot.'

'Yes, I know, they're like brothers. What did he say?'

'Well, it's about the time when you and Christopher went to see your husband in London.'

'Yes?' Melvina was now a little shaken.

'Christopher said that you and he didn't go to London, that you stayed with a lady in Haletown.'

'Really?' said Melvina. 'Oh come Alice, Christopher was just four years old he didn't know where we were.'

'Oh I think he did, I know Haletown and it sounded as if that was where he had been.'

'You know Haletown?'

'Yes, Ben and I used to go there to see some friends years ago and I know from what Christopher said that it was where you were. You weren't in London with your husband, were you Melvina?'

Melvina said nothing. She was trying to think of what she should say. Should she deny it? Should she trust Alice and tell her? She made a decision.

'Alice, if I tell you what happened will you still be my friend and let Albert play with Christopher and Mark?'

'Of course I will, whatever you have done is not their fault.'

'Thank goodness for that,' thought Melvina. 'I will have to tell her.'

Melvina told her the whole story. Alice looked stunned.

'What will you do when your sister finds out?'

'I don't know, I hope that Culbert and I will be married and can live here with our boys. There was a time when marriage was not for me, but now there are the boys... it's different.'

'But what if Mary won't give him up?'

'I don't know, Alice, I don't know, but one thing I do know is that my boys must be looked after, whatever happens.'

'Oh, you needn't worry about that! They can always come and live with Ben, Albert and me. They're already like our family.'

'You would do that, Alice?'

'Yes, I would, they are like my own sons.'

'Well let's see what happens, but please Alice, don't tell a soul what I have told you.'

Alice nodded in agreement and walked back to her home.

Melvina sat back, her mind spinning. 'Now what?' she thought.

Paris, 1906

'You have three lovely girls,' said Adele.

'Yes, they are a joy,' replied Mary.

She and Adele had become good friends in the past year; Adele was now managing the café having spent several years in Versailles, working in a smaller establishment in the main avenue. She had always been ambitious and when the opportunity arose to manage Culbert's café, she had applied. Culbert and Mary were immediately impressed with her knowledge, business sense and diligence towards work. Adele did not expect anyone to do anything she asked if she could not first prove that she could do it. This had earned her great respect among the staff at Café Benedict and had made for a happy establishment. For Culbert and Mary, she was ideal. The friendship between Adele and Mary had developed soon after they met; they had an affinity, which neither could explain but were glad to accept.

'I do miss my sister Melvina.'

'Why do you not go to see her? She would love to see the children.'

'I hope we will soon... Culbert says that we must wait until Gabrielle is at least three before we travel.'

'But why? Children travel well, do they not?'

'Culbert thinks not,' replied Mary.

'But you must see your sister, do you hear from her?'

'Yes, but not so often, she is busy with our Aldwell café so I suppose she doesn't have so much time to write.'

'I think you should go soon, if you leave it too long it will be more difficult, and the bond between sisters should be strong.'

'I agree but Culbert seems against it... It's difficult for me to persuade him.'

'Would you like me to speak with him?'

'Oh Adele, you are so kind, but no, it is a matter for Culbert and me.'

'Culbert goes to Aldwell on his own, does he not?'

'Yes, he has to check on the business to make sure all is well.'

'Are you sure?'

'Adele, what do you mean?'

'Oh you English you are so coy! If my husband went to another country on his own several times each year and would not take me, I would think that perhaps he had a reason for not wanting me to go with him.'

'What are you suggesting, Adele?'

'*Ma petite*, you must know the phrase *"cherchez la femme"*? It is French but applies to all nationalities!'

'Culbert, another woman – never!'

Mary was furious. How dare Adele suggest that her husband would do such a thing?

'Oh, come, come, Mary, all men, how shall we say… dally… with other women now and then, it is normal.'

'It might be for some, but not for us.'

'So why does Culbert not let you and the girls go with him? Why make you wait? After all it is your sister, and do not forget that it is your café as well!'

Mary went silent. He couldn't, she thought, he wouldn't.

'Maybe you are too trusting Mary, but what if it is true? A marriage can continue, it does not have to make any difference.'

'Maybe not to you Adele, but in England we do not behave like that.'

Adele laughed. 'Oh Mary what about your Prince Bertie, now your king? He had many mistresses, and still does even at his age, and size!'

'That's different, Adele, they lead different lives from us. I cannot imagine that Culbert would deceive me.'

'Why don't you ask him?'
'What? Certainly not!'
'Well then, how will you know?'
'I won't!'
'But now you will wonder, won't you, *ma petite*?'

Mary sat looking across the courtyard. Although she had dismissed the idea of Culbert being unfaithful when talking with Adele, she now had a gnawing feeling deep inside her. She thought of all the journeys Culbert had made to Aldwell, how excited he was when he left, how content when he came back to her. Yet he was the perfect husband, he had given her three lovely daughters; their business was thriving; what could be wrong? Why should he want another woman? It didn't make sense.

Mary felt unsettled, Adele had sowed a seed of doubt in her mind, a seed that would grow and grow if she allowed it. There was no option – she must confront Culbert.

'When can we go to Aldwell, Culbert? I really want to see my sister and take the children.'

'When Gabrielle is a bit older, my darling.'

'But why? It's not difficult for her, probably easier than for Jessie and Brigitte, at least she will sleep most of the time.'

'No, my love, I think we should wait.'

'Culbert, I want to go soon – I don't want to wait. Is there some reason why you will not let us all go?'

Mary's voice changed and the sharpness of tone did not go unnoticed by Culbert.

'I have told you why I think we should wait, my love. Why are you so annoyed?'

'Because you go to Aldwell several times a year, but you will not take me or the children. Why Culbert? Why? Is there something you should tell me?'

Culbert looked straight at Mary. 'What would you like me to tell you?'

'What I have asked you. Why can we not go to Aldwell?'

Culbert repeated the reason he had given.

'I don't believe you, I think you have another reason to keep us from Aldwell!'

'And what could that be?'

Mary took a deep breath. 'Have you a woman there?'

Culbert did not expect this question; he hesitated, then said, 'Who have you been talking to?'

'Why, what has that to do with my question?'

'Because it is not a question you have ever asked or something that you have ever thought, so someone must have suggested it to you.'

'And, if someone has, would that alter the facts?'

Culbert knew he was now in a difficult situation and would have to use all his guile to steer out of this awkward conversation.

'I just hope that no one has been spreading falsehoods about me. It is very common here in France, almost a national pastime.'

Mary hesitated; perhaps Adele was a troublemaker. No, surely not – she wasn't sure what to think now.

'Oh Culbert, please can we go to see my sister? I miss her so much, you have never had a brother or sister – you don't know what it's like. We were always together and now we don't see each other, she writes infrequently and I miss her company.'

Culbert realised that he had regained control. 'All right, Mary, we shall go. I will arrange it.'

Culbert went back into the café; he sat in the kitchen. 'I must make plans,' he thought, 'careful plans.' His head ached, it ached often and sometimes the pain was very sharp. It throbbed now and thoughts did not come easily. He reached for his jar of heroin tablets and quickly swallowed two with some water. Previously he had used laudanum but it was difficult to buy now because of the number of addicts it had created. Mary didn't know about these pains in his head; neither did Melvina. When they had first started the doctor said it was because he worked too hard and should take some rest. But Culbert knew this was not the cause. Sometimes he saw bright lights that did not exist, only in his eyes. But what should he do? Now he must make a decision; there was no turning back.

Culbert slept heavily. He had taken two more heroin tablets and fallen into a drugged state.

'Wake up Culbert! It's nearly ten o'clock and the post is here.'

Among the letters addressed to Culbert was one from a trusted friend in Paris. Culbert could not risk Mary recognising Melvina's handwriting so any letters she wrote were addressed to this friend, who then sent them on as if they had come from Paris. Mary had never suspected.

Still in a dazed state, Culbert read Melvina's letter. He couldn't believe it, now they really had to do something. Melvina told Culbert about Alice knowing about them and asked what she should do. 'She sounds desperate,' thought Culbert, who felt the same.

'Bad news?' asked Mary.

'No, no, it is from my friend in the café on the other bank. He has a problem with suppliers, he is warning me about them.'

'Well that's all right, you looked so pale I thought someone had died!'

Culbert felt as though he would like to die. His head weighed heavy on his neck. The heroin, while reducing the pain, left a feeling of heavy numbness, which Culbert often thought worse than the pain itself.

'No, no one has died.'

Culbert washed and slowly dressed. 'Maybe if we all go to

Aldwell, Melvina can arrange for the boys to go away for a few weeks and then we can keep this from Mary. I wonder if she can do that?'

'Have you thought any more about going to see Melvina?'

'Yes, I have, I shall write and ask her when it is convenient then I will make travel arrangements.'

Mary was surprised. 'Oh, thank you! I shall look forward to that.'

Melvina, my love,

We must all come to visit you, Mary insists and someone has been putting thoughts into her head that I have a woman in Aldwell. Can you arrange for the boys to go away for the time we are there, perhaps Alice and Ben could keep them at theirs? Alice understands, you have told me, and maybe she will help. I am sorry this letter is so muddled, I didn't expect all this to happen and I must do something to allay Mary's suspicions, I cannot put her off coming to Aldwell any longer. Let me know what you can arrange. You can write direct to me about this, of course.

Aldwell, Spring 1907

Mary fell in love with Aldwell as soon as they arrived. The short train journey on the branch line from Haletown had caused great excitement with the three girls. They loved the chugging and the chuffing noises and had their faces pressed against the window most of the way.

When she and Melvina had lived in England they had spent all their time in London, never seeing the need to go anywhere else as their home and friends were there. A small fishing town such as Aldwell was something she had read of but never thought she would see in real life.

157

Melvina, Richard Ross and his wife were there to meet them. Mary embraced Melvina and seemed not to want to let her go.

'Come along you two, you will squeeze all the air out of your lungs!' laughed Richard.

'So, this is your lovely wife,' said Richard, when Mary and Melvina eventually separated from their embrace. 'No wonder you have been hiding her!'

They made their way to Richard's home and were soon unpacked.

Mary was so excited about seeing Melvina that she couldn't stop asking questions. 'Now then, I think that is enough talk for tonight,' said Richard. 'You must all be exhausted, the little ones too, why not have an early night and then tomorrow the talking starts in earnest!'

They all agreed and almost collapsed into their beds.

'The air here is so very fresh and clean, I just want to keep taking deep, deep breaths and fill my lungs to the top.'

Mary felt exhilarated and already a colour was coming into her cheeks. Years of Paris air had made her pale, fashionably pale, but now a rosy hue was beginning to appear.

The girls loved the beach and ran along the sand, it was something they had never seen. Gabrielle put some in her mouth.

'No, no Gabrielle, don't do that!'

'Don't worry,' said Melvina. 'All children do that when they see something new in case it's possibly edible! It won't hurt, she'll soon spit it out!'

Gabrielle indeed did spit it out, and they all laughed.

They walked back along the road that was parallel to the beach.

'What is that building in the hollow, Culbert?' asked Mary.

'Oh, that's where they make salt from the sea water, it is a very profitable business.'

'Really? I thought salt came from salt mines.'

'Some does, but there aren't any mines here so it's cheaper to make it from sea water.'

'Does it taste any different?'

'No, but they tell you it does, and if you believe them you will think it's better!'

Culbert and Mary laughed. 'She seems so happy,' thought Culbert, 'I just hope that I can get away with this; I would hate to spoil it all.'

Culbert, with Mary and Melvina on his arms, walked around the corner and along the road where the grassy slope was.

'That's the hill I used to roll down when I was here as a child,' said Culbert to Mary.

'Oh, how lovely, do let the girls do it now!'

'Yes, come on girls, I'll show you what to do.'

Culbert took them to the top of the hill and demonstrated how to roll down it. At first they looked a little scared, then Brigitte lay down and rolled quickly to the bottom. Gabrielle and Jessie followed her.

'Come on Papa, roll down with us again!' Jessie called to Culbert.

He ran up to the top of the hill and bent down. Suddenly, everything went black.

'Papa, Papa! Wake up!'

Jessie tried to shake Culbert, but he didn't move.

'Mama, Mama, Papa can't move!' called Jessie.

Mary, who was walking along the road with Melvina, at first took no notice thinking that Culbert was playing with the children. Gradually, she realised something was wrong.

Mary and Melvina ran up the hill to where Culbert lay.

'Culbert, Culbert, wake up!'

Mary turned white. 'Oh Culbert, what is the matter?'

Melvina bent over Culbert. 'He's breathing Mary, I think we should get Richard.'

'Jessie, darling, run to Mr Ross and ask him to come here straightaway.'

Jessie ran off along the road and startled Richard, who was working in his study.

'It's Papa! He won't wake up!'

Richard did not hesitate; he ran after Jessie to where Culbert lay.

By now, Culbert's breathing was beginning to return to normal. Richard held him by the shoulders and spoke to him. 'Culbert, it's Richard. You'll be all right.'

Culbert gradually came to and gazed around him. 'What's happening?' he asked.

'You passed out. Too much rolling about, I think!' Richard laughed.

They walked Culbert back to Richard's house where he sat in a cool area of the large room. He sipped the chilled water they brought him and seemed bemused.

'Has this happened before?' asked Richard.

'Has what happened before?'

'Losing consciousness.'

'No, I don't think so.'

'Well, I think you should see our doctor and have a check – just to make sure all is well. Probably nothing, just too much exertion on this hot day, maybe a touch of heat stroke.'

Mary looked worried.

'Don't worry, Mary,' said Melvina. 'There is a very good doctor here and I'm sure he will say that there is nothing that a few days' rest won't put right.'

Dr York was a well-respected doctor in Aldwell. Some of his patients were in his 'club' while others paid to see him when they needed to. Richard and his wife were in the latter category, although they fortunately had little need of his services.

He looked at Culbert, remarking what a healthy young man

he appeared to be, and then listened carefully to Mary and Melvina's description of what happened.

'Have you had any illness recently, felt unwell in any way?' he asked Culbert.

'No, I'm very fit, I have to be – I have businesses to run here and in Paris.'

'Oh yes, your café in Duke Street is very popular. Is there anything that's been different recently?'

'No, no definitely not.'

Dr York looked at Culbert. 'I think, Mrs Montaigne, that I should examine your husband thoroughly. Perhaps you would like to wait in the garden?'

Mary and Melvina readily agreed and left Culbert with Dr York.

'Now, Mr Montaigne, what's been going on?'

'What do you mean, doctor?'

'I mean why are you taking opiates in such quantity?'

'Why do you think that?'

'Your eyes, man, your eyes, they show it well. I presume your wife is unaware?'

'Yes, you're right... I have been taking some and Mary doesn't know, I don't want her to.'

'Tell me why you take them.'

'I have bad headaches, they help to ease the pain.'

'How long have you had these headaches?'

'For about a year now.'

'Have you seen a doctor?'

'No, French doctors don't know much, they just want to cut you into pieces!'

'Yes, I have heard that,' Dr York smiled. 'You are a young man Mr Montaigne. Tell me, what do you know about your father's health and your mother's health?'

'I didn't know my father; he died when I was a baby. My mother had lung disease, she coughed blood – consumption, I believe.'

'Your father died very young, why was that?'

'He was a soldier. He was involved in a war in Abyssinia, I think, and died of his wounds. Why are you interested in him?'

'Well, there is thinking now that many illnesses are inherited from parents, or even grandparents, and knowing their history is helpful to us doctors in finding out what's wrong with our patients.'

'I'm sorry I can't help you.'

'You have an eye condition, I notice.'

'Yes, I saw a doctor in France – he said it was strabismus.'

'That definitely can be inherited.'

'So, you think that whatever happened to me on the hill was because of something I have inherited? Really, Doctor, I think I may just have become overheated and over-exerted myself.'

Culbert laughed in a slightly dismissive manner.

'Maybe, but for someone so young, who looks so well, who is not overweight, but who has severe headaches, I must consider an inherited problem.'

'So, what can you do about it?'

'Well... you could go to see a colleague of mine in London.'

'And what would that involve?'

'It would mean a series of tests.'

'No, that is out of the question, I don't have the time... I must soon return to France with my wife and children.'

Mary sat with Culbert. 'What did Dr York say, Culbert?'

'Not much really, he thinks I may have an inherited illness.'

'Why?'

'Because of my eye problem and because I'm too young and healthy to have anything wrong!'

'How odd.'

'Yes, and I can't tell him anything about my father because I never knew him. Maybe he did have something he's passed on to me, but if that is so, there is little I can do!'

'What did he suggest?'

'He said I could see a colleague in London and have tests, but I said no, it would take far too long and we must soon return to France.'

'I agree, but promise me you will rest for the next day or two.'

'Of course my darling, of course.'

Richard and Dr York stood in the garden talking; they had been friends for some years. 'What do you know of this chap Culbert?' asked Dr York.

Richard smiled. 'More than he thinks I know!'

'I think his problem may be inherited, but his father died when he was a baby so we will never know.'

Richard had been told Culbert's background by his parents and knew this was not the case. 'Suppose he had known his father, what difference would that make?'

'Maybe some... he would have known if his father had periods of illness, if he had headaches, dizzy spells and so on, then we might have a better idea of what may be the trouble.'

'I see. But even if you knew, there might not be any treatment?'

'Possibly not.'

'Oh, you doctors never give a definite answer!' Richard laughed and put his arm on Dr York's shoulder. 'Come my friend, let's have some tea, if you have time to stop with us for a while.'

'Of course, Richard, I always have time for you and your family.'

They walked back into the house. Culbert by now had fallen asleep and Mary sat opposite him. 'Shh, he sleeps,' she whispered. 'Let's go back into the garden.'

They sat sipping their tea in the shady area of the garden. It was quiet now; the day had been long and hot, but the cooler air from the sea was welcome.

*

'I think you should rest today. Melvina, the girls and I will go for a walk.'

Culbert nodded in agreement, his head felt heavy and he lacked his usual energy.

'Enjoy the sunshine my darlings,' he said, as Mary and his daughters left the house.

They met with Melvina outside the café and walked into the town. Jessie was fascinated by the shops; so different from those in Paris. Brigitte and Gabrielle were still not quite sure of where they were and stayed close to Mary.

Melvina showed them the large church, much too big for such a small town, she said, and they went inside to admire the stained glass windows. Gabrielle and Brigitte started to run down the aisle but Mary stopped them, saying that they must be quiet and walk with her. They went along the roomy nave, reading all the inscriptions and details of those who had served the church through the centuries. Outside they walked around the garden alongside the churchyard, across the road to the promenade. The girls shouted with delight when they saw the sparkling blue water of the sea and ran ahead. Mary and Melvina walked arm in arm, talking of Paris and times past; both had so much to tell each other after the long separation.

Melvina suddenly went pale and stopped, jerking on Mary's arm.

'What is it?' asked Mary.

In the distance Melvina saw Christopher and Mark with Albert, playing with a ball in the narrow street adjacent to the sea front, near to where Ben and Alice lived.

She steered Mary across the other side of the road. 'I thought there was a hole in the roadway and we might fall.'

Mary looked a little surprised; she could see no hole in the roadway.

'Are you all right Melvina? You look quite pale.'

'Yes, yes, it must be the heat... Come, let's join the girls.'

But luck was ebbing away for Melvina.

Jessie, Brigitte and Gabrielle had also seen the three boys and ran over towards them, asking if they could play with their ball. The boys looked surprised at first, then Albert said of course they could, and threw the ball to Jessie.

'Mama, we have found some friends!' called Jessie.

Mary turned and looked down the narrow street. 'Is it all right for them to play with the local boys?' she asked Melvina.

Melvina swallowed. Her mouth was dry. 'Yes, yes... '

Mary walked towards the children. Christopher and Mark looked at her and then saw Melvina. 'Mama, I thought you had gone to see Papa!' said Mark.

'What did he say? Did he call you Mama?'

Melvina said nothing. She stood transfixed.

Mark and Christopher ran towards her. 'Hello Mama! You're back sooner than we thought, come and meet our new friends!'

'It is over,' thought Melvina. 'It is over.'

The Reckoning

Mary was drained of energy, drained of words, drained of emotion.

Culbert and Melvina sat opposite her, their faces set as if in stone. The girls were in the garden, playing, oblivious to the drama being acted out just yards from them.

'I will make arrangements to sell both cafés immediately, the girls will come with me.'

'Where will you go?' asked Melvina.

'Far away from you two, as far as I can get.'

'And the girls? What about the girls? I have a right to see them... I am their father!'

'You have lost your rights.'

'But you cannot sell the cafés, Mary,' said Melvina. 'When you married Culbert, your inheritance became his.'

165

'But I didn't marry Culbert, did I?'

'What?'

'You must have forgotten, we forged my father's signature, the marriage was never valid, you have nothing Culbert... nothing.'

Culbert had forgotten this fact. Mary indeed was not his wife and he had no claim on her money or property.

Melvina looked at him. 'You fool!' She almost spat the words. 'You said we would have everything when you divorced Mary!'

'Did you ever love me, Culbert?'

'Maybe, I don't know.'

'Well, it doesn't matter now. You and Melvina must leave... I don't want to see either of you again – ever – and you can take those boys with you, bastards that they are, and will always be!'

'But Mary, have some pity, I have been unwell, can you not give me some time?'

'No, the café is closed to both of you. Stay somewhere else. I doubt if Richard will want you both here for long, but that is for him to decide. Just clear your belongings from my property.'

Mary left the room and went into the garden where the girls were playing. She sat on the long garden seat, exhausted.

'What are we to do, Culbert?'

'You do what you want, I shall go to London.'

'What, on your own?'

'You don't think I want you and the boys trailing along, do you?'

'But Culbert, you love me, you said so... don't you want to be with me and the boys?'

'You fool! I never loved you, Melvina. I never loved Mary... It was her money I loved, didn't you realise that?'

'No, but I do now! You are despicable!'

166

Melvina marched out of the room and went into the garden where Mary sat.

Mary looked up but didn't speak. Melvina sat beside her. 'Mary, he has deceived me too, help me!'

'Why should I?'

'Because we're sisters.'

'Not any more, Melvina, I disown you.'

The journey back to France was long and tedious; the girls were restless, Jessie asking where Papa was several times. Brigitte and Gabrielle, fidgety at first, eventually tired and slept.

Adele was waiting to greet them on their return. She had read Mary's letter and knew the situation.

'You were right all the time Adele!' said Mary. 'I should have realised all those trips to Aldwell were not just for business.'

'Ah well, you English are too trusting, are you not?'

'Yes, we are, but I have learned... I am just thankful that we were never legally married.'

'And where will Monsieur Culbert go?'

'He said London, but I don't care where he goes or what he does after what he's done! I never wish to see him again!'

'And you, *ma petite*, you will leave France now?'

'I shall clear my personal belongings and leave as soon as possible. I'm so glad you have agreed to run the café until a buyer is found.'

'Oh, *ma petite*, I think a buyer is found!'

'Really?'

'Why yes, my husband and I, we have always loved the café, we will buy it.'

'Can you afford it?'

'Yes, we have saved money for many years and this is a great opportunity for us. Of course, if you can find someone to pay more than we can pay, you must do so.'

'No, no Adele... we shall agree a price I'm sure! I will be delighted knowing that the café is in good hands.'

'Ah, *bon,* then everybody is happy.'

'Well, as happy as we can be, I suppose,' said Mary.

As the days passed, Mary gradually packed her possessions in the trunks she had bought for the purpose. The girls were blissfully unaware that another journey was soon to be undertaken and that their lives would change forever.

Clearing the bedroom, Mary found the satinwood box, with key, under the bed. She looked at it, remembering that Jessica had said it was for her first born. 'I wonder what's in it?' she thought. 'I don't suppose it matters now. Culbert isn't here so I might as well open it.'

She sat back in the bedroom chair and opened the box; there were several diaries, all dated, a photograph, and some other papers, which looked like legal documents.

She looked at the photograph; it was of a young boy with golden curly hair, taken by a photographer in Port Hamon in England. The boy must have been about five or six years old.

A legal-looking document of thick vellum was rolled neatly the length of the box; Mary unrolled it and started to read. She was stunned; the deed of assignment detailed the legal transfer of ownership of a property called Berg House from Jessica to Theo Harcourt. Mary didn't recall Jessica having mentioned Theo Harcourt; he certainly wasn't her husband, who had been killed in a war in Africa when Culbert was a baby. The property was a grand house and stood in many acres. Why on earth should she have given it to someone? Maybe there would be some clue in her diaries.

She read carefully through each diary; some of the events she remembered Jessica telling her about, her dear Papa and how sadly he died from a lung disease. She read about her dear friend Mrs K and her wonderful cakes. Mary smiled, what a lovely friend she must have been. But surely there was something missing? No mention of Jessica's husband, or of her son Culbert. Maybe later on. But page after page, there was no mention of either. Then the mood of Jessica's writing changed. Theo was mentioned many times; his visits to Berg House were frequent. Mary became more and more puzzled. Who was Theo? Then came the first shock. Jessica wrote of her pregnancy and plans to have the baby away from Berg House. Mary wondered if Theo was the father of another child of Jessica's. 'I'm sure she never mentioned another child. But she didn't marry him,' thought Mary. When she met Jessica, she wasn't married and there was only Culbert. She read on; it suddenly all fell into place. Theo was Culbert's father! The soldier killed in Africa may have been a real person but he never fathered a child of Jessica's. So why didn't Jessica marry Theo and live in Berg House? Why give it to him and leave England with Culbert to live in France? There was more. 'The people here don't like Theo. They say he is trade, he is beneath me and I could never marry him. I would be ruined socially if anyone found out that he was the father of my son. I will say the child is my cousin's; no one will question that.'

So that was it. She gave a huge property away just to keep Theo quiet and then left England so no one would ever know. How strange that her social standing was so important, she would give away such a large estate to protect it.

She read on and in the fifth diary, suddenly there it was. There was the real reason. Jessica must have been in tears when she wrote it. The page was stained but it was still clearly there.

Mary dropped the diary, her face ashen. 'My goodness,' she thought. 'So that's what had troubled Jessica, poor woman... She must have died a tormented soul.'

8

Aldwell, 1920

The First World War had at last ended and Aldwell had its share of casualties, including those falling victim to the Spanish Flu in the last few weeks of 1918.

Albert, now in charge of production at the textile factory, which was expanding each year, had lined up to enlist but was told that his presence was needed at the factory. Instead of the fine knitwear sold in London, the factory had altered its machinery to make uniforms and undergarments for the soldiers. Albert had become an expert in ensuring the smooth running of the machines and his diligence had increased production. He was popular with the workers; he was a local man and well respected.

At first Albert had worried that he would be sneered at because he wasn't going to fight, but he need not have worried. His male colleagues at work, although few as most employees were women, also were exempt because of their essential contribution to the war effort at the factory. One of these colleagues was his brother Christopher, who had joined as an apprentice, just seventeen at the outbreak of the war.

Ben, Albert's father, was fifty-seven, too old for service and still making frequent fishing trips, although Albert's pay more than kept them. Ben and Alice were proud of their son; he was single-minded and applied himself well to all he was required to do at work and at home.

Alice was pleased that Albert had been walking out with Blanche, a young lady who also worked at the factory, in the office. She lived with her parents in the road adjacent to the factory. She was an only child and she too was able to keep her parents at home with the wages she earned. The threat of the workhouse still loomed large but for these two families at least, a safe future was assured.

Blanche had lustrous black hair; it was long and she wore it swirled around her head to form an arrangement that resembled a turban. Many young men admired her but it was Albert she was attracted to. He had kept his lean figure, slightly angular, but he was tall, well over six feet, which was unusual for young men in that town. He dressed smartly and was very particular about his appearance and cleanliness.

Each Sunday, Albert and Blanche would walk along the promenade dressed in their best clothes. Blanche also liked to follow the latest fashions. She was fortunate that she was able to buy from the factory and most years she was one of the female workers photographed in clothes that were to be sold in London. The factory produced a catalogue each year featuring these pictures. As a reward, the women were given the outfits they posed in, so the competition was strong. It was essential to have a slim figure and as a result, the female employees at the textile factory were the slimmest in the town.

But it wasn't just her figure that attracted Albert. Blanche was a free thinker, she read books, newspapers, magazines, and anything she could find to try to 'improve herself', as she described it. Her parents had little education and she, like all the other children, went to the local school until fourteen. After that came work, usually an apprenticeship for the young men, and a life in service for young women. Blanche had no desire to be in service, she had higher aspirations and so far her self-education was paying off. She was an only child and she knew that her parent's house, which they owned, would eventually be hers. The property was old, it had belonged to her grandparents, but it was solid and well built and Blanche was sure it would last for many more years.

This Sunday, they walked back through the town along Duke Street. They passed the former Café Parisian, now a fish restaurant. Albert had told her about the café and how it had suddenly closed, and about the woman who owned it who went away. He also had told Blanche about his two brothers, who had lived in this café with the woman who had gone. Albert said that he never knew exactly who the woman was or if she was their mother; they had called her Mama but didn't seem upset when she left, so he often wondered who she really was. However, Christopher and Mark were his brothers as far as he was concerned and he, as the eldest brother, would make sure that no harm came to them.

Blanche was full of admiration for Albert. He was everything she could have wished for, and she only hoped that he might seek her father's permission to ask for her hand in marriage.

'It's so peaceful now Albert, the war seems a long while ago.'

Albert smiled. 'No more fighting but plenty of hard work to pay for the war.'

'Well, we're doing our part at the factory. I hear we're now exporting over half our production.'

'We're lucky that the owners have found new buyers. It should secure our future, and our children's.'

Blanche blushed.

'Oh, I meant the nation's children,' said Albert looking embarrassed.

Blanche giggled. 'And perhaps ours, Albert?'

Albert was not experienced in the ways of young women; Blanche was his first and only young lady. He did know, however, that he was very happy in her company and that he would like to be with her more. Life with his parents and brothers was happy, but their home was small and becoming cramped now that they were all older. Albert knew that soon he must decide his future. His brothers were able to fend for themselves and no longer needed his guiding hand. Christopher worked well at the factory and his employment was secure. Mark, now eighteen years old, worked for a couple who made and sold furniture, but Albert was a little concerned about him; he seemed to have a wild streak compared with his older, more serious brother. Albert knew that he couldn't tell either of them what to do, they would lead their lives as they chose.

Maybe this was a good time to ask Blanche about their future together. He took a deep breath and tried to talk slowly.

'Blanche, my dear, you know how I feel about you... Do you feel the same about me?'

The sentence came out as a monotone and sounded as if it was from a badly written play.

Blanche laughed. 'Oh Albert, yes, I am very fond of you.'

'Good, well then – may I speak with your father?'

'Albert, are you proposing?'

Albert stammered a little. 'Well, well, yes... I suppose I am!'

'I will ask my mother and father if we can have tea together next Sunday and then you can speak with him.'

'Good,' said Albert.

Blanche was excited. 'At last, I shall be married – we shall have some lovely children and then my life will be complete!'

Ben and Alice were delighted when Albert told them that he had proposed to Blanche. They were fond of her and had been waiting for this moment.

'Will you live with Blanche's parents?' asked Alice.

'There's plenty of room and they're not in good health. They could do with us around the place to help.'

'And eventually, their house will be your home?' said Ben.

'Yes, it will,' replied Albert.

Blanche's parent's house overlooked the marshes, where the narrow river snaked along on its way seaward. There was a long garden with alluvial soil, the river had been much wider in earlier times and the silt left when it shrank was rich with nutrients, perfect for vegetable and fruit growing. Blanche's parents were keen gardeners, although now infirmity prevented them from using the garden to its full potential. Neighbours and friends helped to keep it tidy and it seemed, Albert thought, to be waiting for a gardener to come along and care for it.

There was no garden at Ben and Alice's home, just a rear yard, which housed the toilet. Albert's interest in gardening and growing had come from talking to friends and reading magazines. He felt sure that he would be successful. The future indeed looked bright for Albert.

At work, Blanche was bursting to show her friends her engagement ring. It was an amethyst and shone different colours when turned to the light.

She told them the wedding would take place the following year.

Her best friend Deidre, known to all as Dee, was delighted, especially when Blanche asked her to be a bridesmaid.

'Blanche, can I make your wedding dress? I can make my own dress too!' Dee's excitement was spontaneous and Blanche was pleased to accept her offer; she knew that Dee was an experienced machinist and particularly skilled at some of the intricate features on the clothes they made in the factory. She had her own sewing machine at home and spent hours making curtains and clothes for friends.

Blanche was always surprised that Dee did not have a young man; at one time she thought that Dee was keen on Albert, but nothing had come of it. 'Not his sort, I suppose,' thought Blanche.

Christopher was equally delighted when Albert asked him to be best man, though his enthusiasm was suddenly tempered with apprehension when he realised he would have to make a speech.

'Oh, nothing fancy Chris, just thank everyone and then make a toast!'

So, the date was fixed.

1921

Albert and Blanche were chapel people. Although not as regular in their worship as some, they were part of the chapel family and that was to be where they would be married. The chapel stood in the main street and the area in front of the building had been made into an attractive garden. It was welcoming in appearance and the interior with its gallery was typical of non-conformist buildings.

The parish church was large, very large for such a small town; it had been built in a century when Aldwell was a major fishing port and reflected its wealth. Although architecturally splendid, Albert and Blanche found it overwhelming and so the chapel had become their place of worship.

At the back of the chapel was a schoolroom with a kitchen; here they would have their reception. Because Albert and Blanche worked for the same factory, most of their friends were work colleagues, who on hearing that the date had been fixed had decided to make decorations and bunting for the schoolroom.

'There, what do you think?' asked Dee, as Blanche looked in the long mirror Dee held in front of her.

The wedding dress was delightful; ivory silk with a delicately embroidered bodice, not too fancy but just enough to make it eye catching. The fitted style suited Blanche's slim figure and Dee looked on approvingly.

'It's wonderful, Dee! You are clever!'

'Just a few adjustments here and there,' muttered Dee, her mouth full of pins, 'and then the final fitting!'

Blanche turned and swirled, admiring the way the fabric fell into place with each turn.

'You could make a good living making dresses like this,' said Blanche.

'I doubt it,' said Dee. 'Weddings are few and far between in Aldwell, I would have to move away to a big town or city.'

'Oh, you won't do that Dee, will you?'

'No, of course not! Aldwell is my home and always will be.'

'Maybe soon it will be your turn for marriage, Dee.'

'Maybe.'

'I thought at one time that Albert was keen on you.'

Dee looked surprised. 'Really? I had no idea… '

'Yes, I used to see him watching you, I was surprised that you didn't catch him first!'

'I don't think I'm the marrying kind.'

'Why not?'

'I'm happy in my own company. Since my parents died I've become used to being on my own. I don't think I could change now.'

'But Dee, you're young, there's time to change – that is, if you want to!'

'Exactly, I don't think I want to, I am happy as I am.'

'Well that's good, we're both happy!'

Blanche took off the wedding dress and put her clothes back on.

'Now, let me see your bridesmaid's dress.'

Dee went into the back room and came out with her dress; it was pale cerise, but plain so as not to be the centre of attention.

'It looks lovely,' said Blanche. 'Do put it on and let me see how it looks.'

Dee returned to the front room wearing her dress; she looked radiant and Blanche was quite taken aback at how such a seemingly simple design could make someone look so special.

'You look wonderful. We shall brighten up Aldwell on our wedding day!'

1926

Blanche's parents were now dead; they were buried in the cemetery outside the town. Albert and Blanche tended their grave and made sure there were fresh flowers there as often as possible.

Now living alone in the house, Albert and Blanche felt as if it was a new beginning. After five years of marriage there were no children; Blanche thought that now they had the house to themselves that would change. But as the months went by, there was no sign. Albert couldn't hide his disappointment. He longed for a son, but as time went on it seemed less likely.

Albert had built himself a small shed at the house end of the garden. From there he made ornaments from wood and scraps of metal, which Blanche displayed in their front room. Albert had taken to beachcombing; often he would walk along the beach early in the morning before going to work, looking for anything that had washed up overnight. Sometimes he found useful items, but usually just rubbish thrown overboard. One of his friends had shown him how to recognise cornelian and amber, sometimes found along the beach. In their natural state these looked dull and weren't easy to identify, but soon Albert began to recognise them and passed them on to his friend for polishing.

Albert was spending more time on his own. He had made many plans for a life with children, so when that hadn't happened he turned his energies towards his hobbies and walking.

Blanche seemed content with her life. The lack of children meant that she could carry on working, which was unusual for a married woman, but Blanche couldn't stay at home and idle her time away.

Dee heard the tap on the door, she welcomed Albert and they sat in her front room, which looked directly on to the small side street where she lived.

'Are you happy Albert?'

'Why do you ask?'

'Because I want to know, that's why!' laughed Dee.

'Yes, I suppose so, but… '

'But what, Albert?'

Albert looked embarrassed.

'Is Blanche a bit mean with you, Albert?'

Albert went red and shuffled in his chair.

'Oh come on Albert, I've known Blanche longer than you… is that why there are no children?'

Albert didn't know what to say. It was not a subject that was discussed and he was surprised that Dee should talk about it. But it was true, Blanche, in spite of all her reading and knowledge, had scant knowledge of the intimate side of marriage and had found it difficult. Their union had been consummated but there had been little further intimacy. Albert had let his parents and friends think that it was unfortunate that they couldn't have children, he had begun to believe it himself, but of course he knew the real reason.

Dee had invited him for tea, he didn't know why, but he had accepted. It was unusual not to ask them both and Albert really shouldn't have gone alone, but he was curious. Dee was very attractive and Albert began to feel uncomfortable, he was having feelings that he should have with Blanche. Dee moved closer to him, she stroked his head.

'I can help Albert, I can give you what a man needs.'

Albert felt as he hadn't done for years. He stood and held

Dee close. He embraced her, they looked at each other; nothing was said now. Dee led him up the stairs.

'Blanche thought you were chasing me at one time,' said Dee.

Albert sat on the edge of the bed. 'I've always found you attractive Dee, but you didn't seem interested in marrying.'

'I'm not, but I like doing this!' Dee laughed and put her arm around Albert. 'If we carry on we must be careful... We don't want Blanche to find out and spoil our fun, do we?'

'Do you want to carry on?' asked Albert.

'Oh yes, I don't want to marry you or anyone else... But why should we not have some enjoyment from each other? It won't hurt anyone as long as we're discreet.'

And so the affair started, an affair that was to last as long as Albert's life and marriage, an affair that had the same loyalty and devotion as a marriage but without the legal bond. Blanche was blissfully unaware, and not until Dee's death, long after that of Albert and Blanche, did anyone find out about the long love affair.

Christopher

'It's about time you found a young lady and settled down, Christopher.' Albert still felt a brotherly duty towards his younger siblings.

'You've been seeing that young lady who works at the White House – Edith, isn't it?'

'Yes, she's lovely, but I don't think she feels the same about me... '

'Have you asked her?'

'Not really, she isn't always here. Just in the summer, so I don't know what she does when she goes back to London.'

The White House was the summer residence of a wealthy family who lived in one of London's fashionable squares. Every summer they came with some of their staff, and stayed in their Aldwell home. Edith was lady's maid to Lady Bartolde and always accompanied her wherever she went. Edith liked Aldwell; she was in fact almost a local girl, having originally come from a village about 20 miles away to the north. When a child, she had missed most of her schooling through illness and as a result had to go into service. But Edith was determined to do well and she worked hard so that she had good references. In that way, was able to move up the ladder and each time get a better paid job. Her current job with the Bartolde family was for Edith the pinnacle of her working life; she was well respected in the household and had more time off than most servants. Coming to Aldwell each summer meant that she could see her family, which otherwise would not have been possible.

Edith liked Christopher, he was a thoughtful young man and they had often been out for walks. He had a good job at the textile factory, although he often said that he felt he wanted to do something different. Edith didn't know what he wanted to do – neither, it seemed, did Christopher. She knew that he was interested in her, but she wasn't sure about her feelings for him.

Edith had an admirer in London; Arthur was a soldier, a captain in the Royal Dragoons. Arthur was a man of many talents, as were all his comrades. They were tough fighting soldiers who combined brutal skills with the solemnity and splendour of the ceremonial occasions in London. Edith loved being with Arthur; his smart uniform was as much an attraction as his good looks. But Edith was never sure of him as he was often away and she was certain that someone so handsome would surely attract other young ladies.

Edith's mother, who had poor health, was keen for Edith to marry. Edith was the youngest of six and all her siblings were settled with children of their own. Edith didn't want to be pushed into marriage and had reservations about both Arthur and Christopher. Her mother, like Edith, was smitten with

Arthur's looks and uniform, Christopher she had yet to meet; she knew only what Edith had told her.

'Well, she should be here soon, it's about now she and the family come here for the summer, isn't it?'

'Yes, it is, I'm looking forward to seeing her. Albert, what's marriage like? Is it good?'

Christopher looked straight at Albert. He respected and admired him and always sought his advice.

'It's good if you work at it – always remember that there are two in a marriage and you must give and take!'

Christopher had little experience of women. Most of the young women in his age group worked at the textile factory and while many were good friends, there was no one special.

'I shall walk round to the White House tomorrow afternoon, see if Edith's there and then ask her out.'

'Good, and perhaps you may ask her a little more than that!' Albert smiled and relit his pipe. He had recently taken to smoking a pipe; Blanche liked the smell of tobacco and unlike some women, encouraged him to smoke indoors.

Christopher went to the side entrance of the White House and nervously rang the bell. A rather stern-looking man answered but when he saw Christopher, said that he would call Edith.

Edith looked pleased to see Christopher and went to get her coat while he waited at the door. Christopher had never been inside the White House; it frightened him a little. It was a world of which he had no knowledge.

They walked along the promenade; Edith took Christopher's arm.

'I have been thinking about the future.'

'Really?' said Edith.

'Yes, and I think it's time to settle. Edith, I am extremely fond of you, would you consider being my wife?'

Edith was taken aback; it wasn't the romantic proposal she

had seen on films. She was rather disappointed.

'Well?' asked Christopher.

'I'll have to think about it, Christopher.'

'How long will you have to think?'

Edith laughed. 'I like you Christopher, you're so straightforward!'

'I am a simple man but I work hard, I earn good money and I can provide for us. I have saved and I've enough money to buy a house!'

Edith gasped. 'He is really serious,' she thought.

Christopher had indeed saved all his money, Ben and Alice had insisted he did so; they had enough to live on from Albert's wages while he lived with them, and Ben still fished. They too had been able to put a little away and now wanted their family to have their own homes.

'When will you decide, Edith?'

Christopher was not going to leave this, he wanted an answer and he didn't want to wait forever.

'Can I decide in a few days?'

'Yes, but it must only be a few days, otherwise I will think that the answer is no.'

'Oh Christopher, the answer is not no! I just was taken by surprise.'

'All right, I won't rush you.'

Christopher realised he was being too eager and changed the subject, telling Edith about the new fashions at the textile factory.

Back at the White House, Edith brushed Lady Bartolde's hair. She was attending a reception that evening; Edith had laid out her clothes and was seeing to the finishing touches.

'So, he has asked you to marry him, and what did you say?'

'I said I would consider his proposal.'

'And how long do you have to consider?'

'Not too long, Christopher is very keen.'

'And what of Arthur?'

Lady Bartolde knew of Edith's friendship with Arthur. She knew that whoever Edith chose, she would lose her. Marrying Arthur would take Edith abroad as an officer's wife, while marrying Christopher would mean that she would stay in Aldwell and have to leave her service.

'I am not sure about Arthur, Lady Bartolde, he is so handsome but I fear that he has the eye of other ladies.'

'Yes, I think you may be right, but the life of an officer's wife has its compensations, my dear.'

Edith was undecided; marriage to Arthur would be exciting, an adventure, marriage to Christopher would be safe, secure, but maybe a bit dull. Either way there was no perfect answer.

'How is your mother, my dear?'

'Not too well, I think I will go to see her soon, my brother has written and is very concerned about her.'

'Go whenever you want to, my dear – she must come first.'

'Thank you Lady Bartolde, I will.'

The next day, Edith met Christopher along the promenade. 'I must go to my mother Christopher, there has been a telegram today from my brother... She is very ill.'

'I'll take you,' said Christopher.

Edith was surprised, and pleased. She had been worrying about seeing her mother, so to have him with her would be a great support. Edith's mother knew about Christopher and hoped that Edith would marry him as she said that she didn't trust army officers, they were not the gentlemen they were supposed to be.

They travelled to the village of Edith's home, a hamlet tucked away along the river valley. Their house was small but now there were just her mother and father, all her siblings had gone. Her brother met them; his face betrayed the seriousness of the situation.

Edith's mother lay on the bed, a large pad of wadding on her chest. Edith could see blood soaking through it.

'Is there a doctor here?' asked Christopher.

'We can't afford such luxuries,' answered Edith's father. 'Anyway I doubt there's much a doctor could do.'

'What's wrong with her?' asked Christopher.

'Consumption,' replied Edith's brother. 'That's what it is called, consumption.'

'But how do you know? What is consumption?'

'We have a woman in the village who knows. She comes in to look after Mother.'

Few people, apart from the wealthy, could afford a doctor, and like Edith's parents, relied on someone in the village who had some medical knowledge – someone who usually also delivered the babies, and laid out the dead.

Consumption was the cause of many deaths. Often it was tuberculosis, but sometimes it was cancer, a disease about which little was known. Whatever the cause, they all knew that there was no cure and it would not be long before Edith's mother would die.

'When are you going to marry my daughter?' Edith's mother managed to squeeze the words out.

'As soon as she says yes,' replied Christopher.

'Good.' She smiled and then closed her eyes.

'I think you had all better leave now,' said Edith's brother.

They went downstairs into the small room, which fronted the village street. Edith burst into tears; Christopher put his arm around her while she sobbed.

The rest of Edith's family sat in silence. It was just a matter of time; they all knew that.

Eventually Edith's brother came down into the room. 'Mother has passed away.'

Everyone just sat, saying nothing, taking in the news.

After a while Edith's brother said that he would make all the arrangements and would send them telegrams to let them know what would happen. Edith's sisters all lived in towns far from their parents' home and had to return to their families.

And so they parted, Edith walking along slowly with Christopher to the railway station where they boarded the train back to Aldwell.

'Thank you Christopher, you have been strong for me.'

'Edith, I love you, I will always be here for you.'

Edith looked into his eyes. 'Oh you are so good to me, and I love you too!'

'So is the answer to my question yes?'

'Yes Christopher, I will marry you.'

Edith burst into tears again, but this time tears of joy. Soon they were back in Aldwell with both sad news and glad tidings for their friends and families.

'I shall be sorry to lose you my dear, you know I will give you excellent references – but you will stay until we return to London in October, won't you?'

Lady Bartolde was the first person Edith told of her impending marriage to Christopher. She knew that from now her home would be in Aldwell: no more time in London. She had enjoyed London life but never felt at home there, she was a country girl at heart.

'Yes, Lady Bartolde, I shall stay until you leave, I shall miss you all, it has been a very happy time for me with you, I shall never forget it!'

'Good, well now, there is much to do... We have the Stewarts coming tonight, can you lay out my clothes, my dear? Nothing too flamboyant I think... oh, and don't forget my dear, you can have as much time off as you want for your dear mother's funeral, providing of course that it isn't more than a day!'

Edith laughed. Lady Bartolde always had her priorities, but at heart she was kind and sincere. Edith had learned a lot working as her lady's maid; later in life she would look back and remember the happy times she had in London and Aldwell.

Christopher was so happy, he couldn't concentrate at work and Albert had to reprimand him a few times.

'Christopher, come along, you're making mistakes, it isn't good enough! We will lose money and reputation if you do that.'

Christopher apologised and said that he would settle down and apply himself to his work. He couldn't help but think of Edith and their life together. Since Edith accepted his proposal, he had been to see Mr Danley, a house builder, and asked him about costs and plots. There was a plot for sale in Haletown; it was on the outskirts with three other houses nearby and some across the other side of the road. The plot was long, so there would be a garden and room for a shed. Christopher liked Mr Danley's bungalow and said that he wanted one the same. Mr Danley had told him the price for the building and the land, so Christopher had written down all the details to tell Edith.

1927

As Edith walked down the aisle on the arm of her father, she couldn't help remembering the last time she had walked into this church when her mother's funeral was held. Now her family and friends were smiling, it was a joyful occasion; there were not many weddings in this small hamlet.

Christopher had wanted Albert to be his best man but Albert had declined, saying that he should ask Mark first.

Mark was delighted, although like Christopher had been when Albert asked him to be best man, he was apprehensive until told that his duties were few.

Ben and Alice were pleased to see how the young men had

progressed. At the reception in the church hall, Mark was teased and asked when he would be getting married and settling down.

'I have much to do before that,' he replied. 'I want to see many things, many places!'

No one knew exactly what he intended to do, but he was such a likeable young man that all felt sure that he would succeed. He still worked at the furniture shop but was becoming restless and now at twenty-five years old, felt that his time in Aldwell was nearing an end.

After the ceremony and reception, Edith and Christopher left for their new home. From there, they would travel to a small coastal village further south where they would spend three days' honeymoon, before Christopher would return to the normality of working life.

Edith loved Christopher but often wondered what her life would have been had she married Arthur. Very different, of course, and certainly she would be living in a different society. But she had made her choice and now she looked forward to a family. Christopher travelled each day from Haletown to Aldwell by train to his job and Edith busied herself in their new home and garden. She had enjoyed her work with Lady Bartolde and had been sad to leave her, but that was just an episode in her life. This was the start of her own family. Christopher was a good provider and Edith wanted for nothing, although she felt lonely at times; Christopher's day was long because of the travelling.

It was not long before Edith discovered she was expecting their first child. For Ben and Alice, being grandparents was new and exciting. Having realised years ago that Albert and Blanche would not have children, they welcomed the news and Alice busied herself knitting baby clothes.

Alice and Edith had become very close. Alice loved to hear

about Edith's experiences when she worked in London, and Edith was fascinated by the way Alice and Ben had brought up not only their son, but also Christopher and Mark.

'Who actually were their parents?' asked Edith when she and Alice sat talking one afternoon.

'Oh Edith, it's a long, long story – maybe you should just accept Christopher as he is and not be concerned about where he came from.'

'Of course, but I'm curious, it sounds most mysterious!'

'Maybe it is, but let's leave it there. You've more important things to think of.'

Edith's baby was due very soon and she was booked into Haletown's hospital for the birth. Much had changed since Edith's parents had been born. Now, if a couple had sufficient money, their babies would be born at a hospital; home births were for the poor. Edith would be admitted when she was in the first stages of labour and her stay at the hospital would be three weeks, enough for her to recover and to learn to look after her new child. Ben and Alice had readily agreed that Christopher should stay with them while Edith was in hospital.

Edith boarded the train back to Haletown. She enjoyed her time with Alice, but did wonder why she wouldn't tell her about Christopher's parents. She had asked Christopher but he said that he was very young when he went to live with Ben and Alice and didn't know anything about his real parents; he had always thought of Ben and Alice as his mother and father and of Albert as his brother. Christopher saw no reason to know any more than he already did.

The birth was not easy. Edith's baby was big but the doctor and nurses ensured that he was healthy.

Christopher was overjoyed. 'A son, a son! We have a son!'

Edith laughed. 'Yes – maybe we'll also have a daughter to keep him company!'

The next few days were very warm and Edith and her son,

together with the other mothers and their children, went and sat out on the lawn at the side of the hospital. Some of the children were yellow, baby jaundice they were told, and the doctor said that a dose of sunshine would do them good. He was proved right and after a few days, those with a yellowy tinge looked pink and healthy.

Christopher and Edith had asked Mark to be godfather to their son; he was delighted and readily agreed. He was soon to leave Aldwell but would stay for the christening at Haletown church.

'Where are you going?' asked Edith.

'To London,' said Mark.

'And what will you do there?'

'I've saved money – I'll find some digs and look for work. I think I'd like to make furniture and work in one of the big shops where they make and sell their own designs.'

'Can you do that?'

'Oh yes, I'm well qualified and skilled in the trade, there's plenty of openings for men such as me.'

Edith admired Mark's confidence; it was quite a step. A life in London, after Aldwell, would take some adapting to but she was sure Mark would manage.

'We'll be sorry to see you leave us! You will come back, now and then?'

'Of course, especially now I have my nephew and godson James to think about!'

Mary and Melvina, 1929

Mary sat on the verandah looking out across Table Bay. Harry, her husband, was due home soon from the Governor General's Office where he was a diplomat. She and Harry had met a while after Mary returned to England from Paris.

Harry's wife had died; he had adult children who had gone

their separate ways and he needed the companionship of a woman. Mary, he discovered, also had adult children and was looking for companionship. Harry's position in the South African Office meant that he attended many functions and he needed a wife who could confidently converse with government officials and diplomats. Mary would be perfect. She was elegant and intelligent; she could talk on current affairs and had a charm about her that Harry admired.

Mary's parents had died before she could ask for reconciliation. At first she was very bitter, but realising that she was as much to blame as Culbert, had resigned herself to the fact. All her daughters were living their own lives. Jessie and Brigitte were happily married, living in London. Gabrielle, who had chosen to come to South Africa with her mother and stepfather, was working as an English teacher in one of the local schools.

Before Mary left England for her life with Harry in South Africa, she had deposited the satinwood box and its key in her bank in London. She gave a list of names to the bank separately with instructions that should any of these people ask for the box, then they should be given it without question. Mary knew that one day someone would want to know the truth about Culbert and only someone who could work out where to find it would discover the box.

She had disassociated herself from her sister Melvina. Harry knew briefly what had happened but said that it was of no importance now. Mary agreed and for the first time in many years felt secure, safe and content.

Mary looked at *The Times*. It was delivered each day, flown in from London to the Governor General's Office. 'I can never understand why they have births, marriages and deaths on the front page,' thought Mary.

As if it was in three dimensions, an announcement seemed to jump from the page; MONTAIGNE, Culbert, died suddenly on

June 4th, 1929 in London, aged 59 years. Funeral private.

Mary jumped slightly. Since their parting in Aldwell all those years ago, she had no communication or knowledge of Culbert. 'Just fifty-nine years old,' thought Mary. 'Maybe he had a heart attack. I wonder where he lived in London, and what he did. Oh stop it Mary, you aren't interested in him, remember what he did, forget him.' She put the paper away. 'That really is the end,' thought Mary.

Melvina sat in the small café near her rented room in North London; she sipped her coffee and glanced across as the couple opposite left. On the table was a newspaper, today's copy of *The Times*. Melvina went over and picked it up. She didn't often buy newspapers, she had little interest in what went on in the world; a free newspaper though was not to be missed. It was folded in half and there was the announcement staring out at her as it had at Mary. So, Culbert had died.

Melvina knew he was somewhere in London, but it was a big impersonal city and he could have been on the other side of the world as far as she was concerned. She no longer felt the anger she first felt when he left her and the boys, but now just sadness that her life had been so useless, so wasted. She knew she would never see her sons again, she couldn't tell them about Culbert, how he had deceived her and his wife, her sister, Mary. It was best that they never knew, but she missed them, especially cheeky Mark. 'I wonder how they've turned out,' she thought. Anyhow it was the end, Culbert was dead and Mary had gone to South Africa with her new husband, she had never met Harry and never would; Mary was gone forever from her life.

She made her way back to her shabby room. At least in summer it was dry, but it was stuffy and airless; she hated it there but had no choice, she had little money and lived from day to day earning what she could by cleaning other people's homes. She often thought of the cafés in Paris and in Aldwell, how she had fallen from that lifestyle to one of near squalor by comparison. Maybe it was what she deserved, she thought.

'Hello Mel,' her neighbour called out to her as she wearily climbed the steps to her room. 'You look worn out, are you all right?'

'Yes, Maisie, I'm fine, just a bit tired... this heat doesn't suit me.'

'You look as if you have had some bad news, sure you are all right?'

Melvina smiled. Was it bad news? Maybe not, maybe it was good news.

'I'm fine thanks, Maisie, thanks for asking, you're a good friend.'

Maisie worked in a local shop. She had befriended Melvina from the moment she arrived; she felt sorry for her because she thought she was 'too posh' to live in this part of London and thought she must have had some misfortune in her life.

Melvina had never spoken about her past and Maisie had never asked any questions. There was an understanding between them and from that developed a friendship, which was to last for as long as Melvina was to live.

9

East London, 1930

Mark, now aged twenty-eight, had made the move to London and armed with his bag of woodworking tools, had easily found work with a cabinetmaker in Bethnal Green.

Solly Bernstein was one of the many Jewish immigrants who had set up businesses in the East End of London. He and his family feared the rising surge of Fascism in mainland Europe and had brought their business to what they thought a safe haven. Many of his fellow Jews had also settled in that part of London and were now producing most of the furniture sold there and major towns around Britain.

Mark knew little about Jews; he was only interested in working and making a good living. He had found a room in a house near Solly's works so had only a short walk each day.

Although Solly's workers were mainly Jewish, there were some local young men, and with one, Johnny, Mark had formed a friendship.

The pay was good and Mark enjoyed the work. He was skilful and earned Solly's praise; he liked this 'young man from the seaside', as he called him. Mark told Solly about Aldwell, his brothers and their life there. Family life was of prime importance to Solly and he encouraged Mark to write each week to his family.

'Mark, would you like to make up a four on Saturday night?'

'Yes, all right – who's coming, and where are we going?'

'There's me of course, and my girl Maureen, and my sister Diana.'

'So, are you matchmaking?' laughed Mark.

'Not really, but you haven't a girlfriend and it's about time you did. You're twenty-eight, you don't want to be single all your life, do you?'

Mark laughed. 'No, I don't but neither do I want to be pushed into marriage.'

'Oh come on, it'll just be a bit of fun!'

'All right, of course I'll come but don't give your sister any ideas about me, please!'

They met in the White Hart public house, just along the road from where Mark lived. It was a friendly place, not noisy like some of the East End pubs, and was one where women on their own would sit outside and enjoy a drink without being seen as having loose morals, trying to catch the eye of passing men.

Mark arrived first; Johnny followed a few minutes later with Maureen and his sister Diana.

Mark gasped. Diana was stunning, a beauty. He'd had a few girlfriends over the years, but this one, she really was outstanding.

Johnny introduced them and Mark sat next to Diana.

'Well, Diana, you know what I do, why don't you tell me what you do?'

Diana told Mark that she was studying design and hoped to start her own business designing and making clothes. Mark was impressed. Until now, the women he'd known either stayed at home to look after the family or if unmarried, worked in service.

The evening went well and before they parted, Mark asked Diana if she would come out with him again, just the two of them. He saw Johnny smile in approval, and laughed to himself.

The next day at work Johnny seemed quite excited. 'I'm so pleased you and Diana got on well, I understand you're to see each other again?'

'As you very well know. You were listening, weren't you?' Mark laughed.

'Well, yes, I was, but I'm so pleased, she's a nice girl and you're a nice man, you two shouldn't be living alone for the rest of your lives.'

'Hold on, hold on, we've only just met, don't marry us off yet!'

Solly came into the workshop. 'What's all this merriment in here, what have you two been up to?'

'Oh, nothing we shouldn't Solly, Mark has just met my sister Diana and they seem to have made an impression on each other, we were just talking about it.'

'That's good, nothing better than happy workers! Now let's have some concentration please, we have orders to complete.'

Johnny and Mark grinned at each other and carried on working, both thinking their own thoughts.

Mark saw Diana regularly from then on. He liked everything about her. 'This is the one for me,' he thought. After just a short courtship he asked Diana to marry him; she too felt that Mark was right for her and had no hesitation in accepting, in spite of the short time they had known each other.

They married in the parish church. Mark, being used to smaller chapels, found the building awe-inspiring, but it was Diana's home church and the surroundings mattered little to him. He was so happy.

Christopher, Edith, Albert and Blanche had made the journey from Aldwell, delighted that at last Mark had found someone to share his life with. Johnny was the best man and he seemed as happy as Mark. After the reception, they left for a short honeymoon before returning to London a week later.

Mark had found a flat to rent near to where he worked and

close to where Diana's family lived; it suited all of them. There was a spare room that Diana could use for her study and drawings. Mark was making a large table for her to use for her sewing.

It was a Thursday; Mark came home from work at the usual time and found Diana crying.

'What is it, Diana?'

'Oh Mark, I'm so sorry, I dropped this lovely vase that your brother gave us when we married.'

'Never mind, it's only a vase, we needn't tell him!'

'Oh thank you, I was so worried... '

'Don't worry, accidents happen. You're not hurt, are you?'

'No, no, I'm fine.'

Mark thought no more of the incident and life carried on as normal.

'Shall we go out with Johnny and Maureen this Saturday?' Mark asked Diana.

'Yes, I'd love to. I've been studying so much recently. I'd like that.'

They met at The White Hart. Johnny, now married to Maureen, bought the first round of drinks.

'Well, here's to us all!' said Johnny raising his glass and laughing. 'I can't think of a better toast.'

They all agreed and raised their glasses. There was a crash. Diana had dropped her glass of port.

'Oh no! Oh I'm so sorry!' she said.

'Never mind, I'll get a cloth,' said Mark.

He went over to the bar and got the cloth and another glass of port for Diana.

'Here we are Diana, a fresh glass.'

Diana's hands were shaking as she took the glass.

'Hey, come on, you only dropped a glass. I expect it was wet from washing, no need to be upset.'

Johnny looked across at Diana, then at Mark. He hesitated, then said, 'Yes, it could have happened to any of us, they don't always dry the glasses and they're slippery, forget it.'

There were no more mishaps and the evening continued pleasantly. The two couples eventually returned to their homes.

1932

At work on Monday morning, Solly summoned all his employees to the main work room.

'I need to tell you that we must be prepared for possible trouble. My fellow Jews and my family left Europe because we were threatened by the Fascists there, now sadly there is a movement here, in England, and indeed in this part of London, which is the same that we saw in mainland Europe. They have formed a party called the Blackshirts and say that we shouldn't be here, work here or even exist. We all need to be vigilant. If any of you wish to leave, I shall understand and I will give you excellent references. You are all good workers and will have no difficulty finding employment elsewhere.'

Johnny and Mark looked at each other. They knew about the Blackshirts; they found their ideals abhorrent.

'Well, we won't leave you, Solly!' said Mark. 'We shall stay, and if necessary fight to keep you and your fellow people safe from anyone that threatens you.'

Solly smiled: a smile of relief. 'Thank you, Mark, thank you.'

He walked away. Mark saw that he wiped a tear on his sleeve.

Solly's fears were well founded; the Blackshirts were growing in number and the Jewish communities of East London were their main targets. Most of the skilled workers in the furniture trade in London belonged to a trade union and these were diametrically opposed to Fascism, a political fact that was to prove the salvation of many Jewish communities in that area.

'Johnny, I'm a little concerned about Diana.'
  'Oh, why?'
  'She hasn't been herself recently. You remember that episode in The White Hart when she dropped a glass? Since then she's been dropping things quite often and gets very upset, she even shouts at me when I try to help.'
  'Is she pregnant?' asked Johnny.
  'No, she isn't. We decided to wait a while before we have a family.'
  'Perhaps she has some woman's problem,' suggested Johnny.
  'I don't think so… She isn't the person I married, she's changed, I think she should see a doctor.'
  'If you think so.'
  Johnny didn't seem interested in his sister's welfare. Mark was surprised, they had been so close and now it was as if he didn't care any more.
  'Johnny, I'm really worried about Diana! You don't seem to realise, I think it might be serious.'
  'If you think so then get her to a doctor, but I'm sure you are overreacting.'
  Mark knew he wasn't. Diana had changed so much in recent months, she was irritable, nervy at times and she had been unable to do much sewing as her hands and mind didn't seem to coordinate. Mark knew very little about illnesses but he knew Diana and that whatever was happening to her was not of her doing.

At first, Diana was reluctant to visit the doctor. She grew angry, then her mood changed and she was acquiescent. Mark was relieved and arranged the appointment.

The doctor examined her. 'You seem a very healthy young

woman,' he said. 'I can't find any physical problem, but I think you should see one of my colleagues in the hospital. He knows about more things than I do!'

And so Diana and Mark waited in the small room outside the neurologist's consulting room, Diana nervously pulling at her hair and shuffling in her seat.

'Don't worry my love, we shall soon sort this out,' said Mark.

Diana didn't answer. She was talking less now and sometimes she found it difficult to remember words. She hadn't told Mark this; he just thought she was worried and thoughtful.

The neurologist asked her a lot of questions and gave her some tasks, most of which Diana found difficult.

'Tell me, has anyone in your family had any disease that affected the brain or nerves?'

'I don't know, maybe,' said Diana.

Mark looked startled. The neurologist turned to him. 'Do you know of anyone with a problem in your wife's family?'

'No, no, I don't, we only knew each other a short time before we married.'

'Well, I am afraid I have to tell you that your wife has an inherited disease, it is called chorea.'

Mark went pale. 'What exactly is chorea?'

'It's a disease that affects the brain and limbs. It starts, as it did with your wife, with a tendency to drop things, a lack of coordination, then it progresses and affects the personality.'

'And what is the cure?'

'There is no cure, I'm sorry.'

Mark was devastated. 'You say this is inherited, does it pass to each generation?'

'Not always, but yes, usually, there must have been a case in your wife's family, possibly immediate family… It isn't a disease you can catch.'

'So what do we do now?'

'I will make arrangements, we can talk about that later.'

During all this Diana had sat, not speaking, almost motionless. Mark looked at her, he couldn't speak; he didn't know what to say to her except to take her arm. 'Come on Diana, let's go home.'

The neurologist opened the door for them. 'I shall be in touch very soon.'

A few days later Mark had a letter from the neurologist. In it he detailed the progression of Diana's disease and said that he could arrange for her to be placed in a hospital where she would be taken care of for the rest of her life. He spelt out the danger of Mark looking after Diana; she would become violent and completely incapable of controlling her actions. The second paragraph was a surprise:

Chorea is hereditary and is a disease that must be notified by the family where it is known to exist when a member of that family marries. This is because the gene carrying the disease will be passed on to any children. If the family fail to notify a future husband or wife and the marriage proceeds and the disease is later diagnosed, then the marriage can be annulled.

Back at work, Johnny looked grim. Mark had told him about Diana.

'You knew, didn't you, Johnny? You knew!'

'Well, not really... there was someone who went a bit funny, but we never knew what it was.'

'I don't believe you. Diana hasn't gone "a bit funny", her brain is being destroyed, and you knew this would happen. Is that why you were so keen for us to marry, to get her off your hands, to save you the bother of looking after her and seeing her go into a mental institution?'

Mark was furious; so many things made sense now, how foolish he'd been. But he still loved Diana and this made his anger even more intense.

'You knew I loved her, I will always love her and you still let me marry her. You are despicable.'

'If you'd known, would you still have married her?'

Mark walked away.

Solly put his arms on Mark's shoulders. 'The woman you married, the woman you loved, has died, Mark, her body is now owned by another being, another spirit, it is not Diana. You must grieve for Diana, you must mourn her passing, but above all rejoice in her life and the happiness you had together. Now I want you to have some time away from here. Why don't you go to your brother in Aldwell for a while?'

Mark nodded; wise Solly was like a father to his workforce, always there with sound advice. Solly liked Mark and respected him for the support he gave him and his fellow Jews when the Blackshirts threatened. He knew that now he might lose Mark, he may find staying there too painful, which was why he suggested a break after which perhaps Mark would be able to start again.

'Yes, Solly, I will... Christopher and Edith have asked me to stay with them, I also have a new niece to see.'

'Well then, that's settled, and a new life to celebrate for Uncle Mark!'

Christopher and Edith had been deeply saddened when they heard about Diana, their first reaction was to ask Mark to come and stay with them. When they heard he would come they were delighted, in spite of the sad reason for his visit.

'Do you think he will return to London?' asked Edith.

'I don't know, Mark is a free spirit, maybe he'll try something new.'

James, their son and Mark's nephew and godson, was excited; he had been told about Mark and was looking forward to meeting his uncle and godfather. Frances, just a year old, was blissfully unaware of the sad events of recent weeks.

Since the birth of Frances, Christopher had made changes to their home to accommodate both children who would have the luxury of their own bedrooms when older, something unknown to Christopher and Edith as children. They had both had to share beds as well as rooms with their respective siblings, and were glad that living conditions and wages had improved since their childhood.

'How long will Mark stay?' asked Edith.

'I don't know, he didn't say, I suppose it depends on whether he's going back to Solly's or not.'

'Then I'll make up the front bedroom for him, it's bigger and will be better should he want a long stay.'

'You don't mind him staying for perhaps some considerable time?'

'No, of course not! He's your brother, he needs our support now – he can stay as long as he wants.'

Christopher smiled. 'What a lovely temperament Edith has,' he thought, 'Mark will indeed be welcome here.'

They met Mark at the railway station and after a very heartfelt welcome, they made the short journey to their home.

Mark had not seen Christopher's bungalow before; he gazed at it in awe and walked around the back of the building to look at the garden. Their home in Aldwell had just a rear yard and in London, Mark and Diana's home had about the same space. This was so large: a lawn, flowerbeds and an area for growing vegetables. At the far end, the grass was uncut. Christopher was gradually working his way along and intended to plant fruit trees and bushes in the remaining area.

Mark looked approvingly and complimented Christopher and Edith on such a lovely garden.

'Come inside and see what you think,' said Edith.

She took Mark's arm. 'We're so pleased to have you stay

with us, and James is quite excited!'

James, a little shy, came forward from inside the bungalow. 'Come on James, come and meet Uncle Mark.'

Mark was surprised to see that James had a patch over one eye. He picked the boy up and swung him around, James laughed and immediately the two were friends.

They sat indoors, talking constantly; there was so much to tell. Mark felt tired. Everything that had happened had drained his energy, he felt that he wanted to sleep and sleep.

The next day James, as expected, wanted Mark to play with him and monopolised him for most of the day. No one minded and Edith was pleased that they got on so well together.

'What's wrong with James's eye?' asked Mark.

'He has something called lazy eye, the muscles don't work well together and his focus isn't central. The patch will make the muscles work harder to correct it and hopefully in a few years they'll be stronger. The eye doctor said it's an inherited condition, although you and Christopher don't seem to be affected.'

'No, and we didn't know much about our parents.'

'Christopher seemed to think it had been in the family.'

'Really, I wonder how he knew that?'

'I think Albert must have told him, but it doesn't matter now, it's been dealt with.'

Mark was puzzled. His recollections of his childhood were not clear. He remembered a woman he thought was his mother, who then disappeared; he couldn't remember who his father was. Maybe he too would ask Albert.

Gabrielle, 1934

Gabrielle was becoming restless. She enjoyed teaching at the school for the children of government officials, and they loved her, but life was too easy – it was boring. Gabrielle wanted to do something, she wasn't sure what it was but she was sure it wasn't here in Africa. She knew she was English but knew nothing of the country; she had some vague memories of Paris and somewhere by the sea in England, but remembered very little about any of those places. Mostly she remembered what she had been told. She felt a need to go to her roots and she knew her roots were in England.

When she told her mother and Harry, they were not unduly surprised. Mary knew that Gabrielle's prospects of finding a husband here were mainly limited to the English staff, none of whom appealed to Gabrielle. Even if she chose a life without marriage she needed to spread her wings, thought Mary, and was actually very pleased when Gabrielle told her of her decision.

'Where will you go?' asked Harry.

'There are plenty of teaching jobs in London. My teaching friends have sent me details of several vacancies and there is one in a school in Hampstead in London which I very much like the sound of.'

'Mmm… nice part of London, you should like it there.'

'Do you know it, Harry?' asked Mary.

'Yes, indeed and I still have friends who live there, I can give you their details, Gabrielle, if you like – they'll be able to help you with accommodation.'

'Thanks Harry, that is kind!' Gabrielle accepted her step-father's offer, and already she was making plans for her future.

The time came. Harry and Mary waved farewell to Gabrielle as she boarded the Imperial Airways aeroplane at Cape Town. Mary was apprehensive about Gabrielle flying but Harry reassured her it was safe and much quicker than by sea. There were just twenty passengers, and like Gabrielle, all were excited at the thought of air travel.

They landed at Croydon Airport and Gabrielle took a taxi

to Hampstead, where she had arranged to meet Caro and Philip, Harry's friends.

Caro had found several flats for Gabrielle to inspect, all nearby and within walking distance of Gabrielle's new place of work.

After a few days' rest, Caro and Gabrielle started their inspection tour and eventually found one that suited in a long tree-lined avenue. It was a quiet area and Gabrielle loved it as soon as she saw it. The flat was spacious, much like Caro and Philip's, and the rooms were light and airy.

'Oh this is wonderful, Caro, I feel as if I've come home! Isn't that odd, because I've never been to London before.'

Caro laughed. 'Must be something in the blood.'

'I loved South Africa but it was so hot sometimes, and the shops are not like these here in London.'

'Well, you won't want for shops, that's for certain!'

Gabrielle had seen pictures in magazines of clothes and loved the styles; the cinema and what the stars wore influenced designers. She was not far from the large city stores and planned to spend many hours buying her new wardrobe.

Gabrielle's sisters had been in England for some years. They wrote but hadn't met since she had left for South Africa.

Gabrielle knew that she must visit her sisters; it was expected of her, but she had no desire to renew any links she had with them. They were both married with children. Gabrielle had seen photographs of their children, her nieces and nephews, and felt that sufficient.

Harry made Gabrielle a very generous allowance. She had no need to work but liked to do so in order to make acquaintances with like-minded people. There were several schools in the Hampstead area and Gabrielle had contacted the one she felt most suited her, a small school for children with parents abroad, much the same as the school she had taught at in South Africa. She knew that the children's parents were mainly diplomats and hopefully her pupils would be well behaved and easy to teach. Of course, if the school did not suit, then Gabrielle could look elsewhere, or indeed not work at all. Harry's allowance was for her lifetime and would only stop if she married someone who could provide her with a higher income. Her mother had told her to be discreet about her finances because there were many young men who would see her as a very desirable wife, one of independent means. Gabrielle however had no plans to marry; she knew that her mother had previously had an unhappy marriage and this had frightened her. Mary had told her a little of their life in France, from which Gabrielle understood that men could be deceitful, and she was happy to live without them. That was until she met Patrick, Caro and Philip's son.

Patrick was a tea broker, like his father, and mainly worked abroad. It was a lucrative business and Patrick had his own flat near his parents. It too was very large, and furnished with modern furniture, the walls hung with large paintings of a mainly abstract nature.

Gabrielle met Patrick one weekend when she was visiting Caro and Philip. No one had mentioned their son and she was surprised when she saw him sitting in their lounge; she thought he was a visitor.

It was obvious from their first meeting that there was a mutual attraction. Patrick, like Gabrielle, was well-educated, well read and a good conversationalist. His travels around the world had broadened his thinking and knowledge. He was intrigued to hear about Gabrielle's life in South Africa, one of the few countries of the British Empire that he had yet to visit.

Caro and Philip could see how the two were enjoying each other's company and conversation and were pleased. Patrick was a dedicated hard worker: Caro often thought he left little time for relaxation and enjoyment. Maybe Gabrielle would change that.

'Where are you off to next?' Gabrielle asked Patrick.

'Nowhere for a while, I'm working in the business in the City, we have some important contracts to develop and complete.'

'Oh good!' said Gabrielle. 'I mean it's good that you have some important contracts.'

Patrick laughed, Gabrielle looked a little embarrassed – then she too laughed.

Caro and Philip exchanged glances. 'Maybe,' thought Caro, 'maybe something is developing.'

And indeed something did develop; very soon Patrick and Gabrielle were engaged. Caro and Philip were delighted, they had hoped that Patrick would find a wife but never believed it would happen so suddenly.

'Patrick, our flat is really too big for the two of us, why don't you and Gabrielle have it when you are married? It has a ninety-nine year lease so would hopefully last your lifetimes and it would be our wedding present to you both.'

Patrick and Gabrielle were very grateful and thanked Caro and Philip for their generosity.

'Why don't you take over my flat after we're married, Mother? It would suit you and father and you wouldn't have to move away. We would rather you stayed near, wouldn't we, Gabrielle?'

And so it was arranged, both families would live in Holly Hill. Gabrielle by now was losing interest in teaching and asked Patrick if she could help in the business.

'You can do more than that, you'll be a partner when we marry!'

Gabrielle was overjoyed; she couldn't believe all this was happening. Thank goodness she had decided to come to England.

When Mary and Harry received Gabrielle's letter telling them of her engagement and future plans, they too were overjoyed, their happiness being slightly tempered by the distance between them.

Gabrielle also wrote to her sisters and received replies from each congratulating her and Patrick. She still had no desire to make any permanent connection with them and felt it sufficient to invite them to their wedding when the time came. Patrick asked about them and understood Gabrielle's reluctance to renew contact that had been almost non-existent for so many years.

'Our family has a strange past Patrick, I know little about it and when I asked Mother she said it was best to forget about it, which is what I've done.'

'But I expect you're curious?'

'Yes, of course, very, but sometimes you can find out things that are better not found out – that's what Mother said.'

'Aha, skeletons in cupboards!' Patrick laughed.

'I wouldn't be surprised Patrick, but you know all about me, I have no skeletons, that's what's important.'

Patrick drew her towards him and kissed her tenderly. 'I don't care if you have, I will share everything, including skeletons!'

1936

It was the first time for many years that Mary had all her family together; Gabrielle and Patrick's wedding had provided not only a time for celebration but also of reunion.

Jessie and Brigitte with their respective husbands and children had arrived, as had Mary and Harry. The wedding was to be held in the local church in Hampstead with a reception in a nearby hotel.

Gabrielle had taken the opportunity to browse the city's finest shops for her wedding gown, a fashionable Empire line ivory satin creation which was the style worn by many famous actresses in films she and Patrick had recently seen. Patrick, of course, was kept in the dark about the dress but he had guessed that Gabrielle would choose something elegant and modern.

After the service, the families and friends gathered in the banqueting room of The Heath Hotel for the reception. Mary was overjoyed to see that Gabrielle was so genuinely happy; hers was a true love match. Patrick was a charming young man, thought Mary, not only handsome but also intelligent and a good businessman, he would make a fine husband and father.

Patrick came over to her. 'Thank you for your beautiful daughter, Mrs Baron, it is the best present I could ever have had!'

Mary embraced Patrick. 'Please, call me Mary, and I'm delighted that you chose my daughter, I know you two will be very happy.'

Mary sensed that she needed to talk with Patrick. 'Has Gabrielle told you anything about our family?'

'No, not really, she said she knows little.'

'Patrick, you must know that all families have secrets, things they want no one else to know about. There are such secrets in my family. Gabrielle doesn't know about them and I hope she never will. The most important thing is that you are both happy. I think you have an enquiring mind and I have guessed that you have already tried to find out what happened in our past, but I ask you, please do not, leave the past where it belongs, live for today and look forward to the future.'

Mary was right; Patrick had been interested in the family's past, not because it would affect Gabrielle and him, but because he had an interest in mysteries, especially those which were real. In what spare time he had, he studied ancestry, and Gabrielle's family had been difficult to research – in fact he had come to a dead end.

'All right Mary, I won't do anything to upset you or Gabrielle, rest assured.'

Mary sighed with relief. Harry came to join them. 'We are so pleased for you and Gabrielle, Patrick.' He handed him an envelope. 'We couldn't bring you a wedding present, there wasn't room on the aeroplane, so you can choose for yourself from this.'

Patrick took the envelope and thanked Harry; it contained a substantial cheque drawn on a London bank.

'You still bank in England?' said Patrick, rather surprised, assuming it would be cash.

'Of course, both Mary and I kept our bank accounts in London, oddly enough at the same bank. You never know – we may return here one day when I eventually retire.'

'Good thinking,' said Patrick. 'And thank you, both of you, we will make good use of the money, you know that.'

Patrick and Gabrielle would spend their honeymoon in Italy; when Gabrielle had told her mother of their destination, her eyes had misted over. They had chosen Lake Garda, the same place that Mary and Culbert had chosen for their honeymoon. For Mary it brought back the one truly happy memory of Culbert, those days spent together when the future seemed so exciting. It was a memory that Mary had tried to erase from her mind but it would not go away. How strange that their love, so strong and vibrant then, should turn into something so black. But Gabrielle knew nothing of this, she thought that her mother's reaction was because she imagined it a romantic place, somewhere she had read about.

November 1936

'I'm going to Spain.'

Edith and Christopher looked first at each other, then at Mark who had uttered these words.

'Um… What exactly will you do in Spain, Mark?' asked Christopher.

'I'm going to join the International Brigade.'

Edith and Christopher had read about the war in Spain, where the Republicans were fighting to stop Nazism taking over but it was far away – another world to them.

'Why should you support their cause?' asked Christopher.

'When I worked at Solly's, I saw what the Blackshirts were doing and the threat they and their like pose to the Free World. They must be stopped or all Europe will be under Nazi control, I have to do this.'

Mark had told Edith and Christopher about various episodes in East London when the Jewish community was attacked and businesses burned. Now they realised the connection.

'Don't they want younger men?' asked Christopher.

'They're not fussy – if we want freedom in Europe then we can join, it's not a question of age but in what you believe.'

Mark had stayed with Edith and Christopher in Haletown for two years, returning to work at the textile factory in Aldwell. He hadn't wanted to go back to London because he knew he would constantly be reminded of his time with Diana. His marriage to Diana had been annulled; now he needed an aim in life. The Spanish Civil War was an ideal opportunity and Mark had found no problem in enlisting. When the recruiting officer discovered that he could play the trumpet he was even more enthusiastic, much to Mark's surprise and amusement.

'But you will return to England eventually?' asked Edith.

'Yes, eventually, but not here – you have your family, your life, I can't stay with you forever, as much as I love you all.'

James and his sister Frances had grown to be very fond of their Uncle Mark and Edith was pleased that such a bond had been formed; she hoped that it would last.

'Will you tell Albert and Blanche?' asked Christopher.

'Yes, I must, I'll go to see them both at the weekend.'

*

Albert and Blanche were not completely surprised by Mark's announcement, he had been restless for over a year. They knew he would leave Aldwell but joining the International Brigade was not what they had expected.

Blanche, who as always took an interest in all that went on the world, was knowledgeable about the situation in Spain and admired Mark for the stand he was taking.

'If we're not alert, Nazis will be a threat the like of which we have not yet seen in Europe,' she said.

Albert looked at her. 'Do you really think so, my dear?'

'No, I don't think so – I know so. The German Chancellor, Herr Hitler, will be someone to reckon with sooner rather than later, it's all about Nazis and their hatred of the Jews and Herr Hitler's wish to dominate Europe. Good luck to you Mark, do what you can to stop this evil spreading!'

Mark was surprised at Blanche's eloquence and indeed grateful that she was so supportive. He had wondered if he would be laughed at and thought mad for what he was about to take on.

Blanche went out into the kitchen, leaving Mark and Albert together.

'Albert, before I go, there's something I must ask you about my family.'

'Mmm… what's that?'

'Well, I don't know really, but just who am I, and who are my real family? I know Ben and Alice brought Christopher and me up from childhood, and for that we're thankful, but who were our real parents? Do you know?'

'Mark, I was just a young lad myself when it all happened and I wasn't told what it was all about – all I know is that your mother and father were from Paris and then opened a café in Aldwell. For some reason they fell out and then they left you and your brother, my parents looked after you and you were brought up as my brothers.'

'Yes, but who where they, my parents, and why did they

leave Christopher and me – were we bad children?'

'No, no, of course not! I suppose they couldn't agree as to who you and your brother would live with, so you stayed here.'

'I see.'

Mark didn't see at all, in fact it made no sense to him. Either Albert really didn't know, or just didn't want to tell him. Whatever the reason, he wouldn't get any more from Albert.

The day came to leave and Christopher, Edith, James and Frances, and Albert and Blanche stood on the station with Mark.

Mark got on the train for London and Edith handed him a parcel. 'Here, you'll probably need this, Mark!' she laughed. 'Open it later.'

Mark settled down and put his luggage in the rack. He sat and looked at the parcel Edith had given him then carefully he unwrapped it – inside was a shiny bugle. Mark laughed. 'Edith is a gem,' he thought, 'I shall have to have a photo taken of me with the bugle once I have my uniform.'

'So little brother has gone off to Spain,' said Dee to Albert.

'Yes, he needs to get something out of his system I think – it will do him good, providing of course that he doesn't get killed!'

'Well, I admire him for fighting for what he believes in. These are strange times Albert, we may all be at war soon.'

'Oh I don't think so, we aren't ready.'

'We will see... Anyway what does Blanche think? She's a great reader and thinker.'

'Blanche thinks that war will come, she says that all wars are about land, getting more territory, and that the Nazis will resort to violence to get what they want.'

'She's right and we're lucky here in our sleepy little Aldwell that we're not in the firing line.'

'Let's hope so,' said Albert, 'let's hope so.'

213

1938

Albert and Christopher still worked together at the textile factory. Albert knew that Edith would like Christopher to work in Haletown so that she and the children would see more of him. Christopher still felt a strong attachment to Aldwell, and to Albert. His marriage to Edith was happy, and their children were a joy, but Aldwell felt like a magnet from which he could not easily pull himself. Betsy, who worked in the office, often chatted with Christopher; she was married to John, a mechanic who had the ability to mend, repair and rebuild most engines, most of his work being with agricultural machinery. Christopher had been surprised when Betsy and John married, they seemed so different, but they were happy.

'Does Edith want you to get work in Haletown, Chris?' asked Betsy.

'Yes, she does, and I would like to spend more time at home but there isn't much work there except the sort of work your John does, and I can't do that.'

'Why don't you buy a car, you wouldn't take so long getting to and from work then?'

'Yes, I suppose I could, I hadn't really thought of it.'

'Well you should, and you could take Edith and the children out at the weekends, it would be fun! My John says that the Morris 8 is a lovely car – you could afford it Chris, why not?'

Christopher had read about the Morris cars and had secretly imagined driving one; Betsy's mention of it sparked a renewed interest.

'If you like I can ask John to arrange for you to have a drive in one – he knows car mechanics as well as tractor mechanics!'

'Yes, but let me speak with Edith first.'

'All right, just let me know and I'll arrange it.'

Betsy was so practical, and she was a great organiser, which was why she ran her section of the office so well. She was in charge of finding buyers for the factory's new lines and had a list of contacts that read like a fashion magazine's advertisements. Christopher always puzzled as to how someone whose work was with such elegant people could be happy married to someone whose hands were always covered in grease.

'You look very thoughtful all of a sudden, Chris.'

'Hmm... how does John get all that grease off his hands?'

Betsy burst into laughter. 'Whatever made you ask that?'

Christopher looked a little embarrassed. 'Oh sorry, Betsy, association of ideas I suppose... cars, grease, you know, that sort of thing!'

'I can assure you that he does have skin under all that grease.'

They both laughed. 'I will find it difficult to leave here,' Christopher thought. 'I have my work, Albert, Ben and Alice, my friends. Betsy's idea is a good one, I shall buy a car then I can stay here at the factory and also get home sooner – everyone will be happy.'

Edith welcomed Christopher's idea to buy a car, realising the difference it would make to all their lives. She told James and Frances, although she wasn't sure if they understood what a real motorcar was.

In spite of the excitement, Edith realised that Christopher would never leave his job in Aldwell. She had hoped that he would work in Haletown now that there was more work available, but Christopher was still invisibly attached to Aldwell. At least now she would be able visit Albert and Blanche more easily, but first she must learn to drive and then take her test.

The Morris 8 was a beautiful car, thought Edith. It was dark green, with leather seats and a shiny wooden dashboard. Christopher had a licence before driving tests were compulsory, but for Edith it meant learning and then meeting an examiner for the thirty-minute test.

Christopher sat with her while they drove around country lanes for practice. Edith was a quick learner and she soon was able to drive with confidence. They arranged to meet the examiner at a garage in Haletown and Christopher could see from Edith's face when she returned that she had passed. James and Frances jumped about waving and laughing, Christopher told them that they had a very clever mummy and now would be able to go out for rides and picnics.

But soon the happy carefree days became blighted by talk of war. Mr Chamberlain had been to visit Herr Hitler and had reached an agreement with him; he said there would be no war. Sadly, it was not to be and as the year progressed it became clear that Herr Hitler was not a man of peace, but wanted to conquer Europe. Jews and minority groups were fleeing Germany to escape persecution and in spite of Mr Chamberlain's pact with Herr Hitler, war seemed unavoidable.

10

1960

Albert and Blanche, now in their late sixties, spent their days immersed in their own individual interests.

The textile factory in Aldwell had closed; synthetic materials now replaced natural ones, and their products were no longer competitive.

Because they had no children, Albert and Blanche had been able to save and now had a comfortable retirement ahead. The local library provided Blanche with ample material for studying, a pursuit which had become all absorbing for her. Albert enjoyed making a variety of objects from wood, these being given to family and friends for Christmas and birthday presents.

Ben and Alice had died during the war, both having lived well into their eighties. They were buried in the cemetery outside Aldwell.

Christopher and Edith, slightly younger than Albert and Blanche, were now on their own, James and Frances both having moved away.

Christopher had to retire early when the textile factory closed but he had been thrifty and managed to save. He and Edith also looked forward to many happy years of retirement.

The two couples were meeting more often now, Christopher

217

and Edith being able to drive to Aldwell. They now owned a Ford that had replaced their Morris 8, a vehicle that had served them well for many years. Edith and Blanche had formed a firm friendship. Both women enjoyed discussing current affairs, especially politics, and met regularly each week. Edith, being able to drive, enjoyed an independence that few women had, and made full use of it.

Albert and Christopher spent time admiring each other's gardens. Now with plenty of time, both produced ample vegetables and fruit for their needs.

'I do wish Albert would stop smoking that pipe,' said Christopher to Edith. 'He coughs and coughs, it can't be good for him.'

They sat in their garden in Haletown enjoying the summer sun and warmth; their garden, now mature, provided great pleasure for them.

'I've been reading that smoking cigarettes is good for calming the nerves,' said Edith.

'Well that may be so, but Albert's pipe doesn't seem to calm his lungs.'

'It's very fashionable now for women to smoke – all the famous actresses do, and they all look very glamorous with their long cigarette holders.'

'I hope you won't copy them!'

'Certainly not, I don't believe all I read and I have no desire to inhale smoke and puff it all around, seems most unpleasant to me.'

'Good, I'm glad you are more sensible than those who write such articles.'

'Are you very worried about Albert?'

'Yes, I am, but I'm not sure what to do.'

'What about asking Blanche?'

'Yes, I could, but maybe it would be better if you did when you two are alone. Would you, Edith?'

'Yes, all right, I shall see her in a couple of days. I'll tell her we're concerned.'

Blanche and Edith sat on a seat on the cliff overlooking the sea at Aldwell. It was a clear day and the sun sparkled on the water like drops of silver.

Edith came straight to the point.

'Blanche, I hope you don't think me interfering, but Christopher is rather concerned about Albert, he said he coughs a lot.'

Blanche didn't seem surprised. 'Yes, he does, I'm worried too, I think it may be the pipe he smokes and I feel awful because I almost encouraged him to smoke it when we first married.'

'Oh, don't feel bad about it – all men smoked then, and lots do now, but all the same Albert really shouldn't cough that much.'

'Edith, I've seen specks of blood in his handkerchief at times, at first I thought it was from his hand – perhaps he cut himself when he was woodworking – but now I'm not sure.'

'Can you ask him to see a doctor?'

'Well I can, but whether he will go is another matter.'

'What if Christopher asks? They are very close.'

'Yes, but let me try first. If that doesn't work then perhaps Christopher can talk to him.'

Mark and Betty enjoyed Sundays. They drove from their home in Wallington towards the Thames, each time stopping at a different place to enjoy the scenery, watch the rowers, and stroll along the river's bank.

Mark had returned unscathed from the Spanish Civil War and his service with the International Brigade had exempted him from call up in World War II. But Mark, like Christopher and Albert, who were also exempt, was determined to do his duty and was one of the many fire watchers who also became first aid helpers during the war. Solly's furniture business had been destroyed in the Blitz and there was just a heap of rubble where once there was a thriving industry. The intensive bombing of London had flattened most of the East End buildings. Now new flats stood in their place.

Mark had found work as a manager in a paint factory. It was special paint, and as far as his friends knew it was just ordinary paint for walls. It provided Mark with a good income and he had bought a flat in Wallington. It was in a café there that he met Betty and her daughter Annie. Betty was a buxom blonde; not really Mark's type, so he had always imagined, but she was everything that the stereotyped image of a blonde was not.

Betty had been married to Fred, an American cattle farmer who she had met when he was visiting Yorkshire, where Betty lived. They married and went to the USA to live on Fred's ranch. About three years later Annie, their daughter, was born. When Fred was just forty he had a stroke, which incapacitated him so much that Betty struggled to keep the ranch going. Annie was young and unable to help physically; Betty had to carry Fred everywhere, wash him and feed him. It was exhausting and there was no help. Their ranch was so isolated that no one would stay there long. Just when Betty thought she could no longer carry on, Fred died, leaving Betty and Annie alone. Betty was a tough businesswoman and knew that if she told potential buyers she was selling because her husband had died, the price would drop. She waited for several months then successfully sold the ranch for a good return and she and Annie decided to move back to England.

Betty's family had not approved of her 'American husband' and had broken off all contact with her, so Betty had no wish to return to her native Yorkshire. Instead, she and Annie decided that the suburbs of London would be their new home and Betty bought a flat in Carshalton. They both loved the area, its nearness to London and even more so the Thames, and the lovely little towns and villages that ran alongside it.

Betty had no thoughts of marrying again, she was financially secure and Annie was settled in her new life.

Mark sometimes called in at the café in Wallington on a Saturday morning. This particular Saturday it was very busy and hc had to share a table. Betty and Annie smiled at him when he asked if he could sit at their table and said yes, of course he could. Mark noticed Betty's northern accent and was surprised. Few northerners lived in this part of London.

Betty fascinated Mark; the way she spoke, her appearance, and the very fact she was a northerner in a London suburb.

He couldn't resist it. 'I can't help but notice that you are from the north – do you live here?'

Betty laughed. 'Yes we do! This is my daughter Annie, we live in Carshalton.'

'Rather different from the north!' said Mark.

'Oh yes, but I don't want to go back there... we like it here.'

'So what made you come to this part of the world?'

Mark found himself questioning Betty, but she didn't mind.

Betty told him about her life in the USA, Fred's death and their move to England.

'What about you, ducky?' asked Betty.

Mark wasn't used to being called 'ducky'. Betty saw his puzzled look and explained that it was a common address in the north.

So Mark told her about Solly's furniture business, about Diana, about the Spanish Civil War, and that he was living nearby. It was the first time Mark had told anyone outside the family about Diana, but telling Betty was easy. She was so down-to-earth, she made Mark feel comfortable.

They arranged to meet again and soon were enjoying each other's company. Annie was a lovely girl, quiet and very courteous, Mark thought them a lovely family.

Mark didn't actually propose to Betty, they just knew they should be together and arranging their marriage came automatically; they both knew it was right for all of them.

Mark's flat was the bigger of the two so Betty sold her flat in Carshalton, and once she and Mark were married, she and Annie moved to Mark's home.

'There is one piece of furniture I must bring with me Mark, only one, the rest I shall sell, but if you agree I must have this one piece.'

'Fine, fine, of course you can.'

Mark laughed. How strange she should almost ask permission to put a chair or table in the flat.

The piece of furniture was a piano.

Mark's mouth dropped open when he saw it. 'You said I could!' said Betty.

'Yes, of course! I just didn't expect a piano!'

And so the piano was carefully transported the few miles to Mark's flat where it was placed in the lounge. Betty was an accomplished pianist; she played a style called 'stride', popular in the USA and also in the north of England but not often heard in the south. She played without music, her hands always going to the correct notes and chords. Mark loved to hear her play and marvelled at the speed her hands travelled the keys, especially as her wrists were always laden with heavy charm bracelets.

Annie had started courting Jeffrey, an ambitious young man who worked in the City in the foreign department of a large bank. They were well matched and it wasn't long before they announced their engagement.

Mark was happy, content, and now felt that his life had begun. The past was just that, never again needing to be told.

'We must contact Mark,' said Christopher.

Albert's health had deteriorated rapidly. He had consulted a doctor who had sent him to a specialist; there was a growth in his lungs, which was well advanced.

'Yes, we must, he'll be devastated. They're so close, you remember how happy he was when Mark and Betty married?'

When Christopher told Albert that Mark was coming, Albert's face, now drawn and almost skeletal, showed a smile; his eyes, now cloudy, seemed for a moment to sparkle.

Mark was horrified when he saw Albert; the growth inside his lungs had taken over his body, as an invader would conquer a country.

Albert managed to put out his hand. Mark took it, being careful not to squeeze – it was so bony and fragile.

'Thank you Mark... thank you for coming.'

Mark desperately tried to hold back the tears, but he couldn't. Albert smiled again. 'Don't be sad Mark, we've survived a lot, but now it's over for me. Be thankful for all we've had.'

It was as if Albert had waited for Mark to come before he died. His head fell to one side – he gave a small gasp, then all was quiet.

Albert was buried next to his parents, Ben and Alice; he hadn't quite reached his three score years and ten, which he had always considered his allotted time on earth.

Christopher, Mark, Edith, Blanche and Dee stood at the graveside and each threw a single stemmed flower on to the coffin in the ground.

'How are Betty and Annie?' asked Edith.

'Oh, they're very well. Annie is marrying Jeffrey next year, Betty and I are very happy for them,' replied Mark.

Blanche and Dee stood arm in arm; they had become close friends in recent years and now Dee was proving to be a tower of strength to her friend.

'Dee never married?' asked Mark.

'No, she didn't, she's just not the marrying kind,' said Edith.

'Pity, she would have made someone a good wife.'

'Oh you men, is that all a woman is good for?' Edith laughed as she said it, but there was an underlying annoyance in her voice.

'No, of course not Edith, I just meant that she's such a caring person, seems a shame not to have anyone to share that with.'

'It's all right Mark, I know what you meant, and anyway it's not a day for disagreement.'

They gathered at Blanche's home to say their final farewells to Albert.

'Will you be all right, Blanche?' asked Edith. 'Would you like me to stay with you for a few days?'

'No, thank you, Edith, very kind of you, but Dee will be here. She is so near, but you know you're always welcome, do please come and see me whenever you want!'

Edith looked at Dee; if she hadn't known better she would have thought it was Dee's husband who had died. She must have been very fond of Albert.

Gabrielle and Patrick

'Philip is coming at the weekend for a few days,' said Gabrielle.

'Good, I'm not too busy next week,' replied Patrick.

Gabrielle and Patrick had a son and daughter, Philip and Caroline. Both had attended university and achieved degrees. Philip was studying for a PhD while working part time for his father in one of their branches in the Midlands.

Caroline had chosen a career in archaeology and was currently in Turkey, part of a team working on one of the many ancient sites. She visited her parents when she was in England but this was becoming less often. Gabrielle worried about her but knew that she would find her way in life, as she herself had done.

*

Philip arrived on the Saturday evening; he greeted his mother with the usual bear hug, in spite of her protestations that he was squeezing all the air from her. The rest of the weekend was spent relaxing and talking, doing nothing in particular.

Monday came and Philip and Patrick sat in the large lounge, looking out onto Hampstead Heath.

'I know about your work in our branch, but how's your study progressing?'

'It's going well Dad – actually, I need your help with a section of it.'

'Really? I thought you were doing a thesis on societies and their interactions.'

'Yes, I am, but part of it is discovering our own roots, to see how we compare with our ancestors.'

'Well that should be interesting, although you may have difficulties on your mother's side.'

'Really, why's that?'

'Well, there seems to be a gap, or rather gaps, in the family line. Your mother doesn't know and her mother sort of warned me off finding out.'

Philip's eyes widened. 'Wow! A real mystery!'

'Could be! Could be a challenge for you.'

'Mum, can you tell me about your parents and your sisters?'

'Well, dear, not a lot… you know Aunt Jessie and Aunt Brigitte of course but they know as much, or rather, as little as me. I can't remember much about my early childhood, I know what I was told, which was that we lived in France, then came to England to some place on the east coast. Then something happened and I went to South Africa with my mother and father. My sisters didn't come with us.'

'Do you know what the "something" that happened was?'

'No, but I don't think it was anything pleasant. There was

another man, not Harry; I'm not sure who he was. Harry isn't my father, but you know that.'

'Do you know who your father was?'

'Not by name, but I think he may have been the other man in England at the coast.'

'Can you remember where on the coast?'

'It was a small town, I didn't see much of it, I was very young and it didn't make a big impression on me, but I may remember if I see some names.'

'Well, we will find it easily then, but you have a birth certificate of course?'

'No, I haven't, my mother must have kept it, she and Harry died a few years ago as you know, so I really don't know where it is. But there must be an entry in a register somewhere in France. I imagine I can get a copy, I haven't thought about it until now.'

Philip's interest was alight. Not only would this be a part of his thesis, but also he might solve a family mystery.

'Dad, how did Mum get a passport without a birth certificate?'

'She didn't, she's on my passport, as were you and your sister when you were children. It was called a family passport.'

'Oh, I see… Things were different then, weren't they?'

'Yes, indeed they were!' Patrick laughed, thinking how much society had changed since he was a child, and for the better, he thought.

'Can I contact Aunt Jessie or Aunt Brigitte about where they were all born?'

'Yes of course you can, they should remember.'

Philip's aunts were able to tell him that they were born in Paris, as Philip had thought they might have been. Now he knew how to get his mother's birth certificate; he must write to the Mayor's Office in Paris.

When the envelope with a French stamp and postmark arrived, there was excitement. 'Come on Mum, this is about you!' said Philip.

It was the birth certificate of Gabrielle Montaigne, born in Paris in 1905.

'Let's see who your parents are,' said Patrick, just as curious as Philip.

Mother – Mary Montaigne; Father – Culbert Montaigne, businessman. Their address was Café Benedict, Place du Tetre, Paris.

'Goodness, what a mouthful your father's name was!' laughed Patrick. 'Did you know that was his name?'

'No, I told you, I never knew him, I only knew of him. I was very young when he and my mother split up. The only father I knew was Harry, my stepfather.'

'Culbert is an Irish name I think,' said Patrick. 'A bit unusual but I'm sure I've heard of it.'

'Well, whatever, we make progress!' said Philip.

'So, what will you do next?' asked Gabrielle.

'I'm not sure... I have to find out who Culbert Montaigne was, but if he was French then it will be difficult.'

'Oh, he wasn't French,' said Gabrielle.

'Are you sure?'

'Yes, that's the one thing I do know! He was English, at least he was born English, I think he had dual nationality which is perhaps why he had a French surname, My sisters may know more but they have never wanted to talk about him, so I stopped asking.'

'That's a start. Looks like a long visit to Somerset House and maybe a trip to Café Benedict in Paris!'

A few days, later Philip was called back to the family business, so his investigations were temporarily halted.

Mark and Tommy

'Hello Betty,' said Tommy.

Tommy liked Betty instantly. 'A good down-to-earth northerner,' he thought.

'So you're Mark's friend from work. He's talked about you a lot.'

'All good, I hope, Betty!'

'Yes, of course ducks, and if you're Mark's friend, then you're mine too!'

Mark had brought Tommy to meet Betty; they had been discussing a proposed sideline to earn some extra money and he wanted Betty to know about it.

'Tommy has an aeroplane, Betty, a single-seater Cessna.'

'Single seater, he can't take me for a spin then!' Betty laughed.

'No, afraid not Betty,' said Tommy, 'but that's not what Mark and I had in mind.'

'I am intrigued!' said Betty. 'Tell me more.'

So Tommy and Mark told Betty of their plan to bring small amounts of what they described as 'luxury items' into the country on Tommy's plane.

'You mean smuggling?' said Betty.

'Well, yes... we do.'

'But why? You earn enough Mark, why do something illegal?'

'It will mean we can have a better car, a better lifestyle... but it's exciting as well, isn't it Tommy?'

'So you're doing it for the thrill?'

'Yes, partly.'

'You do what you want, I won't say anything, just be careful. Especially you Tommy, you presumably will have the risky bit, but what's Mark's part?'

'Mark will sell the goods.'

'What sort of goods?'

'Brandy, cigars, perfume mainly, all French.'

'Perfume you say, what sort of perfume?'

'It will be the best. Not the sort you can buy here, it would be too expensive, but we get it without the duty so we can sell it for a good profit, still much cheaper than buying it in a shop with duty added.'

'But who will buy it? People will know it's smuggled.'

'Yes, but we have many friends who will happily pay for it – don't worry, they can all be trusted.'

'Well, I hope so, but as I've just said, be careful you two!'

'She's a gem, your Betty,' said Tommy to Mark.

'I told you she'd be OK about it, but I needed her to know, wanted her approval I suppose... Betty and I don't have any secrets.'

'Good, well that's settled, we can make the first run soon! I'll contact my friend in Paris and we will be away.'

Tommy had obtained his civil pilot's licence after the war. It was easier than driving a car, he said. He bought a second-hand Cessna that he could land on a short runway or field – getting past Customs was no problem.

And so Tommy and Mark formed their 'partnership', with Tommy making flights into France at irregular intervals, landing in different airfields so that he didn't create a pattern for anyone to follow or find suspicious.

Mark sold the goods at local pubs and clubs, never saying who he was or where the goods came from. Between them, they well covered their tracks.

With the proceeds, Mark and Betty were able to move to a large house on the Thames, something they had always dreamed of but had been unable to do on Mark's legitimate income. Mark also bought a larger car. He was careful, buying at intervals so that he wouldn't arouse suspicion.

Aldwell 1962

'Betty, would you like to visit my brother and his family in Haletown? We haven't seen them for some time, it would be nice to pay them a visit.'

'Yes, I'd love to, and to go to Aldwell too, it's a cute little place.'

Mark laughed, he had never thought of Aldwell as 'cute', although it was now a popular holiday resort for the wealthy, especially those from London and the Home Counties.

And so it was fixed. Christopher and Edith were delighted to welcome Mark and Betty. James and Frances were living in Kent and London respectively, but Frances was home for a visit to her parents during a well-earned break from her studies for the period of Mark and Betty's visit.

Edith was very proud of Frances; she had excelled at school and then achieved equally well at university. She now worked for a bank in London but continued studying for a post-graduate degree part time.

James had proved to be a difficult boy; his eye problem, although almost completely resolved, was always an anathema to him. Edith was saddened by the way he had progressed from childhood. He had found studying difficult, blaming his eyesight, and had struggled to gain his few qualifications. He had left Haletown and found work with a small business on the Kent coast that shipped goods to France for distribution to other countries in Europe. It was a clerical job; the pay wasn't high but the family who owned the business provided James with accommodation, for which they didn't charge. Since moving there, James had written home less and less and Edith sometimes wondered if he would break contact completely.

Christopher, now retired, was enjoying his new-found spare time pottering about in the garden and finding more unusual plants to grow. Edith read more and more and had found a new interest in studying antiques. Her local library was always pleased to order the books she requested and her weekly visits were always greeted with anticipation from the librarian, who regarded Edith's requests as exciting challenges.

'You've done well for yourself, Frances,' said Mark.

'Thanks Uncle Mark, I think you have too from the sound of things!'

Mark smiled. Frances knew what he and Tommy did but she too saw it as exciting and said that as long as no one was hurt, then it was all right. She was also very appreciative of the French perfume that Uncle Mark gave her; perfume that she couldn't buy in London, even if she could afford it.

'So, what is it that you're studying now?'

'It's a postgraduate degree. I have to write a thesis on something I choose that is within the bounds of the subject.'

Mark looked a little puzzled.

Frances laughed. 'Sorry Uncle Mark, I am being obtuse. I'm studying anthropology and for my thesis I've chosen connections between Europeans and how this affected trade and so on. I have to go to Somerset House quite often as a result, so I thought that while I'm there I would also do a bit of detective work into our family! It seems shrouded in mystery... do you know anything of interest?'

'Well I wish you luck with your thesis Frances, but I can't help much with the family history. I know that your father and I lived with Albert and his parents, but who our real parents were, we don't know.'

'Oh, that's a shame!'

'You could ask Blanche, Albert's widow, she may know more.'

'Really, do you think she would talk to me?'

'Why not? I'm sure she would love to chat with you. You're an academic, she loves anyone like that.'

'Great, then I'll contact her and see if we can have a chat.'

'Yes, you do that, you'll enjoy it!'

'Why is James the way he is?' asked Mark.

'You tell me, Mark! I despair of him, I must have done something wrong for him to want to distance himself from us.'

'Come now Edith, what on earth makes you think that you have done something? I know that you and Christopher brought him and Frances up exactly the same. Look at her, she's achieved so much, if it was anything you had or hadn't done then both of them would have been the same.'

'Yes, I suppose you're right. James always felt that his eyesight problem was worse than it was, Frances didn't have it so that didn't help, then Frances did so well at school while James struggled. James couldn't even contemplate university; it would have been quite beyond him – that hurt him too. From then on, he just seemed to blame someone else for all that happened in his life.'

'Well, I think it's best you should be happy with the way Frances has turned out. By the way, she's going to talk to Blanche, she wants to find out about our family history and I suggested Blanche might know something from what Albert told her.'

'Really? That's interesting, I would like to know too if she discovers anything. I've always been interested to know your family's history.'

'Would you like me to speak with James? We do keep in touch by letter, but that has become less frequent.'

'Oh yes Mark, would you? I know he thinks a lot of you.'

'Of course, and, apart from being his uncle, I am his god-father so I have a responsibility towards him. Leave it to me, I'll contact him.'

Blanche and Frances

Blanche, now in her late seventies, had developed arthritis and walking was painful. She managed to look after herself but struggled to get up her stairs and now had a bed in her former sitting room. The front room, a showpiece, as in so many houses, was now her sitting room and was used more than at any time during her life, or those of her parents when they lived there.

Frances had always liked Blanche; she admired her and knew that if she had been born in this decade, she would have been able to go to university. But Blanche still read. She relied on friends and neighbours to collect books from the library, sometimes tut tutting at their choice, but always grateful for their consideration.

'Auntie Blanche, do you know anything of my dad's parents? I'm doing a thesis for my studies and part of the work involves looking at our own ancestors.'

'I know some, my dear, your Uncle Albert did tell me a few things but he didn't know everything – you may have to be a detective to fill the gaps!'

'That's fine, Auntie, fire away! Tell me what you know from the start.'

'Well, my dear, Uncle Albert's parents were Ben and Alice. I expect you've heard mention of them, they took your dad and your Uncle Mark in as their sons. They were brought up together and were always regarded as one family.'

'Were Uncle Mark and my dad adopted?'

'Goodness no, they didn't bother with official things like that in those days. They just lived with them as a family. When Alice was in her last days, she talked to Albert and told him about the times when she was a girl – I think the mind goes back when you are near the end of life. She remembered a lady, at least she described her as lady, I don't think she was titled, who came to stay with the Ross family. She had a son. He had a strange name, Alice said, Culbert – we thought she meant Cuthbert but she was quite emphatic it was Culbert.

'She went away but came back some time later when the boy was older. Alice used to play with him and his mother used to teach Alice to read and write. They eventually went away to France. Alice was fascinated by the thought of that, but she never saw the lady again.

'Then many years later, another lady came to Aldwell. She owned a café in Duke Street where Alice used to help. She had two boys, but no one saw their father – she said he was in the army in Africa.

'Alice said she knew the husband in Africa didn't exist and that she had proof, so she asked the woman about it. This woman told Alice that the father was someone else, a married man. That wasn't too unusual and Alice thought no more of it until another woman arrived with a man she called Culbert.

'The woman with Culbert knew the woman in the café, it seemed they were friends. This woman had brought their daughters, three of them, and one day they played with the two sons of the woman in the café. Something happened then and the café closed and the woman disappeared. The two boys went to live with Ben and Alice – they were of course your father and your Uncle Mark.'

'Wow, so who was this woman with the café?'

'I don't know, but she seemed to know the woman with Culbert very well and there was, I heard, quite an argument!'

'So what happened to Culbert, the woman from France and the daughters?'

'I don't know, they all went their separate ways. Your father and uncle were too young to know anything, Albert was a bit older and didn't know all this until his mother was near the end of her life, not that it did her any good.'

'Do you think there was something untoward going on, Auntie Blanche?'

'Yes, I do, otherwise they would have been told who all

these people were. They must have had something to hide to keep it quiet.'

'But what could that be, I wonder?'

'Well, remember it was another era. Morals and ethics were different, so what we accept now may not have been accepted then. To us it may seem nothing important, but then it may have been quite different.'

'Hmm... I see.'

Frances pondered on all this. She was moving in the right direction, but slowly.

'Auntie Blanche, you are a marvel! Now I shall have to be the detective, as you said, but at least I have something to go on.'

'Don't let me tell you your business, dear, but if I were you I would start with the Ross family – they probably know more than anyone. They used to live in a house on the cliff and their son and daughter-in-law lived in that long bungalow at the corner of the road to the harbour.'

'But are any of them alive?'

'The Ross seniors won't be, but their son and family will be. I don't think they use the house themselves now, it's let out, but you could find out where they are from the letting agents in town.'

'Thanks Auntie, I'll let you know how I get on!'

'Yes, dear, I would like that, it's quite a mystery isn't it?' Blanche laughed, something she did very infrequently nowadays. Her life had changed since Albert died, with no children she was alone and the visits from Frances always cheered her.

Philip's Research

Philip had never visited Somerset House until this moment; the name of it had always conjured up visions of rolls and rolls of ancient papers and records in a dusty basement. In reality, it was just the dusty basement that was inaccurate; there were certainly many rolls and boxes of papers and documents, all carefully labelled.

The starting point for Philip was to find the birth certificate of Culbert Montaigne; he knew he was English from what his mother had told him, so somewhere there had to be a record of his birth. But the surname was a problem. To Philip, it sounded as if he had chosen a French name and changed his birth name, probably for business reasons. Was it a straight-forward translation of 'montaigne'? That seemed the most likely, but the word didn't translate – the nearest was 'mountain' but his search came up with nothing. He tried 'mount', 'hill' and everything connected with the word, but still nothing.

The curator was very sympathetic. 'Why don't you try another way?'

'What way?' asked Philip.

'Well, somewhere, someone must have left a record... think about it, young man, what do people in business always have?'

'I don't know what you mean,' said Philip.

'They have a bank account.'

'Oh, I see!'

'And, outside business they have a doctor; very few people go through life without consulting a doctor. You could try both of those avenues.'

'Thanks very much! I'll have a word with my parents to see if they can help.'

Philip left the building, and as he approached the door a young woman came towards him. He held the door open for her; she thanked him and walked to the desk. 'I wish to make a search,' said Frances.

'Dad, I'm stumped on finding a birth record for Culbert Montaigne. The curator suggested tracing him through his doctor or his bank.'

'Well, I don't know about his doctor, but wait a minute...

your mum's mother had a bank account in London. When we married, Harry gave us a cheque and I remember him saying that his wife also had an account at the same bank. Now, she was probably in partnership with Culbert, her husband, so maybe the bank account will tell us something.'

'Do you think you can find the cheque? Surely it must have been thrown out by now?'

'No, Philip, the bank always sends paid cheques back to the customer with their statements. Now most people do throw them away but being a businessman and a bit of a hoarder, I keep all such documents, so it must be somewhere!'

'That's great Dad! Let's see if we can find it.'

Patrick and Philip were immersed in boxes and papers. Gabrielle brought them some tea. 'Any luck, you two?'

'Not yet, but it's here somewhere... the writing on these labels has faded so it's a bit difficult to decipher, but we'll get there!'

Eventually, they did get there and the cheque for Gabrielle and Patrick's wedding gift was in Philip's hand.

'It's a London bank,' said Philip.

'I remember Harry saying that they kept an account in London in case they came back here.'

'Right, well, I'll go and make an appointment to see the manager!'

Frances's Research

Frances stood outside the house on the road to the harbour in Aldwell. There was a gate at the side of the building and standing on tiptoes, she could see a large wooded garden behind it. She had collected the parcel of diaries from Aldwell Post Office and it was in her bag. She hadn't opened them yet but just wanted to take a look at the scene – this, she thought, was where something had started.

The agents had been very helpful and given her the address of the Ross family. No one that Frances was researching was now alive but there was a granddaughter of Mr and Mrs Ross who used to live in the big house on the cliff, whose name the agents had given to Frances. She knew little of the people Frances wanted to research but said she would look out anything her grandparents or parents had kept and passed on – none of them were people to throw anything away.

She had found some diaries, now faded and not easily read, but there were some discernible names. She said that it seemed her grandparents kept a diary at the time when the railway was running between Aldwell and Haletown, not so much for the people involved but because they thought the railway might one day be of interest. They had recorded dates and times of trains, meeting people from the trains and taking them to catch the trains.

Back at Haletown, Frances opened the parcel. There were several diaries, neatly written, almost like a train timetable – but it was the added notes that were of interest to her.

Frances only knew one name, Culbert, but as it was unusual she thought they may have recorded it, and indeed they had.

When Frances read the entries she wasn't sure what to make of them. There was a mention of meeting Jessica, then Jessica's name appeared again when she left, but she also had a baby with her, her son Culbert. A few years later, their names appeared again, clearly, Jessica and Culbert.

'That must be him,' thought Frances, 'there can't be two people named Culbert, and the era is right.' The surname was Warner. 'Common enough name,' thought Frances, 'but it's a start. I shall have to go to Somerset House.'

Frances thanked the young man who held the door open for her and walked to the desk to ask to make a search. She had no idea where to begin so had to rely on the advice of the

Somerset House staff. They couldn't have been more helpful.

The census records provided the answer; there she was, Jessica Warner, listed as living in Berg House.

Frances was amazed. It was unusual for a woman to have a 'seat'; she must have been very wealthy, normally a seat would be in a man's name. Frances knew that to have a 'seat' meant that a person had status as well as wealth. To own property she must have been an only child who inherited from her parents, or a widow, or even both. Frances knew that in the nineteenth century a woman could own very little and on marriage all she had would become her husband's property. At least she had an address; perhaps someone in East Leah where Berg House was might know of Jessica Warner, or have records of her, or of course of her son, Culbert.

Frances realised that she was now on the track of someone who might well turn out to be her relative, a daunting thought. 'Just who will she be?' she thought. 'Do I really want to know?' Then she smiled. 'Of course I want to know, I have come this far, and Auntie Blanche will be fascinated!'

Mark and James

'Thanks so much for coming, James,' said Mark. 'Betty has been looking forward to seeing you so much – she thinks of you as a son, you know.'

James looked a little embarrassed. He had received his uncle's letter and invitation to stay; he had a few days' holiday so felt that he had to go as he couldn't find an excuse not to.

Betty had indeed been looking forward to James's visit. She had a good daughter in Annie and a good son-in-law in Jeffrey, but they were away a lot and led such busy lives that they met infrequently.

'Now James, come and look around the garden, it's right lovely this time of the year!'

James smiled at Betty's dialect, still retained after all these years in the south. 'Good for her,' he thought.

They sat in the garden, which was long and tapered at the end where it met the river. Mark had been careful to buy a property that did not have a wide boundary on to the river, knowing that he would be responsible for it. As it was, the narrow strip that formed the boundary would cause little concern and any damage or wear from river craft would be minimal.

Mark was obviously eager to talk with James about the family but Betty was having none of it.

'No family talk until tomorrow, you two, just enjoy the day and relax.'

What Betty said was not to be questioned. She was not authoritarian, but she had a definite firmness and those who knew her well would know that if Betty had made a decision, then there would be no further discussion.

James looked relieved and sat back in his comfortable chair.

'I love it here, Aunt Betty, you two have done really well! This is a smashing property.'

'Well, you know that your uncle has a sideline, that has made this possible.'

'Oh, yes, the smuggling!' said James.

'Shh James, you'll get us arrested!'

James laughed. 'I doubt it, Aunt Betty, if anyone will get arrested it'll be Tommy.'

James knew about Mark and Tommy's other business and although he admired them as likeable rogues, he knew the risks and just hoped that soon they would decide to end their 'sideline'.

The day ended happily, with promises of serious discussion to come.

'I shall speak openly and bluntly,' said Mark to James. 'Your mother is very upset that you don't keep in contact with her, she thinks she's done something to offend you, or upset you. I have told her that the fault is not with her but with you and it's about time you made peace with her and started behaving like a normal son would to his mother. Don't forget that you have a sister too who has missed having the company of a brother... she also thinks she's done something wrong, when of course she hasn't. You have caused much unhappiness, James, you must stop it and put things right before it's too late.'

Mark sat back. He had amazed himself with that speech; it was something always in his mind but never before said out loud. He was glad that he had managed to say it – rather eloquently, too, he thought.

James said nothing for several minutes; he looked shocked. When he did speak, he said, 'What shall I do, Uncle Mark?'

'You must contact your mother, and your sister, tell them you're sorry, tell them you love them, ask their forgiveness. They will forgive and welcome you, you only have to ask.'

'Oh wow, I just don't know what to say, I've always felt so apart from them all... Frances is so clever, I was awful at school. Mum is clever too, she didn't seem to have time for me, Dad wasn't there a lot when I was young, I just felt so left out.'

'Well it takes two James, you weren't treated any differently from Frances, you weren't left out, you chose to be left out. Now you're old enough to behave differently, as the adult you are, so do so, and don't take too long about it!'

James smiled at Mark. 'OK Uncle Mark, I just hope that they won't reject me.'

'They won't do that, I promise you! Now come on, let's go and have a drink in the pub. I could do with a pint and I bet you could!'

Mark put his arm around James's shoulder and they walked out of the garden into the road.

Betty was watching from the window. 'Good, Mark excelled himself,' she said quietly to herself. She had spent the previous evening 'rehearsing' with Mark, pretending to be James; Mark had been a good pupil. Now Betty felt at ease, the family would be happy again and if they were happy, then she and Mark would be happy.

11

Revelations

Philip sat in front of the bank manager; it was a merchant bank with its foundations in South Africa, provided for UK citizens to use its services.

Situated in the heart of the City in a street made up solely of banks and financial institutions, the area had a solemnity about it. Not far away was the Bank of England and all the famous buildings so often photographed by tourists.

'We did indeed hold an account for your mother's parents, and now that you have proved who you are, I must check that you are on the list of people able to access items held in our strong room.'

Philip looked puzzled, but didn't dare ask why there was such secrecy.

The manager returned with a handwritten list. 'Mmm… seems that you can have access, your name is on this list – not your actual name of course, but as a son of the daughter of the account holder.'

Philip felt even more confused but kept quiet; the manager was a man for business only, and chatter was not to be indulged in.

'If you will wait here, I shall fetch the item.'

Philip was feeling nervous; whatever could it be? Presumably documents, but why had his grandmother drawn up a list of who could look at them?

The manager returned holding an oblong wooden box; it was orange-brown in colour and on the front in gilt were the initials WJG. There was also a key, kept separately in a small envelope. He handed them both to Philip.

'There, you can take them away but you must sign for them, so that we know where they are. If anyone else on the list asks for it, you must allow them access.'

'But how shall I know who they are and if they're genuine?'

'They will only contact you if we send them. No one else can know, can they?'

Philip blushed, feeling rather foolish. 'Yes of course… I wasn't thinking.'

'No, apparently not. Now, I'm busy, so I bid you good day.'

The manager stood holding the door for Philip, showing that the interview had ended. Philip put the box and envelope into his bag and walked along the street to the underground station, where he caught the tube back to his Hampstead home.

Patrick couldn't believe his eyes when he saw the box. 'It's satinwood!' he said in amazement.

'Yes, Dad, I thought it was. It's rare, isn't it?'

'Yes it is, and you realise that whoever owned this box was in the same business as we are? This is a presentation box given to a tea broker or trader, but it must have been someone very highly thought of, the craftsmanship is exquisite.'

He stroked the wood and turned it around several times.

'Come on Dad, let's open it!'

Inside were diaries, small, but every page of each one filled with tiny writing. A document rolled and tied with a ribbon laid the length of the box and there was a photograph of a young boy.

Patrick and Philip looked at it all, not knowing where to start. 'It looks like someone's life is contained in this box,' said Patrick.

'Well, maybe it will unlock the mystery of Mum's parents,' replied Philip, eager to discover the contents of the diaries and document.

'Let's unroll the document first, that won't take long.'

Philip carefully unravelled the scroll; it was a deed of assignment. He read it out to his father. 'It's an assignment of property drawn up by solicitors, giving a property called Berg House to Theo Harcourt, free of charge. The donor is Mrs Jessica Warner.'

'How extraordinary!' said Patrick.

'Let's read the diaries, then we will perhaps understand what it's about and how it relates to Mum's parents.'

Frances met James in London. Since his meeting with his Uncle Mark, James had been anxious to meet with Frances. When she told him about her research and what she had found out so far, he was fascinated and asked if he could help. Frances was delighted at his reaction. 'Now at last he is the brother I always wanted and knew was there,' she thought. His eyesight had greatly improved since Frances last saw him; he now only wore spectacles for reading.

They had tickets for East Leah, the nearest station to the property called Berg House that Frances had discovered through her research. She and James chatted during the journey, just as would friends who had been reunited after years. They decided that their first call should be to the library, where there would be local records. Such a large property should be well known in the area, Frances had told James. Hopefully it would still be there.

The librarian was very helpful and gave Frances and James a copy of a paper written by a local historian, which was specifically about Berg House. They were amazed when they read about how large the property was, and were pleased to discover it still existed, now as a sanatorium for people suffering from lung diseases and those convalescing after surgery.

They read the details carefully, but something didn't seem to make sense.

'Look here Frances, Mrs Warner owned the property, then later it was bought by a Mr Harcourt – but he didn't live there, she did. That's odd isn't it?'

'It's also odd that a woman should own a property in those days, James. She must have inherited it and been the only child of a wealthy family, or been the widow of the man who owned it. Women couldn't own property if they were married or had older male siblings or relatives.'

'Thanks goodness that's all changed!' James laughed.

'But she had a son, we know that Culbert was her son, and yet there isn't a husband. I wonder who the father was?'

'Perhaps it was this Harcourt chap.'

'Yes, but why didn't she marry him or stay with him? Why sell the property and then go to Aldwell? Seems most odd.'

'Well Frances, I think we need to understand the times they lived in, we can't puzzle it out based on today's morals and ethics, things were very different then.'

'Good thinking, James. Let's start from a different angle, one set in the nineteenth century, and see where we go from there.'

After much searching among various papers and leaflets, James and Frances discovered that Jessica's father had lived at Berg House and was the owner before Jessica. This was in the historian's paper. There was, though, little information about Jessica but James pointed out that her surname was different from her father's, so at some stage she must have been married.

'I know,' said James, 'let's go and talk to some locals. We can go to the village pub, you always meet someone in a pub who knows the history of a place, or if not, someone will tell us who we should talk to – and we should go to Berg House, there should be records there.'

And so James and Frances walked to Berg House, a large, imposing building tucked away behind trees, with a large garden running down to the river.

They went to reception, explained who they were and what they wanted to know, and were then shown into an office to wait for the matron.

A nun walked in, much to their surprise; she introduced herself and told them that the sanatorium was run by an order of nuns who specialised in caring for patients with lung diseases.

'Do you have any documents which relate to the history of this house?' asked Frances. 'We're researching previous owners, as one may have been related to friends of ours.'

The nun smiled. 'Have you seen the paper by our historian?'

'Yes, we have but there seems to be gaps which we would like to fill.'

'And what are those gaps?'

'Mrs Warner owned this property after her father died, but she sold it to Mr Harcourt who didn't live here straightaway... and the other thing, well, there was a boy, Culbert, who seems to have been the son of Mrs Warner but we're not sure who his father was.'

'Goodness me, it seems you already know quite a lot! I don't know if I can tell you any more. The only fact I do know is that Mr Harcourt owned other properties in the area, and I believe he originally came from Lancashire.'

'Do you know where in Lancashire?'

'Not exactly, but somewhere it is recorded that his family were in textiles, that's why they had so much money and could afford to buy these properties. Maybe you should start in Lancashire? There aren't many textile factories left so you should be able to find archival material quite easily.'

James and Frances thanked the nun and continued on their walk around the village.

*

'What do you think, James? Should we go to Lancashire and try to find the Harcourt family?'

'Yes, why not? We can do some research first to narrow down the possibilities, that won't be difficult.'

'OK, I'll do that and then we can plan our next move.'

They had found a small pub near Berg House called The Fishermen. They were both tired and hungry so decided to stop for a drink and some food.

'On holiday here?' asked the landlord.

'Not exactly,' said James. 'My sister and I are doing some research on a local property and past owners.'

'Oh, and which property would that be?'

'Berg House.'

'Berg House, well you're in luck! Old Sammy over there is the local unofficial historian – what he doesn't know about this place isn't worth knowing.'

James and Frances looked at each other. 'Just what we wanted,' said Frances.

'Can we join you?' James asked Sammy.

'Harcourt, now he was a funny sort, no one liked him.'

'Why was that?' asked Frances.

'Put on airs and graces, tried to be posh, you know... but he was working class like the rest of us.'

Sammy's family had lived in East Leah and around for as long as anyone could remember and the facts, gossip, and anything else of interest were passed down the generations. Few of them were literate so relied on the spoken word and had detailed memories as a result.

'What do you know about him and Mrs Warner?'

'Oh there was talk at the time. She had a boy, funny name, Culbert, she said he belonged to her cousins who were killed in some accident but everyone knew the boy was hers. She was a lovely lady, when the boy was about four or five they left – no-one knew where they went, they weren't seen again.'

'And what about Mr Harcourt? He was something to do with the textile business we heard, is that right?'

'You are right, indeed you are, his family had a business in Lancashire, near Preston. Loads of money they had but they didn't have breeding, no, they didn't have breeding.'

'Was that very important?' asked James.

'Was it very important? My word it was, in those days it was everything! Round here, money alone couldn't get you in with the posh people, oh no, breeding was what you needed.'

James and Frances smiled, knowing what Sammy meant.

They thanked Sammy, finished their meal and then walked back to the station to catch their train back to London.

'Next stop, after research, Preston?'

'Definitely!' said Frances.

Patrick, Gabrielle and Philip had spent days reading through the diaries of Jessica Warner. Although the writing was tiny, it was clear, detailed and also gave an insight to the era in which Jessica lived.

The one written before leaving England was now in Patrick's hands.

I have to leave this country, the one that has been my home since childhood. I shall return to France, the country of my birth.

I cannot stay here, what I have done is wrong. I did not know that when it happened, but what is done is done.

Culbert must be protected, he is all I have now, but he must not know the truth.

If only I had known then what is the truth, I would not have committed this act, I am no more than a common criminal.

If I am ever discovered then I will surely spend my life locked away, I must go.

'Wow, what's all that about?' asked Philip.

'I don't know, but it must have something to do with Culbert – maybe it has something to do with his parentage.'

'What do you think, Dad?'

'I'm not sure Philip, but remember this was the Victorian era, things were very different, not just morals but also the law. We need to find out what she could have meant by being a common criminal for whatever she did.'

'Well, looking at it at face value, it would seem that Theo Harcourt was probably the father of Culbert. That can't be a crime, surely?'

'You wouldn't think so would you, but that depends on just who Theo was.'

'She says that his family were wealthy textile merchants from the Preston area who came looking for property in the area… Can't see how that can be criminal.'

'No, doesn't seem so but we don't know. I think Mr Harcourt from Preston needs some research.'

'Interesting stuff about their life in France, Mum, isn't it?'

Gabrielle, who had been browsing through the diaries, agreed. 'I was very young when we left France so I don't remember too much. It's fascinating reading all this, it's so well written, really lifelike.'

'I think we should investigate the Preston end of the subject. How about I go there and have a hunt around? I can look a few things up first so I know where to start, but I can't go for a few weeks. Business first, Dad!'

'Good idea Philip, the change of air will do you good. Go when you're ready!'

Dear James,

We are so happy that you and your mum and dad and Frances are friends again; there is no need for people to be unhappy. Us northerners make up quicker than you southern folk do, don't fall out again, there's a good lad.

I'm afraid the news here isn't so good; Tommy has been

arrested. You know he used to land on airstrips all over the place to avoid being discovered? Well, last month he had to land in a hurry because a storm blew up and he finished up on the outer part of Croydon Airport. You can imagine the fuss that caused. Unfortunately, the authorities searched the plane and found all the stuff – he hadn't bothered to conceal it because he always landed where he knew he wouldn't be searched.

He will go to prison I'm afraid, but Tommy is a brick and said that no one else was involved. Of course they can't prove that anyone was, so your Uncle Mark and his friends are safe, thank goodness.

I hear that you and Frances are doing some 'detective work'. I hope it is going well and that you find out what you want to, though sometimes things are best left in the past where they belong.

Would be nice to see you and Frances if you have a few days spare. You are always welcome here, you know that.

Lots of love from Auntie Betty.

Frances and James sat in the large lounge of Mark and Betty's riverside home.

'How is Tommy?' asked Frances.

'Tommy's a survivor, he'll be all right,' replied Mark. 'I just feel bad that he has had to carry the can for us all, but you know Tommy, he wouldn't drop us in it.'

'You are lucky, Uncle Mark,' said James.

'I know, I know, James, but we'll give Tommy a good homecoming when he finishes his sentence. It isn't long now, the courts were lenient with him.'

Frances and James updated Mark and Betty on their research. They were both fascinated, Betty particularly when the Lancashire link was mentioned.

'I knew some of the mill owners, not in that area but where I lived in Yorkshire, they were all the same though. There were two types, the ones who treated their workers like they were family, and the ones who treated their workers like slaves, that's where the saying "satanic mills" comes from – that's what some of them were, dens of Satan, worse than the workhouses.'

'Goodness, Aunt Betty, I never knew that, I always had a rather romantic vision of young women working in the textile mills surrounded by beautiful countryside!' said Frances.

'Well, as I said they weren't all bad, let's hope the family you are looking for were the good ones.'

Mark sat quietly, looking thoughtful.

'All right, ducks?' said Betty.

'Yes, fine, just thinking.'

'Oh, do tell!' Betty laughed.

'This research you are doing about our family, have you asked your father what he knows?'

'I have, but he said he was too young to remember.'

'Mmm, I think your father knows more than he will tell.'

'Really, why?'

'I'm not sure, but I have always had the feeling that there was something odd and Christopher may have known. He is five years older than me and although he was young at the time, he wasn't too young to understand. Then of course there was Albert, now he was ten years older than me, so he would have understood whatever it was.'

'It all sounds very mysterious,' said Frances.

'Doesn't it, and I'm not sure why but your father used to seem almost afraid when the subject was raised, he sort of backed off talking about it.'

'That has really whetted our appetites, hasn't it Frances? Now we must investigate. We intend to go to Preston and see what we can find out about the mill owners. Frances has been doing some research, so we have an idea where to start,' replied James.

'Good luck to you both, I shall be most interested to know what you discover.' Mark looked thoughtful again.

Philip sat on the train, gazing at the passing countryside. He hadn't travelled much to the north of England, certainly not this far north; most of his life had been spent in London and overseas when business required his presence there. The north had always seemed a distant place, somewhere grimy and dark, but Philip knew that this was just an image and that soon he would see the true face of the other part of England. It was autumn now, September 1963; everywhere was mellowing, a time for rest and recuperation.

He knew that the Harris Library was just a short walk from the railway station; he slowly walked along to the Market Square and looked up at the imposing building. He took a deep breath. 'This is it,' he thought. 'Here I may find an answer, but what then, what then?'

He walked in and approached the large reception desk. He had written to the librarian and requested information about the textile mills and in particular any reference to the Harcourt family. The receptionist asked him to wait while she contacted the librarian.

'Delighted to meet you, we have the information you require – at least, some of it.'

The librarian shook Philip's hand and led him into an office; on the desk was a file.

Philip stared at it.

'Everything all right?' asked the librarian.

'Yes, fine thank you, just fine,' replied Philip.

'Well you can sit here and look through this file. I'm afraid you can't take it away but if you want anything copied, then we can arrange that.'

'Fine, just fine, thank you,' said Philip.

The librarian smiled. 'These southerners, they do have a way of expressing themselves,' he thought.

Philip read and reread all the papers until his eyes grew tired. The Harcourts were a well-known family in the area, they were respected and treated their workers very fairly, by all accounts. Theo was one of their sons; nothing seemed odd there. What was the connection with Jessica that wasn't right?

'I shall have to return tomorrow, if that's all right?' asked Philip. 'My eyes are getting rather tired.'

'Yes, of course. We'll leave the file here, come when you like.'

Philip walked back along Lune Street; there was much excitement and noise. It was September 13th and a queue had formed along the street.

'What's going on?' Philip asked one of the young women in the queue.

'Don't you know, ducks? It's The Beatles – they're doing a concert tonight, we're queuing for tickets, seven and six they are!'

'Oh yes, of course.'

Philip was aware of The Beatles and the following they had, but hadn't witnessed it first hand before. He walked quickly along the road, glad to get to the peace and quiet of his hotel.

As he went to the reception desk and asked for his key, a man and woman stood in the foyer. He glanced at them; 'Strange,' he thought, 'that woman looks familiar.' The receptionist gave him his door key and he turned to go towards the stairs. The woman turned and he saw her whole face. 'Now where have I seen her?' thought Philip.

Breakfast was a large meal. 'It'll set you up for the day!' promised the waitress.

Philip smiled and thanked her. It wasn't what he was used to, but when in Rome, he thought.

Then Frances and James came into the breakfast room. Philip looked up when they walked in, still he couldn't place her.

He could hear Frances and James talking and realised they were not northerners. 'I shall have to ask,' he thought. 'I'll wait until they've finished their breakfast.'

'Excuse me, but I'm sure we have met somewhere – I know it is awfully impolite of me to butt in but I'm positive I know you from somewhere!'

Frances looked at Philip. 'I can't think where, we don't live around here. We're from the south of England.'

'Yes, so am I,' said Philip.

'Are you on holiday?' asked James.

'No, I'm doing some research on my family and staying here for a few days.'

'Really, so are we!'

'What, staying here or doing some research on your family?' asked Philip.

'Both!' said Frances.

'Goodness what a coincidence, but then life is full of those, I'm told.'

Frances laughed. 'Well actually, I am writing a thesis and the family research element just happened as a sideline.'

'I can't believe it, me too!' said Philip.

'What family are you researching?' asked Frances.

'My mother's family; the connection with this area is the Harcourt family who used to own a textile mill in the area.'

Frances and James were stunned.

'What's the matter?' asked Philip, looking concerned. 'Have I said something to upset you?'

'No, no, you haven't… it's just so strange… we're also researching the Harcourts!'

They all sat back, bewildered.

Eventually Philip broke the silence. 'Have you been to the Harris library? That's where I'm going through some documents.'

'Yes, we intend to, we only arrived today.'

'That's wonderful, we can share the research, but what's your connection?'

Frances explained what she and James knew of their grandparents. Philip sat open mouthed. 'You're not going to believe this but we are researching the same family, this means that we could actually be sort of related.'

'Wow!' said James.

'Do you know about the contents of the satinwood box?' asked Philip.

Frances and James hadn't any idea what Philip meant so they decided to move into the lounge, ordered more coffee, and then Philip explained.

Now all the known facts were on the table, though Frances was still puzzled as to the identity of the unknown woman who was the mother of Mark and Christopher, the one who had left Aldwell and her sons after arguing with Culbert and his wife.

'It looks as if the woman was Mary's sister, so Culbert's sister-in-law,' said Philip. 'Her name was Melvina – have you heard that name anywhere?'

'No,' said Frances, 'but I still have the train list, she may be on that.'

Frances explained to Philip about the details Mr Ross kept of the trains to and from Aldwell and who the passengers were.

'If Melvina went to Aldwell, that is the only way she would have arrived. If there's some connection with the Ross family then she will be on the train list.'

'Do you have it with you?'

'Yes, I'll get it.' Frances left the two men and went to her room.

James and Philip waited, both realising that soon they would find the answers they had been seeking.

Frances returned. 'Here's the list. I only looked for Culbert, see – his name appears several times, as a young boy, again as an adult. Now let's see if a Melvina appears.' She checked the lists, and there it was; three entries, one when she first arrived, another a few years afterwards followed by another about three weeks later.

'So, this Melvina was having an affair with her sister's husband, had two sons, our father and our uncle, then Mary, her sister, discovered what had been going on and that presumably was why our dad and uncle were fostered. No wonder it's been kept quiet!'

'Mmm... but that's not all.' Philip showed James and Frances the entry by Jessica and the details of the property transfer.

'Whatever can she mean, I wonder? What could she have done that was so bad? And giving away that property – James and I have seen it, it's huge – the locals said she sold it, although it was strange that she still lived there for some time after it was sold.'

'Yes, that's because she didn't sell it, she gave it to Mr Harcourt.'

'But why? Because he fathered her child? That wasn't a crime, which is what she suggests; the locals said that she told everyone the boy was her cousins' child, who she took in when they were killed in a train accident – although no one believed that, but it seemed no one was particularly bothered!' Frances was becoming more and more puzzled.

'Let's go through this slowly and carefully,' said Philip.

'First, Jessica, who owns Berg House, is presumably widowed, inherits the property from her father. She must have been an only child with no male relatives otherwise she couldn't have inherited.

'She meets Theo Harcourt, they fall in love, she has a son, she says she can't marry him because he is socially lower than her, she wrote that in her diaries, and for some reason gives him the property, presumably to keep him quiet.'

Frances agreed. 'But, if Jessica was so well thought of, which we heard she was, and Harcourt wasn't, wouldn't she have been believed if she said it was her cousin's child? And if she wasn't believed, no one liked Harcourt so why should he get away with what amounts to blackmail?'

'I don't know,' said Philip. 'But I think there is more that we haven't yet discovered, something else is there, something we yet have to find, it just doesn't make sense... Giving away Berg House is surely too high a price to pay to buy silence for a "social misdemeanour", it may have been the Victorian era but it still doesn't add up.'

'I agree,' said James. 'There must be something else, let's go to the library and see what we can find.'

'Great idea, I feel exhausted already,' laughed Frances.

'Tell you what, let's have dinner together this evening and perhaps have a look at Preston by night!'

'Splendid,' said James.

'Oh there's three of you now,' said the librarian peering over his glasses at Philip, Frances and James.

'Yes, afraid so, hope you don't mind, we are all researching the same thing so we might as well do it together, save you getting the documents out separately for us all.'

'Good, I like to make life easy if I can!' The librarian smiled and showed them into the office where the documents were.

'We particularly need to research the Harcourt family who had the textile mill here. Have you any more information on them, please?' asked James.

'The Harcourt family, yes indeed, a very well-known and well-respected family, owned one of the largest mills around. You may have heard some mill owners were tyrants while others were very caring. I'm glad to say the Harcourts were the latter.'

'Well, that's good to hear,' said James.

'Yes, isn't it? Now I shall go and find what I can and then leave you to your researching.'

'I think he's quite enjoying this,' said Frances as the librarian left the room. 'He looks like a librarian out of one of Charles Dickens' books!'

'Probably the most interesting thing that's happened in here for years,' laughed Philip.

After some time the librarian returned. 'Here are some to go on with, I'll be back with more later.' He put a pile of dusty files on the table.

'What are we looking for?' asked James.

'I don't know really, let's start with Theo, there must be something there,' said Philip.

Apart from the rustling and turning of papers, there was a silence from all three. The librarian came back with another pile, smiled and left them to carry on.

'James, I've found the record of the Harcourts' marriage, Theo's parents that is, somewhere we should find records of their children and details of what they did. We know Theo probably worked in the mill, all the owners' families did then, so he must be listed here.' Frances was thumbing through the files.

'Here we are, they had a daughter – but that's odd, there isn't a son listed.'

'There must be!' said Philip. 'We know Theo was their son, at least we think we know.'

James was looking through another file. 'Here we are, Theo is listed as a partner, so he must have been their son.'

'Well if he was, he doesn't appear here as being their son… oh, this doesn't make sense!' Frances said.

'Wait a minute, let's look through the other documents,' said Philip.

'What other documents?' asked James.

'These ones, they're not with the business or family ones,

there are some separate ones here in a small folder.' Philip held it up.

He opened it and read the contents.

'Theo was adopted by the Harcourts,' said Philip.

'What?' said James. 'So what does that mean?'

'More research I'm afraid!' laughed Philip. 'Come on, you two, let's have a break. We'll continue this tomorrow, let's go and change and see what Preston night life is like!'

Preston was undergoing changes; high-rise buildings designated as cheap housing were appearing, dotted throughout the area. The closure of the textile mills had led to large gaps in the community, gaps that were not just spatial but also economical.

Frances, James and Philip wandered around; it seemed like a town being rebuilt after a war.

They found a pub and decided to go in for a break in their walk. Frances and Philip chatted about their academic work; James listened.

Frances was conscious that James might feel marginalised by their talk, so changed the subject to more general matters.

'When we've discovered whatever there is to be discovered, will it make any difference to anything or anybody?' asked James.

'Good question,' said Philip. 'No, I don't suppose it will, so why have we done all this, we should ask ourselves?'

'Maybe we all have a curiosity about our roots, our past, especially if there's something that appears to be odd, or perhaps sinister.'

'Do you think we'll find something sinister?' asked James.

'I'm sure we will, but whether it was sinister at the time it happened, or sinister now, that is what we will discover. But whatever it is, we can't change it.'

'Come on you chaps, I am getting hungry, let's find somewhere to eat. I don't fancy the hotel restaurant again, let's find somewhere to have a steak.'

Frances got up and put on her coat, Philip and James followed.

Luckily they found a Berni Inn a few streets away, one of a new chain of steak restaurants that was opening across the country.

The next day was their last in Preston and concluded their research. The records showed that Theo Harcourt had indeed been adopted as a very young baby, just a few weeks old. It had been difficult to trace his birth parents, but persistence on the part of Philip had paid off and now they had the facts. Now it made sense.

They exchanged addresses and telephone numbers and said their goodbyes; quietness had fallen over them, not a sad quietness, but an air of finality.

James returned to his home in Kent, having arranged to visit Mark and Betty to tell them what had been discovered.

Philip had a few days before returning to work and would spend the time at home with his family, likewise passing on all the information they had.

Frances arranged to visit Blanche. She, after all, said Frances, had given them the vital information that led to their discoveries, and she should be told everything.

Blanche greeted Frances as she always did, as if she was her own family. She now had very limited mobility and relied on people calling in to help with the everyday routine of life. She had good friends and neighbours; they brought her shopping and made sure she ate properly.

'Tell me what you've discovered!' said Blanche. 'I'm getting quite excited.'

Frances laughed. 'It's a long story, I warn you.'

'Never mind, never mind, we have plenty of time. Now leave out no detail, I want to know everything.'

'Very well,' said Frances. 'It started in the 1870s when Jessica Warner met Theo Harcourt at East Leah. Jessica lived in a large property called Berg House in East Leah, James and I went there, it's now a sanatorium but still a grand building with large grounds.

'Jessica's father was a retired tea broker; his wife had died and Jessica had been married but her husband was killed in one of the many foreign skirmishes of Victorian times. She moved in with her father to look after him.

'Theo and his family were owners of a textile mill near Preston, they were very wealthy and wanted to buy property in the area, seeing it as a move up the social scale, and of course an investment.

'Jessica and her father met Theo and his parents purely by chance and discussed properties and so on, but Jessica and Theo were attracted and started a relationship. The result of that was a baby, a boy named Culbert, who Jessica told locals was her cousin's child, saved after a train accident, who she had taken in to care for.'

'Did they believe her?' asked Blanche.

'I doubt it, but that didn't really matter, Jessica was highly thought of. Theo wasn't, he was seen as trade with airs and graces, so whatever she said was neither here nor there. The locals we spoke with seemed to know who the father was and it didn't bother their ancestors at the time. Jessica then assigned Berg House to Theo, free of charge.'

'What!' exclaimed Blanche.

'Yes, that's been the sticking point all along. Why should she give away a property that today, in 1963, would cost at least £300,000? That's by direct money conversion, and not allowing for desirability, which would probably make it worth nearer half a million. It just didn't make sense!'

'So why do it? Why not just tell this chap to clear off?'

Frances laughed. 'Oh Auntie Blanche, always practical, that's what you would have done I suppose?'

'Yes, I would, certainly, I wouldn't have given away a property like that unless there was a very, very good reason.'

'Well, there was, at least there was then... The law was different, so what happened then wouldn't apply now, but we have to understand the law of that time.'

'Oh, I am intrigued!' said Blanche, leaning forward slightly in her chair.

'This is what we discovered, which is the reason for Jessica giving the property to Theo. Jessica's father, William, had been married before he met Jessica's mother. When he was a young man, he worked for a time in his company's office in the north of England, one they were about to close prior to his being sent to India and Ceylon. While there he met a young woman, fell in love and they married. His wife became pregnant almost immediately and gave birth to a boy. Sadly she died shortly after the birth, not uncommon in those days, she had a post-partum haemorrhage and her life literally ebbed away from her, there was nothing that could be done. William was trauma-tised and didn't know what to do; he was about to go to India, with wife and child so he thought, but now he had a baby boy and no wife. His parents took over and put the baby in a chil-dren's home for adoption. It was the only option at the time, they were too old to care for the child and because the baby boy was so young, there was no chance of William forming a bond, so he was taken away and William was encouraged to forget the episode.

'Not long after, a couple who had a daughter but were unable to have male babies due to a genetic disorder applied to the home to adopt a boy. They had a textile business in Preston and desperately needed a son and heir. So they adopted the boy and named him Theo.'

'Oh my goodness!' said Blanche. 'So that was why Jessica gave Berg House away?'

'Yes, Theo was Jessica's half brother, and although she had been innocent of the fact, later when she found out she knew

263

that it would be considered a crime to have a child with him, but this was not the only reason.'

'There is more?' asked Blanche.

'But of course, it couldn't be that simple could it? After Jessica had her son, she had a visit from a relative of her father's, she called him a cousin – he wasn't actually a direct cousin, a few times removed but nevertheless he knew about her father's first marriage and the son, they had been friends while William was in the north. He was the only person who knew about Theo and his true parentage. He had heard about Jessica and Theo by a rather roundabout grapevine of the day and knew that he must tell her the truth.'

'What was the rather roundabout grapevine of the day?'

'One of the staff at Berg House, Mrs K, had always kept in touch with this cousin, his name by the way was Culbert, and she told him what had happened. She of course had no idea of the consequences of her revelations, she just thought she was doing the right thing.'

'Oh I see, but why? Surely no one would have believed that of Jessica, and Theo didn't know she was his half sister, did he?'

'No, he didn't but what was known to solicitors of the Harcourt family was that Theo was the rightful heir to Berg House; he was the legitimate son of William Gilman. Cousin Culbert knew this and told Jessica that Theo would find out at some point so she should give the property to him, as by law it was his. The law at the time only allowed males to inherit property, so Theo was the rightful heir to Berg House.'

'Oh my goodness, you have done well to discover all this,' said Blanche, 'and thank you for coming to tell me!'

'There's so much more to tell you, Jessica's diaries were detailed and fascinating – she wrote about when she and her son Culbert were in France; the family they stayed with, the Juliens, whom she had known from childhood; of everyday life there – she even kept recipes as she did in England, I have them here. She wrote of Culbert's marriage to Mary, about Melvina, Mary's sister who became a good friend to Jessica. She also mentioned the eye problem Culbert has, the same problem that my brother James has, an inherited condition, there is so much Auntie Blanche! It's a history in itself. Now we know the truth, but there is something else.'

'Really?'

'Yes, my Dad, Christopher, I'm sure knew some of this, whenever I asked him about his parents he changed the subject. Now why, I wonder? It's not anything to do with him.'

'Your father and my Albert were great friends, Albert knew quite a lot and I'm sure he told your father. For some reason, your father thought it brought shame on him, although he didn't know what it was all about, and that your mother might not have married him if she had thought there was something bad in his past. She did have other boyfriends you know, your dad did well to win her!'

'And that's all?'

'Yes, I'm sure of it. Are you going to tell your father all this?'

'I don't know Blanche, what do you think?'

'I think your father and mother should stay as they are, happy and content, this is of no consequence to them, just tell them you have discovered all you need for your thesis.'

'I think you're right, James is going to tell Uncle Mark and Aunt Betty, though.'

'That's all right, Mark is curious by nature, if you don't tell him he'll know there's something going on. He'll cope with it, but Christopher won't.'

'Wise advice Auntie Blanche, thank you.'

'Why don't you write about all this Frances? It would make a wonderful book.'

'Yes, it would, wouldn't it? But would anyone believe it?'

'Oh, you can embellish it, add a few characters, make it interesting for today's readers.'

'Yes, I might just do that!'

They carried on chatting for a while until Blanche grew tired. Frances kissed her aunt on the cheek and left her house to go to her parents' home, where James had already arrived. James had stayed with Mark and Betty and told them what they had found out. Tommy, now out of prison, was back working with Mark and had been fascinated by the history that James related.

Christopher and Edith were delighted to have their son and daughter with them; it was a rare occasion for them all to be together.

'So now your research is finished you can get back to the present!' Christopher said to Frances and James.

'Yes, I have plenty to do and I am sure you have too, James.'

'Back to the grind as we say!' replied her brother.

Frances and James walked into the garden. 'James, Blanche said something a bit odd about Dad – I always thought he knew more than he said about all this, Blanche did too and thought he was embarrassed about it and that Mum wouldn't have married him if she knew he had an odd past.'

James laughed. 'I doubt if Mum would worry about that, she takes people as they are, not what their grannies might have been!'

'Quite, which is why it's strange. Blanche said something else; she said that Culbert, Dad's father, was quite a woman-iser, according to what Albert had told her, and she seemed to imply that one of his descendants may be like that.'

'Well, it isn't me, I have the eye defect which is enough! Anyhow, lots of men are like that, and it doesn't have to be inherited.'

'Exactly, so I wonder what she meant.'

'Why don't you do more research? You're quite an expert now at finding out about the past, and don't forget Philip is still interested – you have his phone number and address, don't you?'

'I have, perhaps I will give him a ring some time… '

*

Philip looked at the satinwood box. 'What a tale you've held for all these years,' he thought, 'and who knows what more still lays uncovered.'